In The Dollhouse We All Wait

by Amanda M. Bake

Published by Crystal Lake Publishing—Where Stories Come Alive!

Website: www.crystallakepub.com

Torrid Waters is the pulp and extreme horror imprint of Crystal Lake. For this book, the author has supplied the following trigger warnings: medical torture, sexual sadism, rape, murder, physical and psychological torture, medical experimentation (extreme body modification, including amputation), drugs, bodily excretions (scat, vomit, blood, pus, etc.), coercion into complicity, human trafficking, forced exhibitionism for voyeurs, necrophilia, suggested incest/pedophilia in past, 'the rich really are different.'

Chapter 1: DREAM HOUSE

Neither the air conditioner nor the heater in her car worked anymore, but it wasn't a terribly hot day. And although no one could call highway air fresh, it was getting fresher by the minute as they left the city, then its suburbs, for the very edge of big-box civilization just forty minutes from where Mr. Lange had interviewed Sam for the nanny job.

Forty minutes from home to nowhere, where trees instead of buildings blocked the sky.

Sam followed behind the black Lexus in her ancient cream-colored Maxima, which Nissan didn't even make anymore, and certainly not with combination lock pads on their doors. The Lexus in front of her was older, too, but not *as* old. Monstrous as a Cadillac and shiny as polished patent leather boots, it put her inheritance-twice-removed car to shame, as though she were a coffin dragged behind a hearse.

What possessions weren't in the back seat or trunk had been moved to a storage facility. She'd given notice at the office and the gas station. Guilt and anxiety fluttered like a wrung, tattered flag as wind buffeted through the car, unsettling wisps of black hair that couldn't be held by rubber band or comb.

She'd given her girlfriend the address, but neither of them had ever been much for calling or texting, and forty minutes away was both close and too far.

"It's just four weeks staying overnight," Sam had said. *"After that, I can come home nights and weekends."*

Lila hadn't looked up from her ramen, but she'd paused the show they'd been watching when she'd heard the words 'nanny,' 'gone,' and 'month' in the same sentence. Lila had frowned—her clown frown, Sam called it, a cartoonish downturned curve—and attempted to sink back into her hoodie like a forgotten body. *"That's still a long time, Sam."*

"It's like a month-long business trip. And we could use the time apart, couldn't we?"

Air and heat didn't work, but the tape deck did. Her grandmother had favored the Rolling Stones, The Who, The Doors, but she'd owned and passed on an eclectic cassette collection. Sam reached into the tape box and picked one at random to replace the last. Rewind. Play.

The Commodores. "Brick House."

Sam could dig it.

Asking whether she and Lila needed a break had been commentary enough on their relationship, even if Lila hadn't wanted to admit anything was wrong.

Maybe two could live as cheaply as one, but two jobs times two women equaled stressed the four-fucks out—not that there was a lot of fucking going on, between their respective hoodies, strewn coffee mugs, and overflowing trash bins. In such a small apartment, it was amazing how they'd managed to grow apart like exhausted spider plants.

The flier in the café situated between Sam's first and second jobs had seemed too good to be true. Five thousand dollars a month to be a nanny for just one child? An extra two the first month because the single father had to go out of town?

Sam knew as well as anyone that if something seemed too good to be true, it probably was. But bills were piling up, along with everything else. Although she and Lila were meeting financial obligations, their checking accounts remained unsettlingly close to zero no matter what they did, and one or both of their cars was going to break down again any day now. Sam was surprised her grandmother's car hadn't just decided to trundle to the side of a road and collapse into parts.

Their apartment was even older than Sam's car. Every time their schedules overlapped enough for them to talk about moving out, Lila would get sick again, and they'd have to decide between Dr. Google and Urgent Care. Then Sam's car would make another funny sound she had to decide whether or not to ignore. Sam's sisters would have another crisis. Lila's previous significant other would test the boundaries of the restraining order or file another small claims suit against her. They'd tell themselves they didn't smell mildew or mold and light another cheap scented candle to make themselves seem fancy.

Seven thousand dollars a month for one job? Seven thousand dollars a month and five thousand every month after? Just to take care of one little girl, when Sam had basically raised her three younger sisters, because her mother sure as hell wasn't going to do it and her older brother had been too busy playing drums in his garage band that would break big any day now.

One year taking care of a little girl was as much as she made in three years. Two could live as cheaply as one when she was making three times the salary.

Too good to be true, but too good to not at least apply.

Then Mr. Lange had called, with his soft-spoken, Southern-gentleman manner, and set up an interview. Public place, a hundred dollars just for her time. Throwing money around like that, she'd expected him to show up with gloves and a top hat.

Instead, he'd been relatively normal in shirt sleeves and jeans, the kind of effortless but somehow stiff casual Sam associated with politicians. When she'd looked him up later, turned out he'd been mayor of the city of Melissa for two terms, then served in the Texas Senate as well, at least when he hadn't been serving as a county judge. None of that should have been enough to retire from public life at forty-five years old fifteen years ago, but from his demeanor, Sam thought he must have come from American Old Money. In Texas, that meant either oil or cattle or both. He wasn't taking her out to oil or cattle country, so it was difficult to say which, if either.

New Money or Old Money, oil money or cattle money or My Little Pony money, it all spent the same. He'd handed her a crisp one-hundred-dollar bill just to sit down with him at the same coffee shop where she'd found the flier. He'd had a coffee, black. She'd had a chai latte. He'd paid.

"If you don't mind my saying, Mr. Lange, you must have gotten five hundred applicants in a week from your job listing. A hundred dollars for each interview, plus coffee, has to add up, even if you only take yours black."

Mr. Lange had set his coffee down and offered her an attractive smile. He'd had work done on his face, but probably just peels, perhaps some Botox. The lines he'd tried to resist seemed mostly sad. It was easier to ask him about the money than why he didn't have a wife.

"Annie has specific needs. They're sometimes too much for people, even experienced nurses. She's a sweet girl, but because

she's older, she's a handful, and when she does lash out, sometimes people get hurt. She doesn't do any of this maliciously, understand. I'm certain if I can find the right fit—someone patient, mature, compassionate—things will get much easier for Annie. And for me, if you'll allow the self-indulgence. It's been hard for both of us for a long time."

He was no less soft-spoken in person, struggling through invisible swamps of grief and weariness. Sam had reached across the table and covered Mr. Lange's hand with hers.

He'd stared at it as though he barely recognized the sight or sensation.

Sam had worried she'd miscalculated and sent the wrong signal, but he'd covered her hand with a gentle pat in gratitude before relieving the awkwardness by taking another sip of coffee.

"Well, if you'd like to know my qualifications…"
"Please."

Besides taking care of her sisters every time her mother had decided to pop out a new one and go on with her life, she'd worked childcare for ten years after high school because they'd offered free care for workers. Once her last sister had made it into public school, Sam had worked as a substitute teacher while getting her teaching certificate. Then she'd been a middle school teacher for three years before her sisters had started needing her again. She'd moved to first and third shifts at nursing homes.

It was around this time that Sam had discovered she didn't particularly like taking care of other people. She was just good at it because she'd had to for so long.

So she'd gone to a temp agency and gotten a boring office job, with gas-station third shifts to supplement the shortfall. That boring office job, while not quite as soul-sucking as care, hadn't kept up with the rising rents. Then she'd been laid off during the pandemic and had to wait for the temp agency to find her a new job—entry level once again. If her apartment could have passed a safety and health inspection, she might have bitten the bullet and opened up in-home daycare, but between cockroaches, mice, and the weird shocks they got on the water fixtures, it didn't seem like the best idea.

But this... She only needed to take care of *one person*. Even if she had to wipe that sweet little girl's ass, it was just one person's ass, not twelve or twenty-five. Away from home, with spotty cell service, surrounded by actual native trees, and if she heard rushing water, it would be from a creek instead of Dallas traffic. Room and board provided.

Seven thousand dollars? She'd do it for two.

Instead of wallet student photographs or phone pictures, Mr. Lange had taken out old-fashioned Polaroids arranged in a special little photo album. One of the first photos was his daughter at First Communion with a woman who Sam assumed was his wife. She had big hair that seemed dated to Sam, but Texas women still sometimes teased their blonde closer to God, and clothes couldn't always narrow down era.

In all the pictures, Annie was dressed like a porcelain doll: pristine white Mary Janes, ribbon round her waist, ribbon throttling her pigtails, rosy cheeks, big smile, sometimes gap-toothed. When Annie was seven, she wept at a funeral. Her mother never appeared in the Polaroids again.

Annie continued wearing the most perfect and adorable outfits until she was ten, when she started wearing jeans and t-shirts. Then, what seemed like a few years later, she transitioned back into dresses, young rather than modern, and not quite the same on an older body, though not tight or sexualized. A little odd, but she seemed happier in the dresses than the jeans.

"An old and young soul. And it's just the two of us in that big house. We have some staff, but we don't interact with them much. She mostly just likes playing with her dolls. Did you ever play with dolls when you were younger?"

"I played with my sisters," Sam had replied. *"I never really just played for myself. But I still have this old dollhouse my grandparents made for me when I was my mom's only daughter. It has a place of honor in my bedroom. No dolls inside, but I decorate it for Halloween and Christmas."*

Mr. Lange had smiled and seemed less sad. *"Annie calls our house the Dream House. I think you'd like it."*

At the end of the interview, Mr. Lange had told her she was a strong contender for the position. He would contact her by the end of the week either way.

Sam had assumed he'd meant it like any other hiring manager and she'd never hear from him again. But that weekend, he'd called to hire her, and when she'd asked for an advance on the first week, he'd been most agreeable, which solved rent for Lila while Sam was gone.

Sam brought one suitcase of clothes and one suitcase of other possessions, like her laptop and her favorite books, although Mr. Lange had told her that their house had a library.

When she imagined the Dream House—with its two little dolls drowning in too many echoes—she thought of the *Beauty and the Beast* castle, with its enviable library that dwarfed cathedrals. She doubted even a man of Mr. Lange's wealth had a library like that, but whatever he had would still be more library than anyone else she knew.

Sam continued behind him down the county road. She was completely dependent on following him, because although he'd given her the address, he'd said it was difficult to find if one didn't already know where it was.

"The online directions are confusing and actually take you to the mailbox bank, not the house. That's further in."

At this point, she'd take a sketchy house in the woods if it meant she didn't have to think about groceries, schedules, double shifts, or guilt trips. She'd informed her oldest sister that she would be completely unavailable for the next month, so any pressing crises would have to wait until she was no longer functioning as sole surrogate parent for her charge. Mr. Lange was paying her more than enough for her full attention.

After Mr. Lange returned from work, she could go home during her own time and reopen some avenues of communication with her family. On the other hand, Mr. Lange had said that her room would be her room for as long as she was employed, so if she'd rather remain a live-in nanny, they would be happy to host her.

Apparently, there were enough rooms in the house to warrant wings, and she would be living in a completely separate wing from Annie's bedroom as well as from where Mr. Lange slept. Honestly, based on the image Sam had of the house by now, she wondered if she should have negotiated for a higher salary. It wasn't like Mr. Lange had denied her anything she'd asked for so far—except for one thing.

"Do you have a boyfriend?" he'd asked. *"A best friend with whom you spend your days and nights? Family that demands much of your time?"*

"My family is sometimes demanding. I've been working on boundaries. I live with my girlfriend."

Sam hadn't elaborated, but she also hadn't hesitated. Mr. Lange's reaction had been no reaction at all, neither overly polite, overly solicitous, nor overly permissive.

"I only ask because I would rather you not have any raucous parties or…"

"Conjugal visits?"

"Annie's sensitive. She'll be completely dependent on you. She can't just be set aside and ignored. That's why I'm interested in employing an older nanny. I'm not forbidding contact with the outside world by any means…"

"But you don't want me throwing a wild kegger in your nice house. I assure you, Mr. Lange, I have no interest in hosting any parties or honeymoon weekends. My girlfriend has two jobs, too. She'll probably just be glad I'm not stealing the covers or hitting the snooze button when she's trying to sleep."

Lila had mostly watched in silence as Sam had packed up her things and moved them out of the apartment.

Mr. Lange turned quite abruptly into a wooded area, an asphalt road Sam might not have noticed if she hadn't been following him. Even her phone's GPS was unclear on where the turn was. It told her it was a few hundred feet ahead.

The street name was too far back from the two-lane county road, or maybe the forest had just encroached and no one had seen the need for an arborist to tell them where they lived.

She followed Mr. Lange.

A mile in, there was a row of locked mailboxes—eight in all—and a package chest. The GPS told her she'd arrived, but there was only one house within view, and only in glimpses between the thick trees: mid-century modern lines, vaguely Frank Lloyd Wright-esque. Beneath the canopy, late afternoon turned to mid-evening, and the road was turning on her, so she couldn't peer too closely if she wanted to not be dead in a ditch.

Disquiet twinged in her gut again as they drove deeper and deeper into the woods. They took the curve, then turned to the right, then to the left. There were no markers on most of these roads, only *No Trespassing Violators Will Be Shot* signs, somehow discordant against the large compounds she could barely see through the trees. Rich people seeking solitude in the woods sometimes meant armories instead of just gun cabinets.

Sam switched on her headlights to make sure Mr. Lange's black Lexus didn't leave her lost between curves.

Finally, the road reached its end at a stone wall and large iron gate, which Sam had thought only existed in storybooks and European estates. The elaborate, old-fashioned doors swung open to allow Mr. Lange and Sam to drive through and clanged when they closed behind.

The asphalt transitioned into gravel to a roundabout around a working fountain. The trees here had been thinned out but not cleared entirely. Sam's nose stung with mild allergy against the pine and cedar. Still so much fresher than exhaust.

The undergrowth was slowed by tree cover and probably a groundskeeper or two, less work in general than maintaining a lawn. A garden grew next to the greenhouse, and there could have been a yard behind the house, which sprawled so much through her vision that she couldn't see anything beyond it.

Most fancy dollhouses were of three types: Craftsman, Victorian, or castle. This one tended toward Tudor-style castle in variegated grayish brown brick, with turrets that made Sam's heart happier than it had been in months, possibly years. It certainly wasn't historically accurate, and the accents of stone and wood paneling were too clean for the house to be old, but it screamed 'fairy tale come to life.'

She couldn't believe she was getting paid to work in a place like this.

Sam stepped out of her car with her purse and opened the back door to pull out her two suitcases. Her life, in a crumbling vehicle, made small and shabby by this towering place. She'd felt smart in a simple white t-shirt and high-waisted tan trousers from her capsule wardrobe, but the castle rendered her casual, a city bumpkin in need of gauntlets. Even Mr. Lange appeared more at home in sweater and slacks, wouldn't be out of place lounging in some study with a pipe and a brandy.

He took one of her suitcases. The wheels struggled on the gravel, and both of them grunted getting them to the top of the stairs to the front door, but the poured concrete on the vast front porch was kinder.

"I'll get you one of these gate controls and a set of keys," Mr. Lange said as he fumbled in his pocket. "We keep other full-time workers on the estate, too. The groundskeepers stay in a converted barn. The cooks stay in the servants' wing next to the garden. Housekeeping does regular rounds to keep dust at bay in our more active rooms, but if you or Annie make a mess, the linen closet outside the kitchen has cleaning supplies. By and large, the staff aren't supposed to interact with Annie, and vice versa. Meals are regimented for Annie's sake—breakfast at 9:00, lunch at noon, dinner at 7:00. Kitchen staff serve in the dining room, and groceries are delivered every week, so you won't need to leave for that, although you can make requests."

Mr. Lange continued chattering as he opened the door and led them inside. Sam tried to listen, but she was quickly overwhelmed by the interior of the house.

The design inside was almost brutalist in density but avoided ugliness with natural finishings—decorative and polished stone instead of concrete, dark wooden paneling on the walls to warm the cold marble. A staircase out of a Cinderella dream split the grand foyer, arising from a medallion inlaid with wood and other stone in an elaborate motif. If the stone felt like Versailles, the walls felt medieval, with portraits and paintings of all kinds between panel frames like tapestries—from American primitive creepy little girls and their cats to what might have been a real Degas.

"Just one more flight of stairs to reach where you're going to stay. We don't use much of the upstairs rooms, so the housekeeper opened one for you in the east wing. West wing is primarily for staff, south wing is the master suite. The solarium is Annie's studio and where she sleeps. She likes all the windows and watching the sunset, and it's still dim there in the morning. Service stairs in the east wing can get you to her room faster if she calls out in the night. Here we are."

Mr. Lange opened the door to her bedroom.

Awash in sky and royal blues, it looked like it was made of Lambeth cake. Curtained windows overlooked the shady grounds at the front of the house. She'd get more morning sun than Annie, but there were so many windows in the main house, brightening what should have been an oppressive interior, that it didn't matter whether she preferred sunrise or sunset.

Hers was the bedroom of a grown-up princess; Sam could only imagine how much more opulent the master suite and Annie's bedroom were, if this was how they furnished for a nanny.

Sam took a picture of her room with her phone, considered sending it to Lila, then decided otherwise. She'd wait until she settled in with Annie's routines and with her own, alone. Determine whether she missed Lila. Let her decide if she missed Sam, too.

They'd been little more than roommates over the last six months. Not even friends, really. Just two women who shared the same bed because it was a one-bedroom apartment. Stayed together to split increasingly expensive expenses. It wasn't Lesbian Bed Death that rang a death knell for their relationship. They just couldn't address their own needs enough to have time for each other's. Both would rather starve than move back in with their parents, but maybe they just had to find different roommates. Put romance and sex on the backburner until they could finally afford it.

How did people do it? How did they live in all the apartments and townhouses and small houses and big houses and McMansions she drove past every day? What were they doing that they could pay the rent or mortgage, and how could Sam get that job? She didn't need a castle. A two-room apartment would be bliss.

But a castle wasn't all that bad.

She and Mr. Lange rolled her suitcases into her new room.

"You'll have time to unpack this evening after Annie goes to bed," Mr. Lange said. "Closet over there, bathroom next door. You'll be the only one using it. Would you like to meet Annie now?"

Sam left her purse on the bed. She didn't like using phones around clients, young or old.

Back down the massive staircase. She'd have to remember not to run up or down while wearing socks. All it would take was one slip and she'd crack her own skull in a house Emergency Services might not know how to find.

"If anything goes wrong, what do we do?" Sam asked. "I could probably explain to paramedics how to get here, but what if I'm the one who gets hurt?"

"There's a laminated list of numbers on your nightstand. Annie knows how to direct people to the house, too, and knows 9-1-1. We prefer not to take Annie to hospitals, though. The outside world is…a bit much for her. We have an on-call surgeon who knows about Annie's issues. Just dial that number on the sheet for anything short of imminent death. The doctor is primarily cardiothoracic, but she has a lot of experience in emergency surgery and neurosurgery. She can help Annie with everything, even good old down-home country doctor things. While I'm gone, you should avail yourself of the doctor's skills for any of your needs, as well."

There Sam had been a few years ago, feeding Lila chicken noodle between shifts while they'd wondered if she could afford to keep living, and her new charge had a surgeon for the sniffles. The house was pretty enough that Sam could swallow the bile behind teeth in dire need of a dental pick, but at least now she had the self-same surgeon for her own ills.

All for taking care of one little girl.

Mr. Lange went through the foyer and the empty hall behind it—which could have been a gymnasium if not for the massive unused fireplace at one end and the chandeliers hanging over it like massive death traps made for a Paris opera house's vengeful phantom. All the glittering crystal made Sam giddy again, shivering off resentment like dust.

From the open hall, he led her into the south wing of the house. They walked through a dining room, which had a serving hatch—closed—and a door that led to the kitchen, also closed. The dining table could seat two dozen people easily, three dozen if they squeezed. There were two crystal and china cabinets. On the other side of the dining room was a library, with comfortable furniture, a fireplace that looked like it was actually used in the winter, and built-in bookshelves so high that there were also rolling ladders to reach the top shelves.

Usually, when people like this had libraries, they used filler books, even hollow staging props. What surprised and ultimately delighted Sam was that these shelves were filled with the kinds of books people actually read, a sea of spines in all different sizes, shapes, and shades, modern and brilliant against the dark wood. In fact, based on the palette, whole sections were devoted to old and new romance novels, with possibly the entire oeuvre of staples such as Johanna Lindsey, Nora Roberts, and Danielle Steel.

Rather than wanting to appear well read, this sea of literature both pretentious and profoundly unserious suggested that they did, in fact, read widely and well. She couldn't wait to discover what offerings the library had for her—during her own time, of course.

The books distracted her first, then the giant picture windows flooding afternoon light into the room. They framed a palatial porch, which boasted enough outdoor furniture to constitute another room, and a backyard much more domesticated than the front. Surrounded by the same forest, yes, but almost everything from the porch to the tree line was aggressively landscaped, with flowers, non-native trees, a hedge maze, and not a pine needle to be found, the only cedar bark part of the mulch. There was a pool, too, sparkling and clear and as tended as the rest of the tamed property. If not for the extravagance of flowers and what appeared to be a few fig and peach trees, it could have been the backyard of a Beverly Hills douchebag rather than a fairy-tale castle of more modern sensibilities.

The library, though, was comfortable, the curtains cozily heavy like weighted blankets, and in the middle of the living room was a girl on her knees at the coffee table, with every crayon color known to God and man in front of her as she worked on five different coloring books. In three of them, she colored within the lines according to a more conventional palette. In the other two, she colored outside the lines or with a combination of colors neither God nor man had ever intended with the invention of the crayon.

She wore a blue dress. A wide ribbon wrapped around her waist and tied in a bow behind her. Two thinner ribbons wrapped around her pigtails. She wore pearls and black Mary Janes with a clunky little girl heel.

Her brown hair was streaked with isolated grays.

The little girl was not a little girl.

Chapter 2: WITH A CURL

Annie Lange was not a child. She wasn't even fifteen, as the era-indeterminate Polaroids had led Sam to believe.

Annie might have even been older than Sam.

When Annie looked up from her coloring, her expression shifted from furrowed concentration to such emphatic excitement that, for a moment, she really did look like a beautiful young teenage girl with a continued fondness for dress-up. But the little-girl affect jarred harshly with her grown-up features, and Sam would hardly call her young anymore—at least by Sam's standards of young, which did not equal her own age. Sam was too tired to be young.

Annie wasn't tired at all. She jumped to her feet as though nothing creaked her joints, as though she had no trouble sleeping at night, lollipops didn't go straight to her hips or thighs, and she wasn't reaching the end of her fertile years— not that Sam had enough energy for a baby, either.

"Is this Miss Samantha? Oh, Miss Samantha, nice to meet you. My name is Annie Lange, I'm eleven years old, and I'm so excited for you to be here." Annie curtsied instead of offering her hand. The curls of her pigtails and bangs bounced from her enthusiasm.

It was almost caricature, except her smile—despite showing an alarming number of teeth—was genuine all the way up to her eyes. Sam had never seen such joy on a person's features, adult or child. The closest equivalent might have been a juvenile golden retriever.

"Very good manners, Annie." Mr. Lange wrapped an arm around her shoulders to hug her close and kissed her forehead through her bangs.

"Hello, Annie." Sam held out her hand to shake, because she didn't know how to curtsy without a skirt. Annie gamely shook with two firm pumps, ever so serious. "It's good to finally meet you, too. You can actually call me Sam. Only my Nana calls me Samantha."

"I was hoping for a Samantha, like the American Girl doll. Samantha's such a pretty name, and so long," Annie said, her frown not enough to furrow her forehead like her concentration had. "But I guess I can call you Sam. Otherwise, maybe you'd call me something other than Annie. Like Andrea." She stuck out her tongue.

Mr. Lange laughed, though it seemed strained. "Annie, would you like to have dinner with us before I leave?"

"Oh, do you have to go?" Annie wrapped both her arms around his middle and crushed him, her face smushed flat against his chest.

Were she an adult with a full face of makeup, her father might have had to change his shirt, but although Annie's expressions were big, she was startlingly fresh-faced. Both Sam and Lila were pretty lax with their own makeup, but hoodies comprised about eighty percent of their home wardrobes. Annie was immaculate.

She was also freckled by genetics and generous sun time, but despite her labile emotions, her face was smoother than one might expect from someone her age. That didn't, however, make her look younger. If anything, it was harder to ignore that Annie was a fresh-faced *woman.*

There were all kinds of developmental delays and reasons for age regression. Mr. Lange hadn't given a clear diagnosis—but Sam was a caregiver, not a doctor or psychologist. It didn't matter why Annie was the way she was. That was between Mr. Lange and his daughter's doctor.

Mr. Lange hadn't hired her to fix his daughter, just to help take care of her in the safety and security of their home. If that meant treating a thirty-five-year-old (or however old she was) like an eleven-year-old acting like an eight-year-old, then for seven thousand dollars the first month, Sam could absolutely play hide-and-seek, color in coloring books, fingerpaint, read, and teach basic elementary schoolwork to another adult.

That actually sounded idyllic. Even the Common Core math.

"I'm afraid so, pumpkin. But you'll have a wonderful time with Miss Sam. You'll be able to show her the Dream House and tell her all its secrets. You'll go on walks and pick flowers and play with your dolls. I know you like sharing and playing with your dolls."

Mr. Lange led Annie and Sam into the dining room. Surrounded by the higher ceilings and grossly extravagant finishings once more, Sam felt rude, somehow, with sneakers on.

This time, the serving hatch was closed but the door was open, because the chef went in and out the door with plates of roasted chicken thighs, freshly mashed potatoes, and roasted broccoli. For Mr. Lange and Sam, wine glasses had been set out next to their water. Annie had a small glass of white milk and another of chocolate milk.

"Annie doesn't like regular milk much, but she has a rule." Mr. Lange spoke to Annie the same way he would speak to a child—a little slower and higher in register than the way he spoke to Sam. "She has to drink the white milk to grow big and strong, and she can have chocolate milk to help swallow it down. If she doesn't finish her regular milk, her chocolate milk will have to suffice for her dessert. But Annie likes dessert, don't you, sweetheart?"

"I love dessert. I especially like ice cream sundaes with fudge sauce or Neapolitan ice cream with strawberry sauce. Are we having ice cream tonight, Daddy?" Annie stuck her straw into the white milk and drank half of it in several large swallows, then switched the straw over to the chocolate, where she sipped more leisurely.

"What day is it, Annie?" he asked.

"Wednesday, Daddy."

"And what dessert do you have on Wednesdays?"

"Chocolate pudding with whipped cream."

"That's right. You like chocolate pudding, too."

"I sure do!"

"Eat your veggies, Annie."

"Yes, Daddy. What did you do before here, Miss Sam?" Annie asked as she filled her mouth with broccoli. She spoke with her mouth full but chewed with her mouth closed, grimacing against the bitterness of the broccoli. "Did you take care of another girl?"

"I worked in an office putting together and checking spreadsheets. Do you know what a spreadsheet is?" Sam asked between bites of chicken.

"I don't like the computer if it doesn't have games, but I know what spreadsheets are. They're like lists you make up."

"That's right. Checking the lists against other lists to make sure that the first and second lists are aligned. And sometimes at night I worked at a gas station."

"Did you pump the gas for people?"

Sam smiled. "No. I stayed behind the counter."

"And you worked at night? Weren't you scared of the dark?"

"Sometimes it was a little dangerous, but it was mostly just boring. Not a lot of people are getting gas at three in the morning, when most good girls are in bed." She added that last part to taste how it felt to treat Annie like a child. Still felt like a lie to her, but maybe she'd get used to it. She'd gotten used to a lot in each of her jobs.

Don't be a hero. That's what the gas station manager had impressed upon her from the beginning. She'd spent most of her time replenishing inventory when it was quiet, but as soon as someone showed up on the security screens, she got behind the bullet-resistant glass. Not bulletproof, just resistant.

The only time she'd ever really been scared was when a guy had come in smelling of gin but hyped up on something else. He'd damn near lost a hand trying to climb in through the small transaction opening. He'd bled all over the counter and spat at her, slashing at her with his knife. The police hadn't come fast enough after she'd pressed the silent alarm, so she'd just given him money and told him to leave, and he had. The police had caught him afterward. Her manager had said she'd done the right thing. She'd gone for an STD test after and surrounded herself with the scent of Lysol until the results had come back clean.

The rest of the people who'd tried to rob the store were a few eggs short of a brain pan, because they just couldn't get it through their heads that her gas station wasn't one they could rob as easily. Off-brand was more jealous with its profit margin than big-name stations. But at least she'd only had to clean one bathroom, even if it had sometimes been befouled by guests who hadn't had the decency to look ashamed as they'd left. Sam had often considered just lighting a match, grabbing a Hostess cupcake package, and watching the station burn. She'd considered the same thing when one of those big wolf spiders had decided to come creeping in, with its jerky legs and furry butt and babies on its back.

This place probably had spiders and mice and rats and all the things that big houses with lots of humans encouraged, but everything was so spotless, it felt like mice wouldn't dare shit on its nice floors.

As long as there were no bedbugs.

"Are you scared of the dark?" Annie asked.

"I like the dark. It's peaceful. Are you afraid of the dark, Annie?" Sam asked. "Do you sleep with a lamp on at night, or…"

"I like sleeping with a lamp so I can look at my things and feel happy, but I like the dark, too. Dark is when I close my eyes. Dark is when I dream about what I'm going to do in the day, and then I get to do it. I'll dream of you tonight, Miss Sam."

"Well, maybe I'll dream of you, too." Sam continued with her meal while Mr. Lange watched her and Annie interact.

Sam had no doubt that if Mr. Lange thought Annie didn't want her here, he would kick her out at a moment's notice. She'd at least be able to keep the thousand-dollar advance, which could cushion Sam's knees for begging her old jobs to take her back before they had to train someone else to replace her.

But although Mr. Lange seemed weary, drained of half his color and slowly working on the other half, he didn't interrupt.

Sam sipped her wine. She was uncomfortable that Mr. Lange hadn't told her Annie was older. She was also uncomfortable with how far out they were, how winding the roads. It seemed like there was no other place in the world anymore but the Dream House: beautiful, expensive, and empty as her dollhouse now sitting in dark storage because she hadn't wanted to explain to a child that it was for looking at, not touching. She especially didn't want to explain that to a delayed or regressed thirty-year-old.

She'd worked with developmentally delayed and other neurodiverse kids before. They usually had additional behaviors and tendencies, none of which Annie exhibited.

Sam had also worked with elderly clients with dementia. There was childlike fear in their regression. Annie was a bundle of kinetic energy waiting to be released, and she had no fear—perhaps because this was her house, her routines, her rules, with none of the overwhelming interference of noisy city life or nosy rural life.

For better or worse, her skin was good, her hair was better, the tailoring was on point, and she seemed like a happy adult child. So Mr. Lange must have been doing something right.

"Did your dad tell you I have a dollhouse, too?" Sam asked. "It's a beautiful Victorian painted like a gingerbread house."

"I make gingerbread houses at Christmastime. I eat all the icing and get sick, but I put Red Hots on for the red lights anyway," Annie said. "Can I play with it?"

"I didn't bring it with me, but I'll show you a picture later. Do you have a dollhouse?"

"I have all the dollhouses. And all the dolls. Can I show her, Daddy? Can I show her?"

"After dessert, sweetheart. You'll have all the time in the world to play with Miss Sam."

"Do you have any favorite kinds of dolls, Annie?" Sam asked. "I didn't play much with dolls when I was your age, but I liked Polly Pocket, Littlest Pet Shop, and My Little Pony figurines. They still make them now, but they're different than they used to be."

"I've been collecting dolls since I was five." She held up her hand to show all five fingers and her palm, which had marker on it in the shape of a heart broken by a black lightning bolt. "I have Polly Pocket, Littlest Pet Shop, and My Little Pony, too. I have Barbie and American Girl and Bratz and Monster High and antique dolls and dolls that look like antique dolls and Beanie Babies and Beanie Boos and Trolls and a zoo of stuffed animals. I play games and I color in my coloring books and I paint and I learn, but mostly I play with my dolls. I love my dolls and my dollhouses and my Dream House. I can't wait to play with you, Miss Sam."

"I can't wait to play with you, either." Sam was kind of looking forward to seeing how extravagant a rich little princess's playroom could be. She knew how many Polly Pockets she'd wanted as a child, and she'd loved to rearrange her My Little Pony displays every month or so and just stare up at them after she'd finished playing with them. She hadn't had much in her little closet of a room, but what she'd had, she'd admired.

"Annie, would you like to have your dessert in here or the library?" Mr. Lange said.

"The library. May I be excused, Daddy?"

"Of course. Thank you for drinking all your regular milk and eating all your vegetables. Miss Sam will bring you your pudding."

"I'm going to draw Miss Sam a picture." Annie bounded out of the room.

"Mr. Lange…" Sam began.

"I'll need to leave soon." Mr. Lange brought all three plates to the serving hatch, lifting the door only enough to push them into the kitchen. "My flight is in three hours, and even with pre-check, DFW is still a good hour and a half away."

"You're leaving tonight?" Sam had assumed he would leave in the morning at the earliest and that they'd have the rest of the evening to discuss how to properly care for his daughter. Given the revelation for which she'd had no warning, Sam had questions. "Mr. Lange, you haven't given me any kind of schedule or list of allergies or curriculum. If it's so important that she remain on a routine, I should know what that routine is."

"Oh, Annie knows her routine. She'll let you know what it is."

"Sir, with all due respect, she'll tell me she doesn't have to eat the kale and that her bedtime on Fridays is midnight and that she has chocolate cake for breakfast."

From the other side of the serving hatch, Mr. Lange pulled out charmingly old-fashioned ice cream bowls full of chocolate pudding topped with whipped cream and chocolate sprinkles and shavings. "My Annie knows what's allowed and what she needs, even when she doesn't want it. She wakes up at 8:30 for breakfast at 9:00, independent studies until noon for lunch, then playtime inside or outside until dinner at 7:00, then playtime inside or outside until 9:00, when she goes to bed. At that time, she may take a bath or shower, or she may take one earlier in the day. She won't need you for that unless she wants you to read to her. She'll sometimes want you to read to her in bed, too. And she doesn't have any curriculum. She's taken elementary and middle school courses several times over and passed them without struggle. Sometimes she decides to revisit them. Otherwise, she just pillages the library, which has any matter of subjects for her to peruse. I didn't hire you to be her governess, Sam. I hired you to be her nanny—to watch over her, take care of her, and make sure she's happy. Her happiness means more to me than anything in the world."

He set the pudding down on the long empty table and took both of her hands in his, warm and a little clammy to accompany his pale complexion. "Annie isn't normal, I know, but she's all that's left of her mother, and if I spoil her, it's only to see that smile. She looks so much like my wife, except she's still a child in her heart, and she has been for a long time. But she takes care of her things and follows her rules, and she's happy. Can you help me, Sam? Can you keep her happy for me?"

"Happy means a lot of things, Mr. Lange," Sam said. "But whether she's an adult or a child, I can take care of her. I just would have preferred a little more transparency and a lot more information about her needs before you left. Like, a binder or something. I had no idea you were leaving so soon."

"Fair enough. Well, you have the doctor's number and mine on the sheet in your bedroom. I'm not always reachable, but I regularly check my phone. If you have any questions or concerns about Annie's habits, I'll be able to provide you an answer. The rest, Annie should be able to provide you herself. I'm sure you'll be fast friends, especially with your experience taking care of all kinds of people. That's what I liked about you, Sam. Over all the others, I thought you'd meet Annie and wouldn't flinch."

"I'll take care of her, Mr. Lange. I don't see any reason why that would change. I just don't want any more surprises."

He made a face she thought was supposed to be a smile. The man did not look well enough to eat pudding, but he handed hers and Annie's to her and carried his into the library. He must have been really anxious she would walk out just when he needed to leave. The Dream House suggested he was doing more than all right for himself. That didn't mean the burden of nurturer and breadwinner didn't weigh on a person when all he could offer his unique daughter was a house rather than a foundation.

In the library, Annie was drawing a picture of one of the turreted towers at the front of the house, with Sam in one of the windows. In the image, her hair was long instead of practical shoulder-length and hung in a braid down to the ground. The drawing was more sophisticated than the average elementary-school artist, with details like the slats of the roof, each individual stone of the tower, and the fact that the figure was recognizably Sam and not Annie, though they were both dark-haired.

"Tell me the story of your drawing," Sam said as she handed Annie her pudding.

Annie took the bowl in both hands, cradling it like a baby bird down to the coffee table. Then she plopped her big spoon into the custard and gathered a large spoonful of pudding, cream, and sprinkles. It was an ambitious bite, but she'd had many years to practice, so Sam didn't tell her to take smaller bites. After the first few, Annie started taking smaller bites on her own.

"You're trapped in the castle," Annie said between swallows. "You're Rapunzel and let down your hair. You have such pretty hair. Short and shiny and thick. Imagine if it were long and you let it down for someone to save you."

"But no one's there," Sam said.

"No, there's not. Maybe tomorrow."

Annie held out the drawing again for Sam to take. Once Sam had accepted it, Annie went back to her pudding and found another coloring book, with a collection of mandala outlines. Annie decided to stay in the lines here, entranced by how her repeated choices emerged into something floral, although her colors clashed in jarring ways Sam couldn't put her finger on. Like camo in a sanctuary.

Sam supposed that if she'd been drawing in coloring books for several decades, she'd shake up the color palette now and then, too.

As soon as all three of them had finished their pudding, Mr. Lange stacked the bowls for easy transport and stood. "Well, sweetheart, it's time for me to go."

Annie looked up from her work, all big swimming eyes. "No. Don't go, Daddy. Stay. Don't you want to play with me? Don't you want to play with me and Miss Sam?"

"I really can't delay any longer, and I know you'll enjoy playing with Sam far more than you do with me."

Annie clambered up from the floor and attacked her father with a bear hug around his waist. "Why do you always leave me, Daddy?"

Mr. Lange patted her back and her hair, but he looked out the window at nothing, as though seeing where he needed to be rather than where he was. "I know, I know. But I go on these trips so you can keep living in the Dream House and so I can find good people for you like Miss Sam."

"But you're gone for so long, and I miss you so much."

"That's why Miss Sam is here," Mr. Lange said gently, easing from her latch. "I'll come back before you know it, but right now, Annie, I have to go."

For a moment, it seemed like Annie wouldn't let go. Then she frowned and loosened her hold, looking for all the world like she was going to either cry or throw a fit. Two large tears slipped down her face, but she steadied her trembling chin with resolve and nodded.

"Give me a kiss." Mr. Lange met Annie for a firm father-daughter kiss. Then he kissed her forehead. "Now, why don't you show Miss Sam your room?"

"Love you, Daddy."

"I love you, too, sweetheart."

He took the pudding bowls out of the room, presumably to slip them back under the serving hatch, then passed through the library again for the hallway at the other side of the room, which would lead to the master suite. He nodded to Sam as he crossed. Sam nodded back, indicating that they'd be fine.

Annie watched him until he was out of sight. Then she wiped her eyes and held her slightly wet hand out to Sam. "Can I show you my room, Miss Sam?"

"Sure, Annie." Sam let Annie lead her out of the library and through the empty hall.

In the dimmer light, the interior of the Dream House seemed all the emptier—a little haunted.

Sam didn't believe in ghosts, only guilt, and although the house had been built to look old, it was relatively new, like most construction in the area. Every land was a graveyard, stolen by blood or gunpowder, but she personally had yet to see the specter of anything other than eviction.

If Sam had believed her own bedroom fit for a princess, Annie's made it seem intended for a servant girl.

The solarium hoarded as much light as it could from thick glass windows mullioned with metal. They extended from the floor to the top of the wall, then angled in and beamed sunset on more inlaid marble floors, which extended to a series of carpeted stairs up to the bedroom and playroom. A single column in the middle of the room, carved with animals and flowers in a spiral to the top, interrupted the open concept. Between the column, carefully arranged beams, and cathedral arches, the three rooms that comprised Annie's bedroom were the size of a gutted shotgun home on its own.

The solarium section of the room boasted a botanical garden of hanging ferns and vines, waxy leaves following the sun. Air conditioning would have to work extra hard during the long summers, but for now, the room was just cool. Annie flipped some switches on her light plate, which illuminated the chandeliers: one dripping bordello red, one in miniature of the ones in the grand hall, and the third dripping Mardi Gras purple. Some Tiffany-style (or real Tiffany) lamps switched on, too, as did fairy lights draped all over the bedroom, playroom, and over shelves and shelves (and shelves and shelves, with ladders like the library) of toys.

The toys were displayed more how an adult would display them, behind glass panels to prevent excess dust. However, low tables centered on plush rugs all over the room showed the toys she was playing with strewn over in clear imaginative use.

Annie didn't have a kitchen, but she did have what would have been called a wet bar or coffee bar by an adult. There were two mini fridges, one presumably for food, the other clear to display her sodas of choice. Above them were equally colorful and neat baskets and containers of snacks and candies if she got hungry while she played.

A magnificent monstrosity of a four-poster bed, as elaborate as the rest of the house, was tucked in a nook—in storm clouds of purples and blues and gentle rather than aggressive pinks, with yards and yards of curtain mist from the canopy to the floor. Surrounding her bed were poofs and pillows and beanbags for herself and her stuffed animal menagerie: giant lions, tigers, elephants, polar bears, pandas, sloths, snakes. The only thing missing was one of those massive teddy bears three times her size, although she had shelves and shelves on either side of her bed full of stuffed teddies of all shapes and sizes. Her bed itself was home to four or five stuffed animals of choice, but she could toss, turn, roll, and possibly even sleepwalk without stepping off the side of her bed. At least it seemed that way to Sam, who'd shared a full with Lila and who'd been given a queen in her new bedroom.

If Sam wasn't mistaken, there was a place in the ceiling right at the foot of Annie's bed where a TV could slide out. Her father had said Annie needed to go to bed at 9:00, which suggested she didn't necessarily have to *sleep* so much as she couldn't play anymore.

The house was a Dream House; this room was what heaven would be for hundreds of thousands of little girls. Sam's thoroughly neglected inner child wanted to claim a few of the beanbag chairs and just stay and sleep in here. Maybe she could convince the housekeeper to set up a cot under the My Little Pony and Care Bears shelves.

And the dollhouses…

Annie had a Barbie Dreamhouse playset, obviously, but also Victorian, Queen Anne, and Craftsman dollhouses, all under their own protective glass containers. Unlike Sam's, she'd arranged dolls inside them, the miniature furniture meticulously painted, upholstered, and stitched into a cohesive display.

Mr. Lange could have commissioned the dollhouses fully furnished, but Sam suspected they were Annie's darlings, given the elaborate craft section of the room nearest to the solarium windows on the furthest side of the bedroom. Canvases leaned against each other on the walls and the glass, and paints, glues, resins, beads, needles, yarn, and all manner of different options were stored in service to her whim.

From the look of those paintings—especially compared to the crude marker and crayon drawings in the library—Annie was actually an exceptional amateur. She'd had years to practice the skills she wanted to learn rather than what other people would have her develop to become a working member of society.

Must be nice, Sam thought, but without malice. Because it *was* nice. It was nice not to have to fit a square peg into a round hole, which usually meant a certain amount of carving into the meat of the peg.

In addition to dollhouses, Annie also had an entire neighborhood of playhouses in the solarium, as though the ferns and ivy were landscaping. There was a gingerbread house, a two-story castle, a fairy cottage, a haunted house, all custom built for a large child. More dolls and stuffed animals sat inside in little chairs at little tables, suspended in tea parties, games of chess and checkers, or playing with figurines of their own.

Annie settled at one of her low tables to play with Pet Shop figurines, muttering to herself whatever story she'd concocted, but she continued to watch Sam taking in the sheer *amount* of what Annie owned.

Sam could barely conceive of the Dream House as a dwelling, but the building itself was so hulking that it was impossible to deny. Annie's things, however, were small, pervasive, overwhelming. Sam's life had been distilled to two suitcases and a storage unit. She couldn't imagine actually owning this many *things*, more *things* than many toy stores. Staggering, the sheer cost that had gone into everything. Anything and everything for that poor sad man's little girl.

"Do you like it, Miss Sam?" Annie asked as she petted the heads of several little puppies and kittens.

"I think it's magnificent, Annie. I would have loved this room as a kid."

"Do you love it now?"

"I do." Sam knelt on the rug across from her. "What's your favorite thing about your room?"

"It's where my teddies are. They make me feel safe. And all my favorite things are here. I can look at them any time I want. I also like my bed. I like to go to sleep. But I don't go to sleep yet. It's not bedtime."

"Don't worry, I won't make you go to sleep early."

"Daddy's gone, isn't he?"

"If he isn't yet, he will be soon. But while he's gone, you and I are going to get to know each other and have a wonderful time. And I'm sure he'll call you."

Annie turned her attention back to grooming. "He never calls me while he's away."

"I'm sure he wants to. He's just very busy."

"You don't know what he does. You don't know he's busy." Another frown—not the kind that preceded a tantrum or uncomfortable question, but of young anger.

"He loves you," Sam said. "I could tell that much."

"He watches over me, but he doesn't look at me. If I died and Mommy didn't, he would be happier. Then the Dream House could be their honeymoon, the way he planned. The Dream House wasn't finished when Mommy died. She never got to live here. Only I did."

Sam crawled over to sit closer. "Your dad can be sad your mom died and happy you're alive at the same time. You're right. I don't know what he does. I don't know whether he's busy. But I know he loves you, and I know taking care of a house like this ain't cheap."

"You mean taking care of a girl like me," Annie said, still sulky with her pets and not meeting Sam's eyes.

"No, I really mean the house. This big honking house. Kitchen staff, garden staff, housekeeping, doctor on retainer, nanny… It adds up. Living costs money. Do you understand that, Annie?"

"Of course, I do. I'm only allowed to ask for so much every month, and I only get some of the birthday and Christmas presents I ask for. I make some things because they're too hard to ask other people to make, so I'm really good at making things now. But I think Daddy has enough money. He still works because he wants to be away from me." Annie pushed her figurines away from her. "That's okay, I guess. When the cat's away, the mice can play. When Dad looks askance, the dolls can dance. When Dad hides, the toys abide."

"I like your rhyming."

"I like nursery rhymes, Dr. Seuss, Daddy's records. Do you sing lullabies before sleep?" Annie asked.

"I know a few lullabies. I can't promise I'll sing well."

"Can you sing me a lullaby now? I need to tuck my kitties and doggies away."

Sam nodded. If singing "Rock-a-bye Baby" and "Ring Around the Rosie" slightly off-key would make it easier to distract Annie from her father leaving, Sam could sing off-key.

Annie tucked her pet figurines into their spots in the playsets, although she left those out on the table. Then she continued drawing in the coloring book she'd started in the library.

Sam sang all the lullabies she could think of, but when she stopped, Annie looked up with a pout.

On their first night, Sam could indulge a little. So she switched over to other songs she knew and made them into lullabies, like Ed Sheeran's "Thinking Out Loud" and James Blunt's "You're Beautiful"—whatever ballad she could sing from memory like a bad karaoke cover. Sometimes, Annie sang with her as she went from table to table, coloring and playing and putting away what she played with.

Sam's voice scratched like a bad record by the time eight-fifty came around on the big rainbow light clock. Annie yawned and set down her coloring book.

"Can you brush my hair after I get my pjs on, Miss Sam?" Annie asked.

"Sure, I can. Do you need help?"

"Can you come read to me while I get ready? I took my bath before you came."

"Pick a book for me. I can read a chapter, *maybe* two. Then it's time to go to bed, right, Annie?"

The bathroom was right off the craft area. A double vanity, marble everywhere the eye could see, another chandelier over the clawfoot bathtub, a large shower with several settings, a water closet. Another door led into a carpeted closet, which could hold a queen bed and furniture set with room to spare.

Annie brushed her teeth and took her pills from a weekly pill box. Sam couldn't tell what the pills were, but she could probably check Annie's cabinets another day or ask Mr. Lange about it later. Then, after Annie undid her pigtails, Sam brushed her hair.

With her hair down, she looked much more like the adult she was, and although the bathroom had everything else, it didn't provide a single mirror. There were plenty of reflective surfaces in the house, including the marble, but Annie apparently didn't go out of her way to look at herself, either because what she saw didn't mesh with what was in her head or she just didn't want to be reminded.

Sam wouldn't call herself a crone; that didn't mean her eighteen-year-old self would have been okay with everything she saw in mirrors. And her ten-year-old self would have been appalled that she hadn't turned into someone who could be confused for a Disney princess. Not that ten-year-old Sam had had an inkling she wouldn't be looking for a Prince Charming, either.

Annie handed Sam a middle-grade book to read aloud while Annie removed her dress and put on pajamas. Reading the book kept Sam's gaze politely away. Eleven years was old enough to do these things on her own, even undoing the bow and zipper.

Fortunately, there were more cute pajamas in adult sizes than day clothes. Her frilly, pink, Little Bo-Peep nightgown had little doily bows all over it, but Annie seemed happy in it. Sam was more of a tank top and shorts kind of woman—and if it was hot, nix both. The A/C was so good in this place, though, and it would be better if Sam didn't have to put on clothes if she had to get up for Annie in the night.

"One more chapter?" Tucked in bed among her pillows and stuffed animals, Annie appeared swallowed by her elaborate duvet.

"I told you I'd do up to two chapters, and I finished two chapters. We'll have tomorrow to read together, and the next day, and the next. It's time for you to go to sleep."

"Can I show you more of my doll collection tomorrow? It's not just this room, you know. I play in other rooms, too."

"How many rooms do you need?" Sam said with a laugh.

"These are my small dolls and animal dolls. I have other rooms for big dolls, old dolls, dear dolls, dolls I make, dolls I restore, dolls I dress, dolls I dream up. I want to show them to you. You can help me take care of them, play with them, make them even better. Do you know how to sew a seam?"

"More or less." Sam set the book on Annie's nightstand. "Let's save dreaming for sleep, though. With your dad away, do you want me to sleep in here tonight to keep you company?"

"No. I have all my friends with me. You can sleep in your own room. My monitor is here." Annie crawled over the side of the bed to pull out the nightstand drawer and take out a pink and purple walkie-talkie. "Yours is next to your bed, too. If I need you, I'll call."

"Sounds like a plan. Now, if I go to the library, does the light in there keep you up?"

"Nope. I want light on in here tonight, too. Turn off the lamps and the chandeliers, but leave the fairy lights on. Miss Sam?"

"Yes, Annie?"

"Are you glad you came? Are you happy to be here?"

"I think I will be, Annie."

The entrance to the bedroom was too far for Annie to overextend her good night. Sam looked back at her after switching off the lamps and chandeliers, leaving only the rainbow glow of the clock and the multi-colored fairy lights all through the room. It was still bright, especially since the lights reflected off the solarium windows and marble floors, but the bed's canopy shut out much of it, leaving Annie a huddled shadow under the duvet, gathering stuffed animals closer around her and settling in to sleep.

Sam smiled. From a distance, she could almost believe Annie really was a child. A little spoiled? Perhaps. A little sad?

Undeniable. And Sam hadn't yet encountered her first tantrum, her first refusal, her first denial, her first fight, her first attempt to convince Sam something was true when it wasn't.

But worth the money. Worth the time, the isolation, the weight of the Dream House dark around her as she headed to the library, where she read historical romance until the weariness of the day's novelty brought her back to her bedroom.

She almost got lost.

Tucked in her own princess bed, she wondered whether she was allowed to sneak into the kitchen for a snack. A question for tomorrow.

She hadn't even felt compelled to check her phone to see if Lila had texted her. Her nightstand had its emergency number sheet, pink and purple walkie-talkie, and an alarm clock. Sam set the alarm for 7:00 so she could shower in the morning and look around a bit before Annie woke up.

Then she settled onto the pillow-top mattress and within the duvet cocoon in the cool dark and had her first easy and peaceful sleep since she didn't know when.

Chapter 3: **BALLROOM DISPLAY**

Seven on the dot, morning light peeked through the trees and open curtains. Sam couldn't remember the last time she'd slept more than seven hours. She slapped the alarm off because the harsh vibrations disrupted the absolute bliss and *quiet* of the moment. No one vacuuming at five in the morning. No one fighting in the apartment next door or above. No one fucking. No beeping from appliances. No beeping from cars. No honking, no traffic. No yelling.

Just birdsong and a low vibrating hum from the A/C.

She could pause and yawn and stretch and her foot wouldn't kick Lila's leg, and when she brought her sheets back around her because she was cold, Lila didn't pull back the sheets Sam stole. Sam could be as warm and cocooned or outstretched as she wanted, because she was the only one in the bed.

Maybe she'd grow to miss the sound of Lila's soft breathing when Sam's phone alarm didn't wake her, or Lila's frustrated sigh when it did. Maybe she'd miss being able to turn over and press her forehead against Lila's back when she crawled into bed at five in the morning. Maybe she'd miss waking up at two in the morning with Lila tucked against her, arms around her waist. Not from anything Lila had done consciously, but oriented toward her in sleep, muttering nonsense or giggling in the night, which was sometimes creepy and sometimes funny, depending on Sam's state when it woke her.

Maybe having all the space and silence in the world would eventually not be enough. For now, it felt pretty damn good.

Except for the part where she had to get up if she didn't want to drift back asleep again.

Sam whipped the sheets off and braced herself against the cold air conditioning. She'd much rather be under a mountain of covers in the cold than under a single blanket when she was hot. She grabbed her robe to warm her to the shower, which warmed her further, steaming the mirror into a fog.

So, not all the mirrors were gone. Just the ones Annie was most likely to see.

Not that Sam needed a mirror much herself. No dress code, no requirements for makeup or grooming—and even if there were, Mr. Lange wouldn't be able to enforce it when he wasn't home. That didn't mean she'd take care of Annie in pajamas or her sloppiest of sweats. She just didn't have to dress like she had at the office, nor did she have to break out the gas station polo.

She headed out into the house again in leggings and an oversized button-down, with a nice sneaker because she still didn't want to break her neck on the stairs. If Mr. Lange had wanted Mary Poppins, he should have found an au pair. He'd seen what she looked like during the interview, the contract signing, and yesterday without comment.

It was strange, dressing the way she'd dress all the time if she had a choice. No wonder she and Lila had taken refuge in hoodies—just to let their skin breathe when they weren't smothered in other people's expectations.

When she reached the ground floor, Sam expected to hear the kitchen bustling. Excellent insulation meant she could only hear the kitchen staff when she cautiously pushed in the swinging door.

They clattered and chopped and sizzled at the large butcher-block island and stove, but they froze when they saw her.

Wearing an apron too big for her, the short woman who had served them last night rounded the island with a pronounced limp. She looked Sam over head to toe in a motion that oozed contempt, then said in heavily accented English, "I am the chef, Ji-an. We met yesterday. Breakfast will be ready at 9:00, like always."

"I was just coming in to see if I could make a coffee or look through your tea selection…"

Ji-an bustled her out of the kitchen. One of the women slicing apples at the island held her knife so hard that her hand shook, clattering the metal on the board.

Once they were out of the kitchen and into the dining room, Ji-an continued. "You want coffee? I will make you coffee. You want tea? I will make you tea. Order at the hatch. Your side doesn't come to our side, and we do not come over to yours. Only I am allowed in the dining room. You are not allowed in the kitchen. You knock at the hatch if you need something or have a request, although menu is fixed at beginning of the week. You are the new nanny, yes?"

"My name is—" Sam said slowly, more out of confusion than trying to make herself understood.

Ji-an cut her hand through the air. She didn't need or want to hear Sam's name. "You want coffee? How do you take your coffee?"

"Um, with a few dollops of vanilla creamer, I guess."

"I'll get you your coffee. I'll find an electric kettle for your room so you can make tea in the mornings, if you prefer. Anything else you need from the kitchen?"

"There are probably days I can cook something for us. You don't have to provide breakfast, lunch, and dinner all the time—" Sam began.

"Mister wants us to provide three meals. Miss Annie needs three meals. We cook three meals. If you don't want it, send it back uneaten," Ji-an said. "I'll go make your coffee now. This is not your place. Your place is taking care of Miss Annie and keeping her out of the kitchen. You want to do something different with food with Miss Annie, you give us a list of what you need and when you need it and we will provide. But you stay on your side. For everyone's safety. We don't talk anymore now. Give me some minutes for your coffee."

With that, Ji-an bustled back through the door and left Sam bewildered and alone in the expansive dining room.

Some families preferred their help to be virtually invisible, but she'd never heard of help keeping themselves separate from other help. It made sense to keep a child from the knives, but although Sam was a stranger, she wasn't a danger in the kitchen, even a bustling one.

But house rules were house rules, and it wouldn't hurt her to leave the kitchen area to kitchen staff. She had the whole rest of the house in which she was allowed to roam. It would be weird not to be in charge of her own food, but she didn't have any dietary restrictions or allergies, so there was nothing to stop her from taking advantage of the service and not having to think about the next meal, and the next.

The rich are different. This family is different. Just enjoy the perks, darlin'.

She still had a little more than an hour before Annie woke up. There was a dearth of visible modern technology but an excess of clocks, some with batteries and some that were likely wound daily by the housekeeper.

Sam and Lila both liked a neat home, even if they were sometimes too tired to put dishes away. They made the effort in spare moments, but even that seemed Sisyphean some days, and that was just in a bad one-bedroom apartment. As big as the house was, the upkeep needed to maintain the show-readiness of the Dream House seemed an impossible task.

Yet, everything was spotless, with only the most superficial layers of dust. Every slab of marble gleamed, despite an adult child and what were doubtlessly other scuffing shoes, and every window dared not show more than the most minor of water stains. Every clock was wound, every curtain artfully draped, every book dusted.

The serving hatch door lifted. Ji-an or one of the other kitchen workers slid a mug through the opening to the serving side.

The coffee was exquisitely smooth, and the creamer was homemade—so much *creamier* than store-bought. She sat out on the patio and listened to morning creep into the forest and couldn't believe this was her life.

"That's fantastic," she said through the serving hatch as she passed the empty mug back through.

"I know," Ji-an shouted back from wherever she was.

"I'll be wanting that at eight every morning, if you don't mind."

"I will provide."

Sam entered the library to search for a book she could read while Annie was working and coloring. It would take her decades to get through every single book, presuming they didn't add any more or use other rooms to expand. When you had what seemed like a hundred rooms, Sam supposed filling them was half the conundrum—and half the fun of being so rich you could build a castle in the middle of Texas and air-condition it enough to be cold.

If she thought about the staggering excess too much, she almost slipped on the marble in her rubber-soled shoes.

Closer to 8:30, Sam headed for Annie's room.

The sun rose on the other side of the house but insinuated gently into the bedroom, an ever-so-subtle sunbeam alarm, like waking up in morning fog. But as it turned out, Annie had another alarm that switched on the sound system embedded in the wall next to the bed nook. It looked like it could play a hundred different kinds of musical media, but in this case, it drew from a digital playlist of aggressively happy pop music, the kind with an addictive beat. Despite the gratingly nasal and heavily Autotuned singer, Sam couldn't help swaying and tapping her foot along.

Annie woke with the alarm, but like Sam, she was reluctant to get out of bed. With no indication she knew Sam was there, Annie sang softly with the music and played with the stuffed animals around her, making whole conversations between her and them and each other. Teddy bears got into arguments with kitty cats, while the elephant refused to take sides. Sam leaned against the door frame with a small smile before she realized she was smiling.

Annie played like that for fifteen minutes. Then Sam knocked on the door frame.

"Hey, kiddo, I think it's time to get up. Bows don't tie themselves, and I'm afraid I'm useless in that department." 'Kiddo' didn't sit right in Sam's mouth, but it wasn't quite as off as it would have been when she'd first met Annie.

Annie glanced up in surprise and let her animals fall beneath the edge of the covers. Then she climbed out of the bed.

Nope, still unsettling to see an adult wearing a little-girl nightgown that rode up to reveal a patch of spider veins. But Annie showed no stiffness as she clambered to the bathroom to brush her teeth again, still humming along with the music.

Sam perched on the stairs to the solarium and watched sunrise limn the multiplanar edges of the Dream House roof while pretending she wasn't listening to the music. Finally, five to 9:00, Annie skipped out of her closet in black Mary Janes, white frilly socks, a pink dress the color of a dried rose, and red ribbons the color of a fresh one. Instead of pigtails, she'd tied the smaller ribbons to the bottom of braids.

Sam herded Annie out the bedroom door in front of her. "What's for breakfast on Thursdays?"

"Oatmeal with brown sugar, bananas, and honey."

"So…oatmeal with lots of sugar."

Annie giggled. "That's what makes it taste good."

"That makes a lot of things taste good."

In the grand hall, Sam started at seeing three women sweeping industrial dust mops across the floor.

An older woman stood under the massive stairs and supervised, tapping her foot as though in time to music only she could hear. The three younger women stepped in perfect time with the older woman's tapping. Their uniforms were that of an old-fashioned maid, with skirt hems brushing their shoes, but instead of white hats and aprons, all four women wore black on black.

The three women sweeping didn't just keep their eyes downcast. When they noticed Sam and Annie, they lowered their heads almost in a bow, so that they were just black caps and heavy skirts, the whisper of cloth on marble gathering dust, and *tap, tap, tap.*

The older woman, of more matronly composition, kept her gaze upon the maids, her foot steady, but her lips thinned as Annie skipped off-rhythm across the marble—*click-a-click-a-clickety-clickety*—staring and smiling at the older woman, as though daring her to tell them not to scuff her pretty floor. Despite her cold tension, like power lines in a blizzard, the older woman said nothing.

When Sam and Annie appeared in the dining room, their oatmeal had already been placed on their mats, with Annie at the head and Sam next to her like the previous night. The oatmeal was plain and steaming. Bowls of sliced bananas, honey, and brown sugar had been provided for them to add sweetness to taste.

Sam finished the meal a little heavier than she was used to for mornings. It was much tastier than she'd expected, though, as much of a surprise as the coffee. Like she'd gotten so used to a shittier version of things that she hadn't known the shitty things were supposed to taste good when done right. Or when you used real cream and better sugars. This job was going to murder her waistline, make her as lazy and indulgent as a house cat. She'd probably need to start getting up earlier to run the perimeter of the property a few times, just for the self-denial of it all.

Annie finished her milk—no chocolate milk for breakfast—then wiped her mouth with her napkin and pushed her chair back. "Race you to the library."

Until noon, Annie once again entertained herself, this time with a large history biography that was well into college-age reading level. Nevertheless, she curled up in an oversized leather chair that made her seem all the more childlike.

Sam had been reading from the adult section at ten, so she wasn't too thrown by the reading level so much as the content Annie had chosen. But mornings were for learning, and she had endless days to indulge her curiosity on any subject, whether spurious romance novels or historical figures. It was her choice how to enrich herself.

Sam certainly didn't mind. Couldn't, in fact, figure out why Mr. Lange had a nanny problem. Annie couldn't take care of herself like an adult, but she could take care of herself like a child, and she had a whole household arranged to take care of her in more concrete ways than Sam, who basically had to keep her company amidst the traditional class segregation.

It wasn't that hard. Was Annie's physical age really enough to dissuade so many other nannies from such a good salary?

Lunch, fortunately, was light, because Sam didn't think she could eat much more, but she also didn't know if she could make it to dinner without a snack of some kind. Lunch was apples, peanut butter, and raisins and currants.

"Okay, Miss Sam, I got up, got dressed, ate my food, and did all my reading today. Can I please, please, *please* show you some of my dolls now? Can we go to the ballroom?"

"You have a *ballroom*?" Sam asked, laughing slightly.

Annie nodded. "It's like the hall, but underground."

"You have a ballroom in your basement? You have a *basement*?" As though aboveground wasn't enough for a little girl, her father, and their staff, they needed a ballroom for all the company they never had?

The rich are different. This family is different. Annie is different. Keep telling yourself that, Sammie. It's not going to make things less ridiculous.

If the house were just one floor, it would already be unimagined luxury. But three? And based on some of the towers, with a few fourth-story rooms and attics? No one needed it, and who the hell wanted it? *Really* wanted it, not just dreamed about it from time to time, because dreams didn't require maintenance?

The Langes weren't a party family—nothing she'd witnessed had indicated that they regularly entertained, despite chandeliers and a long dining room table and endless guest rooms down the hall she lived in now. Annie wasn't necessarily the mad wife in the attic, but Mr. Lange hadn't brought her into public with him to meet Sam. Sam had had to come to her.

What was it all *for*? Marble and wood and paintings and chandeliers, all for a little girl to play?

Annie took Sam's hand and dragged her along the hall's marble floors to the front of the house and its grand staircase. A door camouflaged as one of the panels swung open at Annie's deft guidance, revealing a wrought-iron spiral staircase.

The massive room below was filled with more curtained windows on the side opposite the staircase, but these windows were frosted, the light a diffused golden glow against fog. Because it wasn't real sunlight, and they weren't real windows, there underground. The illusion was almost seamless, the light a near perfect facsimile.

On the side through which they entered, the paneled walls were lined with preserved animal heads—deer and moose, but also longhorn, alligator, hare, jackalope, horse, zebra… When Annie had said she had a whole zoo of stuffed animals, Sam had thought she meant the stuffed animals in her room, not an actual taxidermized zoo.

Annie let go of Sam's hand to skip ahead and marvel at all the heads, while Sam couldn't find a good word to say. One could make a case for deer, elk, moose, cow—things that were killed for their meat. But a massive elephant head had been mounted in the place of ultimate pride in the center panel, surrounded by rhinoceros, crocodile, maned lion, hyena, Siberian tiger.

At eye level hung pictures of the hunts where these things had been felled—provenance. Mr. Lange hadn't struck her as a hunter, nor as someone who smiled much, but he was younger and all teeth in the pictures. Maybe game-hunting had been a joy before his wife's death or daughter's birth. But if they were the follies of youth, why so proudly displayed?

Sam wasn't vegan or even vegetarian, but looking at those walls made her sick to her stomach. She was pretty sure that species of rhinoceros was now extinct. As long as mild-mannered, world-weary Mr. Lange had a nice conversation piece in his basement ballroom no one danced in.

"This is my stuffed animal zoo. The fur isn't as soft as the ones in my room, but these are real and they're beautiful. Look at how beautiful it is." Annie rubbed her face against a cheetah head. Her laughter echoed through the large space, with its inlaid parquet floors and ceilings painted with cherubs and seraphim between more chandeliers. "Aren't they pretty?"

"I don't know what to say," Sam managed to sew together, swallowing against the wave of uncharacteristic emotion sharp in her throat at the sight of a giraffe, wildebeest, American buffalo, panda.

If she had to spit a compliment, Sam would say that the craftsmanship was exceptional. The forms were well-dressed without leaning into the uncanny. And the eyes…the eyes were bright with life. She expected eyelashes to flutter at any moment.

She couldn't bring herself to touch any of them like Annie, though. Was she curious what a rhinoceros felt like? Yes. Was she going to reward this behavior by leaving finger oil to deteriorate the preserved hide? *No, ma'am.*

Annie skipped back over and grabbed Sam's hand again. "Come to the dressing room with me, Miss Sam. That's where I keep all my best Barbie dolls, the most prettiest with the prettiest gowns. Sometimes I turn on the music down here, dress in my best dress and necklace and ring, and put the dolls out on display turntables to dance with them. We dance until midnight on really special nights, like my birthday when I can stay up late and there's a table over there with every dessert I like, like cake and pudding and pie and petit fours and doughnuts and ice cream. We'll have to find you a dress for my birthday. It's not for another four months, but I can make one for you. Oh, it would be so much fun to make you a dress. Do you like to wear dresses?"

"Not as a rule." Sam believed in encouraging creativity and imagination, but she also didn't believe in lying to kids. "However, I'll wear dresses for special occasions, and your birthday sounds like a special occasion to me. I'm looking forward to seeing what kind of dress you make. Do you make clothes for your dolls, too?"

Annie nodded enthusiastically as she led Sam into a room off the ballroom. Carpeted, no windows, proper for a dressing room. "I make clothes for all kinds of dolls. I make a lot of my own clothes, too. When Daddy buys me things from the store, they almost never fit right, not like when Mommy took me to the store and dressed me up and everything was perfect. So I learned how to make myself perfect, with my dresses and ribbons and skirts and tutus and ballerina toe shoes and tap shoes. I promise you'll like your dress, Miss Sam. Look. Look at my collection of my best beautiful Barbie dolls."

Sam was a lot more in awe of Annie's formalwear Barbie collection than the trophy wall.

Younger Sam had fantasized about ballgowns almost as much as she'd fantasized about living in a castle—unlikely dreams that hadn't figured money or other variables into account. She'd look at Barbies like this and imagine herself wearing their gowns and how pretty she'd be. She'd gone as a princess for Halloween one year, but she remembered a vague sense of disappointment that she hadn't looked quite the way she'd imagined—not in a forty-dollar costume from Party City.

Annie probably didn't know what a Party City was.

Annie switched on the dressing room lights. Every shelf was front-lit golden and backlit with something softer, giving the whole room a sheen and shine of nostalgia over cardboard and plastic containers of glittering, glistening dresses within. The dolls themselves were almost an afterthought, like any mannequin.

Holiday Barbies, glamor Barbies, fantasy Barbies, fairy queen Barbies, Barbies in their Disney princess best, Barbies in their Disney villain best, Barbies from different eras, Barbies from different countries… All of them the kind of Barbies that little girls like Sam, during her Barbie phase, would gaze at in envy, knowing that the thinner containers might be all they ever got, and that was a big if, depending on discounts, thrift stores, garage sales, or the right online auction. Oh, she'd enjoyed the dolls she'd received, but there had been something attractive about toys designed to look at but not touch. Something so pretty that it belonged behind a glass case like in a museum. Something so pretty she could just stare at it for hours and imagine herself that pretty, and then she would sink back into herself and feel that same vague disappointment, which she wouldn't understand until her childish expectations about adulthood met harsh reality.

In addition to the regular-sized Barbies, there were a dozen My Size Barbies that Sam remembered advertisements for when she was a kid—another item she'd coveted and probably wouldn't have known what to do with if she'd actually gotten it. The dresses on the original My Size Barbies would have been similar to Party City quality—cheap-shiny, cheap-glittery, cheap-sheen, rustling like plastic wrap. The dresses on these My Size Barbies were made of better material and tailored to fit the large dolls rather than to be exchanged between doll and girl. There were small errors here and there, even to Sam's unpracticed eye, something slightly off in proportion and drape. But they were ambitious and excellent attempts at sewing—*almost* good and definitely impressive, no matter the age of the hands creating them.

Sam spread a skirt out to its full width in admiration. "Did you make these dresses yourself, Annie?"

"Mm-hmm. I also made the dresses on these." Annie gestured to the far wall of Barbies, which displayed them in clear acrylic boxes rather than original packaging.

These dolls had clearly been altered from their original paint job. Even their hair had been adjusted. Some of the designs were similar to the original, with different eyeshadow or softer lip, but sometimes she'd gone for more dramatic, strange, even unsettling: white eyes, silver shadow, exaggerated or absent features, something more appropriate for repurposed Monster High than Barbie. All the dresses were gorgeous, though, and in keeping with the way she'd redone their makeup and hair, from winter formal to eerily realistic zombie queen, whose eye hung out of a blank socket.

A little gruesome, but Annie had already said she liked the Monster High dolls, too, and there was a horror section in the library. Even these more gruesome dolls were pretty in their own way. One had been adjusted to have four arms and four legs; her long-trained skirt looked like it had been made of cobwebs.

"You're really skilled. Did your mother teach you how to do this? Your dad? One of your nannies? Did you watch a bunch of YouTube videos?"

Annie shrugged. "I don't like online. There are some sewing books in the library, but mostly I just decided what I wanted and figured out how to make it. It takes trial and error, but less than it used to."

"I'll bet. This is really cool, Annie. You'll have to teach *me* some things."

"Oh, I hope so. Dresses for dolls this size are easier, and if you make a mistake, there's plenty of fabric left to correct it. It took longer for me to figure out making clothes for myself. I practiced on larger dolls first, then the My Size bodies. Then on mannequins. Would you like to see the ballroom mannequins? I just need to turn on the music in here…"

"I don't know if I can handle any more magic in this place," Sam muttered.

"There are places in this house even I haven't seen yet. I'm sure of it. I don't mean the places I'm not allowed, but places Daddy built for Mommy that weren't for me to find. But I have my own secret places that only Daddy knows about. Like the ballroom. I'll show you all of them so you can play with me where no one else can find us."

Annie opened a panel on the wall between the dressing room and ballroom. Another sound system. "Clair de lune" shivered clean and clear through the open door.

From the parquet floors arose life-sized mannequins in plastic display cases of their own. There had to be at least two dozen, and more cases yet to be filled. A turntable inside moved the mannequins in time with the slow music. The mannequins themselves looked unsettlingly human but were the unmoving of the inorganic.

The gowns brought to mind a museum of eighteenth- and nineteenth-century fashion or the best fucking prom dresses in the whole world—all made by a thirty-year-old designer who thought she was still eleven.

Someone really should have known about her. If she'd been a real eleven-year-old, the whole world *would* have. She would never have said, 'I don't like online.' She wouldn't have been stuck as a youth from before the internet had crept into every area of life—on the cusp, but not quite there. Back then, the phone every young teenager had wanted was clear with colorful electrical guts, not the newest smartphone that could make a movie and have pizza delivered.

In a place like this, all ties cut, Sam had almost forgotten she had a smartphone. The family room was a library, and the only TV Sam was aware of was in Annie's room. She also presumably had a computer somewhere if she woke up to downloaded or streamed music, but this was a Dream House, not a smart house. A haven, where the world couldn't encroach through a little electronic brick. Where women dressed in the fanciest bespoke gowns and danced in time to a waltz.

They didn't need a man. They didn't even need a soul. Just pretty things on their frozen bodies.

The eyes here were good, too, like the animals. With the glint of movement and fake outdoor light, they could have been real—except that, of course, they didn't blink.

Annie let go of Sam's hand so she could weave through the slowly spinning bodies. When Sam caught her reflection in their static display cases, she once again felt underdressed.

The song slowed to a halt. So did the mannequins, like music-box dancers. The gown on the mannequin in front of Sam enthralled her: gold brocade that wouldn't have been out of place in Elizabethan costume, although this gown had more modern lines. The thread looked like it had been spun from real gold. For all Sam knew, it had been. Seed pearls of different sizes had been sewn to the bodice in an elaborate pattern, like lace from the irritation of gastropods. At the décolletage, there was even a diamond brooch—probably real, because why wouldn't it be?

The mannequins came to a complete stop, skirts rustling like woods in a light wind. Sam stepped closer to the display case to get a better look at the details, the elaborate collar framing red ringlets and 'Queen of Hearts'-painted lips and eyelids. Sam wondered if Annie had made the pearl headdress, too.

The quality of mannequin in the Dream House exceeded that of any boutique or department store. Most places deliberately tried to make mannequins look more stylized to keep them from entering the realm of uncanny. Either these mannequins had already been uncannily human or Annie had made them so to better display the quality of her gowns, similar to what she'd done with the altered Barbies.

Sam took another step closer. She didn't want to leave prints on such beautiful art displays, but she wanted a closer look at that diamond brooch to figure out how real it was, how it caught the light…

The mannequin blinked.

Sam jerked back, just as another waltz started. She didn't know the name of this one, and she barely heard it as the turntables spun the mannequins once more. She struggled to follow, trying to see if she'd seen what she thought she'd seen. A trick of light, maybe from the turntable starting, or maybe Sam herself had blinked, or maybe there'd been one of those stealth power surges that made her wonder if she or the lights had dimmed.

Sam ran around the spinning turntable, daring herself not to blink if she could help it. Maybe it was just her panic and disorientation in basement sunlight, but it seemed like the mannequin's face was sadder, brows low over the dark eyes. Was that a tear running down the mannequin's face, or had the tear always been there, or was it just another trick of the light?

This waltz was faster. Even sprinting, Sam couldn't keep up with the whirling, rustling skirt circuiting in place.

"Miss Sam, what's wrong?"

The waltz slowed at its end; the turntables did as well. Annie came up behind Sam and stared up at the mannequin with her.

"Do they seem too real?" Annie asked. "Sometimes I think they are. Or maybe they're so lifelike that they call ghosts to live inside them so they can dance one more time. Daddy says sometimes my dolls look so real because we make them real. We stand so still that we tremble with our own heart's beating and think it's the doll that moves."

Sam kept staring up at the mannequin, willing it to blink again, willing it not to blink again, not sure which one she was really rooting for at this point.

The more she thought about it, the more she was sure it had just been a trick of eye and brain, and she definitely did *not* want the mannequin to blink. Because then the mannequin couldn't be a mannequin. And that would be a very different kind of wrong.

The mannequin didn't move. Didn't blink.

Sam shook her head, laughing at herself.

Annie skipped back to the dressing room to turn off the lights and music. She also pushed whatever button made the mannequins sink back into the parquet floors.

Then it was as though they'd never been there. Just the dozens and dozens of glass eyes from the mounted animals on the wall.

Chapter 4: BALL JOINT

"You know, Miss Sam, I don't just have pretty things to play with."

Sam was glad to be back on the ground level, where she knew the sunlight refracting through the chandelier crystals was actual sun. "I did notice you like a few spooky things, too."

"Not only that." Annie led her back through the hall. The maids and housekeeper had moved on. Sam couldn't hear them, couldn't hear anything but Annie's shoes clicking. "Broken toys are good to play with, too. You can use them to repair a prettier toy when it breaks an arm, leg, foot, eye, open stuffing in the stomach… Patch it up, good as new. But broken dolls can still play Tea Party with one hand, and sometimes, you need to break something to make something else special, like putting together a collage or mosaic."

They passed the entrance to Annie's bedroom and a hallway of rooms that curved around it. Then they entered the ground floor of the east wing.

To her immediate left were what looked like several large rooms with smaller rooms arranged across from them like satellites. Ahead of her, the corridor continued, and there appeared to be another hallway parallel, with the cross corridor linking them. Most of the doors were closed and everything was quiet, except for a small voice somewhere in Sam's chest that told her there were no windows except one at the very end of the hall. Not enough light. No exit signs.

Everything else in the house was expansive, excessive. The space here was much more efficient. The weight of the house, already prodigious, pushed down on her in otherwise plain halls—beige carpet, basic crown molding and drywall, construction-grade rather than custom. The second floor, where Sam's bedroom was, had more elaborate crown molding and trim in the style of the wooden paneling of the main house, and similar but more textured carpet, with the subtlest patterns.

Sam wondered if these were servants' quarters for the maids—although Mr. Lange had said that the west wing was for staff.

Sam had never considered her instincts particularly useful. She'd had bad feelings about people based on behavior that had turned out to be introversion rather than inherent bitchiness, and she'd had good feelings about people who had disappointed her. She'd trust her instincts as a mother before she'd trust her instincts as Sam, because Sam had terrible instincts. And what Sam had done to parent her siblings hadn't been instinct so much as basic necessities—get them clean, get them fed, get them to bed. Make sure they do their homework, even if they don't have the neatest science fair project, at least it's done. Pick them up after school, forgot Addy, go back for Addy. Call me if you drink and I'll drive you home, call me if you need money for rent, don't call me if you forgot your lunch because I'm at work and can't get it for you, you'll have to wait until you get home and eat it then.

She'd never been herself long enough to develop her own instincts beyond a pervasive sense of dread—and resentment for those who'd never had to feel that dread. But dread was usually dull, unimpressive, just a bill in angry red telling her she was overdue, while her checking account roared at her for being overdrawn. Not the boogeyman of her youth; she barely remembered being afraid of the dark in her closet.

She'd never even really been in the closet, because she hadn't been able to half-consider what gender she was noticing until after the last of her mother's children were old enough to get their own jobs. Before that, it had just been the odd party, the odd experiment, getting drop-dead drunk, playing Spin the Bottle, kissing whatever was on the other end. None of it had meant anything until she'd had to figure out who she was without her siblings making that decision for her.

Then she'd gone a little nuts with a delayed adolescence in her late twenties, which hadn't helped hone her instincts much except to establish that they were actually terrible.

Yet, her instincts were telling her there were monsters in the shadows. Even though there was only Annie in front of her, Sam fought the urge to just run.

Annie stopped in front of a door labeled Repair Room. She took out an electronic badge from inside the bow around her waist and passed it next to the door frame. A surgical-grade crease indicated where a control panel was, and a red light briefly glowed through the plaster, then switched to green as the door unlocked. If Sam hadn't seen it, she wouldn't have known there was a card reader there at all.

Annie stepped into the dark room, grabbed Sam's hand, and pulled her in before Sam could process that *this* was definitely not what it should be. The door locked behind them with a small beep.

Annie tucked the card into her bow—presumably into a pocket in the bow, since satin would never hold the card on its own—then flicked on the lights. "Look at all the broken dolls, Miss Sam."

Sam didn't want to turn away from the plain wall, the plain door, white on white, because her long-ignored and ill-used instincts screamed now in this carousel-ceilinged room, a mechanical whir like the inside of a music box behind her. She wanted to say she'd go to the dining room for another amazing coffee while Annie played with her dolls by herself. She wanted to say that she didn't play with dolls and hadn't for a long time. She wanted to close her eyes and go back to the cool room and warm sheets, when the Dream House had been big and quiet and easy as store-bought pie. She shivered, and still didn't quite know why.

The whimpers behind her weren't from Annie.

Reality was rarely as bad as what a scared mind imagined. The closet was always just clothes and shoes, nothing more.

Annie turned Sam around.

It was worse.

Shelves and shelves of broken dolls lined the walls with as much deliberation as the glamorous Barbie dolls in the ballroom dressing room. Heads, arms, torsos, some naked, some clothed. Sometimes the clothes were in tatters, ruined, moldy, stained. Sometimes a hank of hair had been ripped or cut from the scalp; sometimes the eyes were missing or a hole marred a porcelain face.

The broken dolls weren't the most alarming feature in the Repair Room.

Around fourteen people were slumped on the floor, joints and neck attached to flexible but implacable nylon shackles. They had superficial padding to discourage sores and were thick as bangles to keep from digging into skin, but they were still essentially zip ties. These attached to nylon-coated metal chains that, in turn, connected to tracks from the walls to the mirrored carousel ceiling in the center.

Almost in the middle of the room was another control panel that looked like it had been patched together from a theater sound and light board soldered to the guts of old ham radios and telegraphs, not that Sam could tell one thing from the other.

What it had been created from didn't matter. She kept getting stuck on mechanics to distract herself from the actual people, not dolls, slumped against the wall. Definitely people, not mannequins. They breathed, they blinked, they opened their eyes to squint against the soft light.

They were certainly positioned like dolls, limp like dolls, faces painted like dolls, and in varying stages of dress, like dolls that had been set aside in the middle of play so a child could finish a chore or eat dinner.

Their joints were hinged like ball-joint dolls: wrists, ankles, knees, elbows, mandible, dislocated and relocated over and over again, until pain and looseness of tendon and ligament left them limp. Which explained why—despite tear-streaked cheeks and blood, inflammation, and sometimes pus at surgical stitching around the hinges—no one clambered to their feet or wrenched against their bindings.

Despair, too, kept their whimpers soft. Snot dripped like dried melted wax, coated and crusted facial hair and mouths. Lacrimal sediment gummed heavily kohled or false-eyelashed eyes. Blood dried foul and brown with shit and urine on what were essentially giant bedpans that they rested upon, to spare carpet stains.

Those awake or aware enough raised their heads, as wide-eyed as the gunk would allow. Some shook so hard that their chains clattered against the tracks like coins falling into a vending machine. Those whose jaws hadn't been wired shut became more restless as Annie stepped up behind the board. Their whimpering slowly transitioned into speech—still almost gibberish, as though their words were gummed with mucus as well.

Clearest was *no*.

"No…no, please, *no*, don't, no…please, don't…don't let her…stop her, no, no, no, no, *no*…"

"Annie…" Sam stepped forward, then back, repulsed by the mess, by the smell—more metal than shit, which suggested the pans and people were regularly cleaned. Disgusted by the tears and snot and seepage. Horrified that this was really here, that it had been here while she'd slept and eaten and read and watched Annie sleep. That Annie had known this was here and slept soundly. That Annie was at least partial architect— beyond belief that she was the only one, although with unlimited funds, unlimited time, and a curious mind, anything was possible.

Anything at all.

Annie skipped to the control board platform and jumped onto it with the enthusiasm of hopscotch. "My newest dolls are Jesse and Ann. Ann, like Annie, but she doesn't look like me. When I met her, she had glasses. They broke, like her, but dolls don't really need glasses."

Sam forced herself closer to the metal carousel's center as Annie switched on the control board to whirring life. The broken people grew even more agitated, twitching against their bindings. "Annie, these aren't dolls."

"Of course they are. If they weren't dolls, could we play with them like this?"

Annie curled her fingers around a pair of modified gaming joysticks and pushed both of them toward the center.

Two broken people, a man and a woman, jerked up from their pans. Each of them screamed as their bodies were pulled up by harnesses connected to their nylon collar. Weight would be distributed through their trunk without discomfort, but their damaged parts couldn't hold themselves up and had to be manipulated by the chains and shackles, which disturbed the surgical wounds and pervasive musculoskeletal damage.

"Stop. Stop it. You're hurting them." Stunned as she was by revulsion, Sam was surprised to hear the hitching sob in her voice—but far away, as though her response to broken people's pain was miles from where she thought she was.

"Don't be silly. They're just dolls. Watch." Annie continued to push the joysticks inward to bring the two broken people to the carousel room center, where they hovered and hung like marionettes below a circle of Edison bulbs. They cried, whimpered, tried to plead, but despite their pain, they lacked conviction—in Annie or themselves.

"Say hi to Miss Sam, Jesse and Ann."

Jesse and Ann just hung there in their misery.

Annie pressed her thumbs on the button on top of the joysticks. Jesse and Ann jittered, eyes jerking open and teeth chattering with electric shock. The shackles were plastic; there must have been nodes of some kind on the collars.

Annie pouted at the disobedience. "If you can't say hi, I'll have to force the motion."

"Hi," Jesse said. Thick blood dripped from his cut, swollen lips, black and blue as though they'd been smashed against his teeth.

"Hi." Ann trembled so hard that her voice wavered.

"No, don't just say it. Wave. New dolls are always so stiff. Let me show you." Annie wiggled buttons on the side, forcing their arms to make an exaggerated waving motion like windshield wipers.

Ann started crying anew with each movement that disturbed the injuries to her shoulder, elbow, and wrist. Her hand flapped like a dead bird. Jesse's neck tightened alarmingly under the collar, as though if he tensed any more, he'd choke himself on the nylon by cutting off a pulsating vein. His face turned bright red.

"Annie, stop it." Sam started soft, but couldn't stand to hear Jesse fighting his own impulse to sob. "Annie, you're hurting them."

Annie let go of the controllers and looked at Sam like she'd lost her mind. "Miss Sam, you can't hurt dolls. And you promised to play with me. You're *supposed* to play with me. Maybe it's been a while since you played and you forgot your imagination since the last time. Grown-ups often do. They lose it, like pocket lint or car keys. But I'll show you, Miss Sam. You have to help them move if they're too stiff or not moving correctly. Let me lubricate their joints." She pressed a button on the control board.

"No, no, no, don't do that," Ann begged. "We'll be good. Don't make us…don't, don't…"

"Oh God…" Jesse groaned. "God, don't. *Fuck.*"

"Annie, what are you doing?" Sam said.

A yellowish fluid moved from a container under the control board through IV tubes Sam had thought were just another chain but actually connected to a dock in their arms. Within seconds of it hitting their system, their eyes rolled back and they settled in their shackles, swaying slightly in the swing of them. Their lids fluttered like moth wings.

"Now we're all going to play nicely, like we're supposed to," Annie said. "I'll be Ann. Annie will be Ann. And you'll be Jesse. Jesse's just come home from work. Ann already got home from hers and has been making dinner. 'Hello, honey. How was your day?' Go on, Ann, say it."

"Hello, honey. How was your day?" Ann could barely open her eyes, but to Sam's horror, she smiled a little.

"What did you do to them?" Sam asked.

"That's not what Jesse says. I understand. I'll start for you. Jesse, say, 'Hello, sweetheart. Traffic was hell.'"

"Hello, sweetheart. Traffic was hell," Jesse repeated.

Ann wore a sundress that used to be pretty, but Jesse was only wearing plaid boxer shorts, which did nothing to hide that he was getting an erection.

Sam wanted to vomit, but there was nowhere to turn that didn't make the nausea worse. "Annie, what are you *doing*?"

"Playing with my dolls. I played with my dolls yesterday, too, and the day before that, and the day before that. You saw me. I play with them and I sleep with them and I fix them and I make them pretty again. Dolls do so much better when they're played with. They wear down, of course, but that's what gives them life. Like in *The Velveteen Rabbit*."

"I don't know what you did to them, but you need to stop right now. These are *not* dolls. You don't play with them. Put them down right now, Annie." Sam covered her mouth at the first taste of sour bile on her tongue and forced herself to swallow.

"But I've done my lessons for the day, and now I get to play, as long as when I'm finished I put everything away. Those are the rules."

"And what do the rules say about hurting people?" Sam asked.

"I don't hurt people, Miss Sam."

"Okay, what do the rules say about hurting your dolls?"

"Once they're mine, I can do with them as I please," Annie said simply. "Sometimes that means I have to throw them away because they can't be used anymore. But most dolls that can't be fully repaired can be replaced."

"I don't know what you're doing to these people, but it's not repair or rehabilitation. Don't you see that you're torturing them? You're not taking care of your dolls, Annie. You're damaging them. You're playing too rough."

Sam didn't know how to phrase it in a way Annie would understand. She blinked so innocently at Sam and manipulated the joysticks so Ann and Jesse opened their arms for each other. Then she told them to hug, so they did. They patted each others' backs like a man hug rather than husband and wife, but Ann rested her head against Jesse's bare shoulder like she was nuzzling.

"Repairing dolls is a process. Sometimes they look scary before they're finished, but Daddy always said dolls don't really stare at you in the dark. It's just porcelain and glass, and porcelain and glass aren't scary. Come on, Miss Sam, *play with me.* Ann, tell him you've been waiting for him to come home all day because you have a gift for him."

"I've been waiting all day for you to come home," Ann said blearily. Her pupils were pinpricks under heavy eyelids. Her patting turned into light petting, like on a dog.

"Jesse, tell her you can't wait to see her present."

"I can't wait to see your present, Ann," Jesse said. "What do you have for me?"

"Ann, raise the skirt of your dress."

Even blissed out on whatever chemicals pumped into their veins, Ann's face contorted as new tears flowed through old tracks. Nevertheless, she took the dress hem and raised it over her thighs. She wasn't wearing underwear underneath. Clothes but no underwear.

And on Jesse, underwear but no clothes. Not that the underwear held anything in. Whatever Annie had pumped into them, it had gotten Jesse there in record time. He was fully hard and partially out of the opening in the front of his boxers. He, too, was crying, but silently.

"Ann, tell him you made him cherry pie, but it still needs to finish baking in the oven."

"I made you cherry pie, honey," Ann said through dazed sobs. "But I just put it in the oven, and it needs to finish baking."

"But maybe you can have a little fun until then."

"Maybe we can have a little fun 'til then," Ann repeated.

"Jesse, tell her that you've been thinking about this all day."

"I've been thinking about this all day. I'm so sorry, Ann. I can't— Ah!" A single shock jolted through him. It did nothing to flag his erection.

"Annie, stop it! Annie, listen. Let's go play with some of your Barbies. Your Littlest Pet Shop. Hell, even your Bratz. Please, can we go play with other dolls?"

Annie glanced at Sam. "We'll play with other dolls later. I want to play here." She turned back to the couple. "Now kiss."

Annie brought their bodies flush together and bonked their faces against each other while they puckered their lips, wincing and flinching against the bruises already on their faces.

"Kiss more." Annie was beatific as Jesse made an effort to hold Ann's head in place so Annie didn't have to bump their faces. He held his hips back and Ann held hers back, but they sought a kind of comfort in their kiss, salty and slippery though it must have been. Sam didn't know if they'd known each other before, but they kissed as though they hadn't, timing off. Still, their hands made fists to cling, Jesse to Ann's hair and Ann to her dress, holding it up. She hadn't been told to put it back down.

Sam slowly backed away. She remembered playing with dolls, and she knew how this was going to end, to the mortification of parents when they happened to catch their kids making their dolls do it—probably because the child had accidentally seen them.

There was an illicit thrill, too, in making grown-up dolls do what grown-ups did, even if a child didn't quite understand. Dolls were all about roleplay. Sometimes that roleplay was a fantasy quest, and sometimes that roleplay was adult mimicry, all in the safe space of sexless dolls—who sometimes ended up having more sex than the parents, by a child's reckoning of the deed. The things Sam had made her Barbies do, before she'd even had a conception of sapphism, and the things she'd noticed her younger sisters doing with their dolls, sometimes with Sam there playing with them and trying not to laugh… Because when kids did that kind of thing with their toys, it was anatomically incorrect, almost certainly implausible, and actually impossible with sexless dolls.

These dolls were not sexless, and Annie, although a child to her own mind, was inventive.

Sam backed against the door and fumbled for the knob, but the door was locked; Annie had the keycard. Sam jerked at the doorknob, hoping adrenaline would help her break it. It remained immovable.

"We're not finished, Miss Sam." Annie's happy face slowly transitioned into sullen thunderclouds. "I need your help with this part."

"No, Annie. You're harming your dolls, and I won't help you do that."

Annie slapped one of the larger buttons on her board. "Ann, give Jesse the present you've been saving for him. It's time for Mommy and Daddy dolls to have sex, because that's what mommies and daddies do to become mommies and daddies."

"But are they dolls who can't become mommies and daddies, or are they people who can become mommies and daddies?" Sam continued jiggling the doorknob, even though she knew it was futile. Now she was the one close to tears, because the goddamn door wouldn't *open*.

"It's just pretend, silly."

Annie rounded the carousel's center, where the chains marionetting Ann and Jesse arranged them into an established configuration. Ann flipped onto her back in the air on an invisible bed, her arms splayed, her legs stuck straight up and parted. The chains bent Jesse over her, the harness thrusting his hips forward in a steady, unmistakable motion.

However, he thrusted roughly two inches above Ann's vagina, which meant the head hit her mound or slid along her belly, depending on angle.

Ann cried silently, staring dazed at the Edison lights and mirrored ceiling. She was shaking her head but no longer pleading, drifting on whatever took the pain away. Jesse alternated between *no* and *fuck*, rejection and exclamation, but there was resignation now, and biological helplessness. Sam didn't think this was the first time they'd been made to do this, nor the first time others had been made to do it. Because they stared, dead-eyed, at the merrily jingling, glittering show, dripping, seeping—maybe glad it wasn't them this time, but with no guarantee they would be spared later, or even soon.

"Annie, let me out of here. You've been mistreating your dolls. I think you need a time-out until we can figure out how to better treat our things." Sam grabbed onto whatever she could think of, nonsensical as it was. What Annie was doing to these people was worse than even ordinary torture, yet not out of the question when playing with dolls. So how could Sam get through her delusion that what she was doing was wrong? How could she get the upper hand when Annie had the master key? Mr. Lange had said he needed to get Sam a set of keys, but it hadn't been with her things, and he'd left before he could hand one to her personally.

The windowless room pressed in on her, ceilings lower, walls closer, a cold, cold sweat on her scalp and down her back.

Annie stepped down from the platform toward her. "Miss Sam, I think we need to get a few things clear." Despite her dress, braids, and bows, Annie was too hard to seem childlike anymore—precocious instead, old and young soul. "These are not *our* things. These are *my* things. I can throw them against the wall or crush them with a cinderblock and still not mistreat them, because they're mine."

Annie took Sam's wrist rather than her hand and drew her away from the door. Sam was utterly weak, unable to convince her legs to push her back or her arms to pull away.

"In the afternoon and evening, I am free to play with my dolls however I see fit. You're my nanny. You're supposed to act like my mommy when Daddy isn't here. But I know what I'm allowed to do. You still have things to learn about how to take care of me and help me take care of my things."

"Annie…" Sam shook her head, shook all the way to her ankles the closer she came to the simulated sex between two broken people who couldn't resist the motions or whatever moved in them to make them obey.

"I'm not finished, Miss Sam. As my nanny, it's your job not just to take care of me but play with me. I have many dolls but not many people to play with. All the adults are busy working. They don't have time to play. You're paid, and paid well, to play with me."

"I don't want to play like this," Sam said, voice higher with her own regression—like when Cameron Padilla, a blonde-haired doll-like beauty in Sam's third-grade class, would dangle worms over Sam's head. In retrospect, Sam suspected Cameron had kind of liked her, but Sam hadn't known that back then, and the little girl's efforts to express it had been misguided and squishy. When girls made other girls cry, it was no sweeter than boys making girls cry.

"Whether you play or not, I'll still play." Annie took Sam's other wrist, then slid her hands back to take Sam's in something approaching tenderness. "You either play with me, Miss Sam, or I play with you."

Cold, hard, and heavy as the grand staircase and foyer floor, Sam looked again at all the broken people in the Repair Room—forced herself to really see them, to meet the sight unflinchingly.

They were young, twenties and thirties. As bad as they looked, they had a long way to go to look like prisoners of war, which suggested either a certain level of reparative care after Annie finished playing with them or robust health to begin with. There were more women than men, which was typical in a little girl's doll collection. And in child care professions—but Mr. Lange's promised salary would compel a nurturing man to test their luck.

All those previous nannies…

They quit, but they were never let go.

"Do you understand?" Miss Annie repeated.

Sam nodded slowly.

"Come play with me?" The smile was back, bright and youthful in a less than youthful face, all the way to her eyes—the way she'd smiled when Mr. Lange had first brought Sam to her. Excited. Guileless.

Sam couldn't figure out exactly how much Annie understood what she was doing. Until then, she'd been straightforwardly playing with dolls like most children do, although the method of play had sophistication that, like the ballroom dresses, suggested years of experience. She wasn't a savant. She had time and money on her hands.

That ultimatum, though…

Kids could be cruel. Kids could be sophisticated. Kids could be smart. Kids could be complex and lyrical and complicated and sneaky. But could boredom lead a child to go to such extreme lengths? And how could a child believe that a doll was a doll and not a person, then threaten that a person could become a doll at a moment's notice? An acknowledgment of the delusion or a particular compartmentalization?

Either way, Sam's survival with all her limbs intact seemed contingent upon assuming Annie believed these were all dolls, regardless of how much or how little she suspected Annie truly believed it.

Nanny or dolly?

The choice seemed easy as she let herself be led back to the carousel's center. Less so as Annie knelt on the other side of the two broken people, watching them avidly, her pupils seeming so much more dilated when compared to the constriction caused by the drugs put into their system.

"I always need help with this part." Annie gestured Sam down to the ground with her, just as if they were playing with real dolls. "The program puts them through the motions, but you need to put it in."

"What?" Disbelief stole Sam's air, making the word less substantial than the soft, wet sound of a precum-leaking cock sliding against slickened abdomen.

"I'll hold Ann up, and you put Jesse into her. That's how mommies and daddies make babies. Mommy and Daddy dolls need to make babies the same way."

"You can't... This is... Dolls don't fuck."

Annie giggled uncontrollably, like she'd been caught drawing dirty things in her coloring book. "You used the f-word."

"Dolls don't have parts. If they don't have parts, they don't...have sex. Isn't this enough?"

"I like my dolls when they have all their parts, because playing with them like this makes more sense. Come on, Miss Sam. I'll be Ann and you be Jesse. Put it in."

"Annie..."

"Are you going to play with me or not?"

Jesse let out a groan that expanded into a wail. He closed his eyes. Ann didn't. She stared, almost completely untethered now, bound though she was in every other way.

"I'm so sorry. I'm so sorry," Sam muttered, her hands shaking violently as she reached for Jesse's cock through the mechanical motions maintained by the control board. She threw up in her mouth as she closed panic-cold fingers around his erection. Jesse twitched, clenched his eyes shut, still murmuring *no* and *fuck*, wincing when the head struck Ann's vulva tip-on. "I'm so sorry. I'm sorry. God, I'm sorry..."

Sam gradually shifted the aim of Jesse's hot, drug-enhanced, fever-red erection down through Ann's swollen folds to her vagina, where the repeated motion pushed it rudely in.

The cock didn't bend but was smoothly swallowed, bringing Sam's fingers against Ann with a visceral squish. Ann arched. Sam jerked back, but she wasn't sure she could ever bleach that sensation from her brain, so unpleasant against all other pleasant memories of other vulvas, pussies, and cunts—

depending on the person—that she'd enjoyed and worshipped in the past.

That squish, with the thickened state of Ann's vulva as red as Jesse's erection, suggested a certain amount of vasodilation and increased blood flow in her, too, but it wasn't enough. Whatever was in the drug cocktail wasn't a love potion. Ann's arch hadn't been encouragement but to escape abrupt, blunt intrusion. Whatever haze she'd been chasing didn't pull her away far enough from terrible reality.

She sobbed ugly as Annie held her legs open and tilted her hips up to keep Jesse's cock inside through the steady forced pounding. He reached the base every time and, judging from Ann's reaction, probably struck the cervix because he was in too deep and she was only superficially aroused. What little lubrication she'd produced wasn't enough to make what Jesse did to her not painful.

Worse, someone else was making it happen, with Annie directing this particular scene and someone else with two hands, two feet, and an unclouded brain was helping Annie instead of helping them. Because Annie was about Sam's age, about her size, but entirely unpredictable, and Annie had the key out in a place Sam couldn't reach.

Sam held her hands out in front of her as though they were covered in blood, even though her right was barely smeared with pre-ejaculate.

When Jesse slipped out of Ann, Annie glared at Sam. "You have to put him back in."

"Why are you doing this?" Sam said, afraid she'd faint if she fucking moved. But she didn't faint as she reached to direct

Jesse's cock again, with all the joy of picking a rat out of a toilet bowl. "Oh God."

"Now you have to push. Push him in and keep him from falling out again."

"I don't...I don't know what you mean. I don't know..." Sam's breathing wasn't reaching her lungs. She couldn't catch her breath, even as it hitched through her chest.

"Get behind him and push."

"Annie, you can't... I can't... Oh God." Gasping, Sam crawled behind Jesse, grabbed his hips, the heels of her hands on his ass, and she added her push behind the motion keyed into the chains, propelling him forward so that he stayed inside Ann and fucked her harder.

Ann cried out even more from the firmer jostling thrusts, and she tried harder to get away, but Annie got behind her and pushed as well to keep her in place. Jesse wailed louder, too, interspersed with unmistakable groans of pleasure that made Sam's skin crawl even more than Ann's steady, rhythmic misery.

Sam pushed until Jesse's buttocks flexed on their own in quickening need that overtook his resistance or any ethical discomfort.

"I can't... I can't... What... What are you... Annie, why... I can't..." Sam kept saying that, but she could and she did.

Touching a man after determining she only liked women was repugnant all on its own. Being compelled to help a man rape a woman against his will—raping the man to rape the woman—ripped through her like lawnmower blades, yet nowhere near what Jesse and Ann were feeling, in either pleasure or pain. Sam's shards of protests fell away until all she could do was cry, too. She hadn't cried like that in years, hadn't known she still could.

The only one laughing was Annie.

She pushed up on Ann, her legs parted, too, but with her skirt between her spread legs and tights covering her skin. She giggled as she moved her hips in crude mimicry. Although Ann was in no state to enjoy anything, Annie raised her singsong voice in a childish adult parody, "Oh yes, oh yes, oh yes, oh it's so big, oh it's so good, yes, yes, yes, harder, harder, oh, I'm coming, I'm coming, I'm going to come, oh yes, fill me, fill me, yes, yes, *yes…*"

She laughed even more when Jesse's buttocks clenched again, his thighs tightening, and he jerked forward.

"Smoosh them together," Annie said, pushing up Ann's hips more. "You have to lean him in."

Sam nearly screamed through her tears as she brought herself flush against Jesse's naked back and pushed him in completely. The motion of the program ground him into Ann, but his hips had their own rhythm as he came. Ann screamed discordant to Sam, the accomplice, and discordant to Jesse, with his unwanted pleasure. Ann's mouth was a wet cavern that turned into silence when she wanted to scream beyond her lung's capacity, until she had to gasp it in again, and then her scream was near deafening.

Sam cried into Jesse's back, almost unable to hold herself up, but she was keeping him in, keeping him too deep and too hard, punching Ann's insides with him. She forced herself back again, letting Jesse go entirely. She fell onto her ass on the hard ground, shaking and crying and hating herself even more than she hated Annie. Children didn't understand, even when they thought they did, even when adults thought they did. Annie was just a child pulling wings off flies, because if she really understood…

Annie crawled out from under Ann to return to the board, where she hit the big button that had started the pre-programmed motions, then moved the joysticks apart. Jesse's cock slipped out of Ann's pussy, messy and drooping but not quite soft. When Annie adjusted Ann upright again, Jesse's semen eventually spilled in a slosh down her thigh.

Annie hit the cocktail button. Yellowish fluid entered their bodies once more. Ann settled into quieter and quieter sobs, then pitched forward and vomited on her sundress, but she didn't seem to care. Her heavy eyelids sank lower and lower over glassy eyes. Jesse hardened again, but his head fell back as his limbs went loose in their shackles.

"See?" Annie said. "Such a nice gift. How nice of Ann to give Jesse a gift that makes him feel so good. Even though you're not a mommy, Miss Sam, you're a grown-up. Do you know what it's like to feel good like that?"

As Annie sent them back to their spots, the track that Jesse was on trailed his feet over Sam's body.

She pulled herself out of the way, but she didn't have any drugs, so she couldn't stop crying. She curled her body in on itself, hands in tight fists between her thighs like protection.

Less than an hour ago, she'd been happy. She'd been happy because she hadn't known, and she wished she could have gone on not knowing, wished the job had stayed easy and all she had to do was make sure Annie put away her toys after she was finished so no one would step on them and the maids could do their job.

The maids. The kitchen workers. They had to know. The maids would have to clean up after them. The kitchen workers had to feed them somehow. That's why they needed so many people to take care of one little girl and her father.

Her father.

Mr. Lange had brought her here. Mr. Lange had brought all of them here, because Annie didn't leave the Dream House. Annie needed to stay in the Dream House to maintain the fantasy, the illusion, the delusion. Her father kept bringing her new playmates, kept bringing her new dolls. Either way, she got what she wanted, because Annie Lange was her daddy's princess and always got every doll she'd ever wanted, from a tiny Polly Pocket to human ball-joint dolls.

What about the mannequin in the ballroom? Had it really blinked? What had Annie done to them? Sprayed their skin with resin until they couldn't move, forced them frozen in place forever?

What about every other room in this ridiculous place?

Sam pushed herself upright on the floor, still weak. "Annie, I don't want to play in here anymore."

Annie continued fiddling with the board, making some of the other broken people jerk when their shackles moved, out of fear that they would be chosen next. "The maids deal with the mess dolls make, but you tidy up after me. Wipes are over there. Clean up the mess you helped make first. Then we can go."

Sam climbed shakily to her feet and fetched a container of wet wipes and a plastic bag. She went to Ann first. She'd given adults baths before, but this was different. When she'd had to clean seniors' bodies, it was because of a mess they hadn't been able to control—rarely personal, although sometimes they'd tried to make Sam miserable so they wouldn't be alone in their own misery.

This was different, because she was part of the reason why she had to wipe semen off Ann's thighs and vulva. There was nothing she could do about what was still inside of her or what it could do. But she could make sure Ann was dry. Sam undressed her entirely, working the dress out from under the harness and leaving her naked, then wiped her chest, harness, and neck of the vomit that had spilled over her. Sam looked around for something to cover her, a blanket or another dress.

"The maids will redress her when they come in to clean. Ann shouldn't have thrown up her food."

"Sometimes that's how people react to opioids," Sam said. "She could be overdosing."

But Ann was still breathing—shallow but steady, pulse regular.

While she was under, Sam gently wiped at the surgical marks. In theory, Annie's aptitude with needle and thread in fashion could translate to flesh, but Sam thought about what Mr. Lange had said—that they had a surgeon on call.

Which was more likely: That Annie had done all this intricate body work or that she had help from someone with a medical degree?

After arranging Ann so her legs were at least closed, Sam went across the room to Jesse. Tending to him as someone who couldn't take care of himself was easier than making herself part of his sexual activity. Even so, she fought waves of nausea as she cleaned him of his semen. She left his boxer shorts on after spot-dabbing at the dampness. They'd dry and be mostly fine, as long as he didn't eliminate in them while chasing the dragon into forced oblivion. She also cleaned the surgical work on him as best as she could, but at least one of the shackles had partially opened sutures in his ankle. The flesh there was red. The IV dock looked headed toward infection as well.

"Annie, Jesse needs special help," Sam ventured. "If someone doesn't fix him, he might lose a foot or an arm."

"Dr. Panabaker plays Doctor with me all the time," Annie said without glancing up from her work. "She gives me a fun Band-Aid and a lollipop when she's done with me, but she's also good at doll repair. She's been sewing up my teddies for a long time. She gives them a Band-Aid and a lollipop, too. But I eat their lollipops. Teddies don't suck on lollipops. She's just being silly."

Sam wasn't a doctor or a nurse. She'd just been an aide. She couldn't do anything for Jesse except tuck his half erection back into his boxer shorts like closing a door in the dark, leaving him cleaner than he'd been.

"I'm done, Annie."

Sam sounded almost normal herself, but she just didn't want Annie to decide to play House or Doctor on another broken doll. She needed *out*. She needed to remember that the sun was real and air could be breathed and there was a world beyond this place. Not that one would ever know by taking in the whole three-hundred-sixty-five degrees of the Dream House property—nothing but the house, the grounds, the wall, and woods all the way around.

Annie left the control board and leisurely made her way back to the door.

Sam didn't jump up and hurry after her. She was afraid if Annie saw how eager she was to leave, she'd find a reason to play more.

And it didn't matter how many wipes Sam had used. She was never going to get her hands clean.

Once Annie was a few steps from the door, Sam made herself get up as though calm and in control, although she was neither. Annie passed the keycard in front of the nearly invisible reader, which blinked green. Sam waited for Annie to open the door, then slipped her body between door and frame so Annie could no longer keep her in, but she still followed Annie out into the sterile hallway.

"Annie, I'd like to go to the kitchen for another coffee," Sam said. "Can you entertain yourself for a while?"

Annie smiled. "I'll make tea in my room while you get coffee. Then we can have a tea party in one of the playhouses."

"Sounds good." Sam turned her back to Annie and prayed she wouldn't hear the surreptitious slide of something more dangerous than a keycard out of Annie's bow or braid, a pocket, or the bra that flattened her chest.

Like a syringe of whatever she'd given to those broken people.

She walked past Annie's room and into the empty hall, with its heavy chandeliers and wall of real windows. Grackles grackled outside like they didn't know what was happening within the giant brick and glass cage. No maids or housekeeper. No kitchen staff.

Sam didn't go to the dining room. As soon as Annie's bedroom door closed, she swerved toward the grand staircase, the inlaid foyer. The large wooden front doors.

Locked. No matter which way she turned the deadbolt on the handle, the door wouldn't move. She couldn't find a control panel seam on the walls here, but the area was heavily shadowed, and she didn't have a keycard to wave around to try to find it.

"Fuck," she whispered.

She looked behind her. Still no Annie or disapproving housekeeper.

She ran back to the hall, with its French doors to the porch. The handles opened easily and swung out.

That didn't make much sense, locking the front doors and not the back, if the aim was to keep Sam and others inside the house. Unless the intention was simply to encourage Annie to take advantage of the backyard rather than wander out the gate, which was the kind of sense that was nonsense. Unless it wasn't nonsense at all.

Sam headed out onto the porch. A leisurely stroll, because Annie would be able to see her out the solarium glass, and Sam wanted to seem like she was just getting a breath of fresh air while waiting for her coffee.

The grackles screamed even louder at her intrusion on their world. Or perhaps there was a bobcat or coyote on the other side of the wall.

The fucking wall.

Sam rounded the south wing master suite toward the greenhouse. Windows allowed some light and forest views into the kitchen, and the greenhouse was all window, of course, but there were no windows in what looked like the servants' addition. The garden was attached to the greenhouse. The wrought-iron fence around it that had seemed so charming before no longer seemed charming—just another pen.

Yet, she was on the outside of it, and the kitchen door was a swinging door that didn't lock.

So, what kept people who *could* leave from leaving? Despair, once they saw how solid the stone wall was around the property, with the only gate controlled by a remote Sam had never been given? Or something more concrete?

A barn squatted in the back corner of the property. Mr. Lange had said that was where the groundskeepers lived. The roof edge was potentially within reach of the top of the stone wall, but the large, tall bushes that lined the wall would make it difficult to reach and dangerous to miss, as would the drop on the other side. Had anyone ever braved the sharp leaves and dense foliage? A few scratches seemed worth escape.

Sam reached the front of the property, with its even taller walls and magnificent gate. There was another control panel here, which they hadn't even bothered hiding. It required the remote, a keycard, or a code. Sam had none of those things.

She tried 1-2-3-4. She tried putting in A-N-N-I-E in numbers, like on a telephone. But people with secrets this serious surely wouldn't make it that easy.

They didn't. The light flashed at her in an angry red.

Hitting the control panel didn't help, either. Nor did shrieking at the sky like one of the grackles. She rattled the gate—with its elaborate design that wouldn't support climbing—but didn't expect it to budge.

She continued rounding the property, peeking between branches, like she would just stumble upon the Secret Garden. That seemed like the exact kind of whimsy the Dream House designers would indulge in, although perhaps not at the expense of their less whimsical secrets getting out.

As she parted branches to peer through, cold metal pressed against the back of her head.

"You're the new nanny, aren't you?"

Sam backed away from the bushes and turned around to a pistol pointed straight at her. The safety was off, and the groundskeeper's hands were much steadier than hers. He was a large man, black, his hair close-shorn and none on his face, with a bit of a gut but mostly solid. She knew he was a groundskeeper and not a security guard because of the grass stains on his tan jumpsuit and on his steady, steady hands.

"There are only two ways in and out of this place," the groundskeeper said. "No one leaves through the gate unless Mr. Lange lets them. The groceries get delivered through the utility shed over there. Delivery people have one key. We have the other. When the delivery people are in the shed, our door won't open, with or without a key. You may not have noticed, but underneath their fancy, old-fashioned ways of doing things, they're working with some serious technology. They're old-school in case the technology fails and new-school in case someone disables their more practical deterrents. They know you're out here. They know you're searching. And it's mine and Barry's job to make sure no one gets past the bushes, much less the fence. You hear me?"

"So, what, you're going to shoot me?" Sam said, striking out at the bushes in frustration—which was a mistake, because the sharp leaves cut her hands in the process. No worse than a paper cut, but a paper cut was bad enough. "Even if I got out, this is a forest of about six rich families. How much do you want to bet the other five have their own skeletons? Which means they wouldn't let me into their compounds, much less allow me access to a phone."

"I'm authorized to shoot to kill, especially with outsiders. But with people from inside…" He lowered the bore of his gun to her leg. "If I shoot here, they'll take the limb. What good is a nanny who's recovering from amputation? You get what I'm saying?"

"You'd do that? Make damn sure they could still use me? Why would you do that?"

"That's my job," the groundskeeper said, just as quietly, but a little slower. "That's what they keep me alive for. That's what they keep my family alive for. Do you understand?"

"Are you telling me—"

"As long as I do my job, no one plays with my family." Now his hand wavered, but not off his mark. "Do you understand?"

"I can't do this." Sam rubbed her forehead and shook her head. "I can't *help* her like this."

"There's no way out. No good way. Next time I see you out here, it better be because you're admiring the fig trees or taking a run or walking with Miss Annie. Put escape out of your mind. Because they're watching. They're watching everything."

"Who's *they*?"

"They always know. They got my family, but all you have is you. So if they catch you, *you're* the one she plays with, and it starts over again with someone new. Always someone new. I don't know why I bother anymore."

"How many nannies has she gone through?" Sam asked, out of breath even though she wasn't moving.

The groundskeeper swallowed. The naturally burst capillaries in his eyes became more pronounced as he tried to maintain his composure. His aim, however, no longer wavered. "Mr. Lange finds good people. They never last more than a week."

"Fuck." Sam braced her hands on her knees, wondering if she should put her head between them. "Fuck, how is this real? How is this happening?"

"The key is to not be a good person. Maybe if you're bad enough, one day they'll let you out that gate, because they'd have everything they need to keep you quiet. But no one on the inside's ever been out that gate yet. Except Mr. Lange."

Because all his skeletons were behind a stone wall, razorblade bushes, and an iron gate. No wonder he took month-long business trips.

The question wasn't whether Mr. Lange knew. The question was how much. How much did he let himself see? Mr. Lange found good people—good nannies, anyway—and he was a bad person for doing that. But was he bad because he spoiled his daughter, because he was a coward who didn't try to stop her? Or was he bad because he spoiled his daughter and didn't *want* to stop her? Accomplice or participant?

What kinds of things happen when he's home?

"You've never been on the other side of the gate, even though you do your job?" Sam asked.

"I can't leave my family behind." The groundskeeper lowered the gun entirely. "Am I going to have to shoot you?"

"No. No. I'm going." She turned, but paused. "What do I call you? I'm—"

"Lance," he said. "I know who you are, but it's better not to know names or get attached. We just knew you were coming. Nanny is big here. The go-between. The buffer. Nanny is important."

"But a nanny can't control her."

"No one controls Miss Annie. We serve at her pleasure. Better hurry. They might think we're conspiring."

Sam retreated, then jogged back down to the house—the beautiful, impossible, skulking, forbidding, looming house.

From the vantage point of walking the house's perimeter, the east wing was a tumor. Windows, her own included, mostly lined the second floor. The rest of it was brick, wood, and stone, stylized in such a way that the lack of windows wasn't immediately noticeable, because the turrets were windowed and there was otherwise nothing to compare it to from this angle.

Aside from the grackles, everything was so quiet out here. The only screaming anyone would hear was animal. Brick, cinderblock, and insulation blocked out sounds from the inside.

Sam touched one of the bricks. She didn't want to know any more, but she suspected that if she agreed to Annie's terms, there wouldn't be much she didn't know about what happened on the other side of that wall.

She would be the conscience holding Annie's guilt while she danced through life with a child's lack of care.

The key is to not be a good person.

Sam didn't think of herself as a good person. She was a caregiver. She was sympathetic. She was empathetic. But she was sometimes so tired, and because she was tired, she could be hateful, dull, bored. She was good at jobs, but she wasn't good at being a good person, or else she would have broken up with Lila before coming to this job rather than leaving it up in the air.

Sam blinked, then ran the rest of the way around the east wing, Annie's room, back to the patio doors, which were still open. Annie stood in the empty hall, holding one of her ragdolls by its leg, the dress flipped upside-down over its face. Her sullen look had returned.

Sam froze. "I'm on my way, Annie," she said carefully. "I still need to get that coffee. I got distracted by the beautiful day."

"Do you want to play outside?" Annie looked at Sam like a suspicious, hungry dog at a mean man's open hand of treats.

"After I get my coffee." Glancing back at Annie to make sure she didn't cut off escape altogether, Sam went to the serving hatch and opened the sliding door. "Ji-an?"

"What?" Ji-an snapped back, sounding far away and impatient.

"Could I have another coffee, please? Same way."

"Give me a minute. Jesus H. Christ."

Sam closed the hatch again and turned to Annie. "I need to go get something from my room. I'll be right back for my coffee. Then I can play Tea Party with you. We can even play outside if you like. I'm still getting settled in here, and I forgot to do something. Okay?"

Annie rocked back and forth, her heels clicking on the hard floor. Then her lips, her jaw, her whole demeanor, relaxed. "Okay."

She skipped back toward her bedroom.

Sam waited until she couldn't hear Annie's Mary Janes. Then she sprinted across the marble floors to the stairs and rushed up to her bedroom, where she locked the door, although she doubted that would really keep Annie out.

Her purse was at the foot of the bed. She hadn't wanted to use her phone before because she'd been enchanted by this place, by the illusory lack of technology. If *they* were always watching, there was probably so much more technology she didn't know about, couldn't see, cameras where they shouldn't be. She'd slept, dressed, undressed, showered in complete ignorance she didn't have anymore.

But the one piece of surveillance technology she wanted—her goddamn phone—was nowhere to be found. She dumped out her purse, hoping it was hidden at the bottom. It wasn't lost in her bedclothes, wasn't in the bathroom drawers or counter, wasn't on the dresser, wasn't on or inside the nightstand.

There were other things missing from the nightstand, too. Like the laminated sheet of contacts Mr. Lange had promised.

No phone number for Mr. Lange. No doctor's number. Not even the obvious emergency services or poison control. All she had was Annie's walkie-talkie—because Annie, at least, kept her promises, no matter how terrible.

Then she heard her ringtone. Under the bed.

She might have kicked her phone there by accident, but Sam didn't think so. She knelt and lifted the sheets.

Her phone wasn't there, but an old toy phone was. Using the ringtone of her phone.

"Fuck."

Sam pulled it out from under the bed. It wasn't connected to a phone line. She hadn't expected it to be.

She picked up the red receiver and brought it to her ear. "Hello?"

"Come play with me," Annie said brightly.

Sam dropped the receiver and jumped back, but she could still hear Annie on the other side.

"Come play with me. Come play with me. Come play with me."

Not a phone. Another fucking walkie-talkie, technology stitched together like she stitched a ballgown. *Like she stitches a person?* There were medical texts in the library, after all, and an endless number of people to practice on.

"*Fuck.*" Sam fought the urge to cry again, pulling at her roots. Then she darted to the phone and picked up the receiver. "Annie, where's my phone?"

"You're talking in it, silly."

"No, *my* phone. Where's *my* phone?"

"I don't know what you're talking about, but your coffee's going to get cold, and so is my tea. Come play, Miss Sam."

"Annie, it's not nice to take people's things. It's mean to play tricks on them like this. Did you hide it?"

"It's also not nice to accuse people of taking things when they didn't, and it's mean to say you're going to do something, then don't. Are you a liar, Miss Sam?"

Sam stared at the phone, at the happy face of the cradle staring up at her. "No, Annie, I'm not a liar," she said more carefully. "I told you I needed to get something. I needed my phone. I was waiting for someone to check up on me after I got situated, and I wanted to see if they had."

"I don't know where your phone is, Miss Sam, but I know where you're supposed to be."

Chapter 5: JACK-IN-THE-BOX

Sam didn't hurry. She didn't want to seem afraid, although she was. Didn't want to seem like she was at Annie's beck and call, although she was. If they were going to maintain this charade, she needed to pretend that being a nanny meant something, that she was the adult and Annie was the child.

And if she was the adult who'd just lost her phone, she definitely needed her coffee. It had been put into an insulated cup and everything, and it was still really good. Sam closed her eyes, giving herself the moment.

"Thank you," she said through the serving hatch. No one replied, but that was okay. They probably couldn't hear her over the multiple blenders.

Annie had made herself real tea with an electric kettle from her snack bar and was pouring it for a teddy bear and monkey stuffed animal in the gingerbread house. In an ordinary playhouse, Sam would have to crouch or walk on her knees, but in the custom build, she only had to bend over to get through the door, then keep her head bent before joining Annie at the parlor table with her friends. Annie had also unpackaged some snack cakes and was fake serving them to her stuffed animals, then eating them herself and speaking for the animals about how good it was.

When Annie handed Sam a little porcelain plate, too, Sam accepted it with only a tremble.

"Don't you think this will spoil your dinner?" she asked.

"It hasn't yet," Annie said. "Do you want some tea or just the coffee?"

"I'll finish my coffee first."

The snack cakes weren't spiked. Neither was the tea after her coffee, although it didn't taste like much. Annie was literally just playing Tea Party with her stuffed animals and nanny as though she hadn't played House with two broken people who she thought were dolls.

She'd transitioned seamlessly from horror into typical child play as though there was no transition for her at all. As though one was the equivalent of another. Other than Sam's residual nausea and hyperawareness of every fairy light, every gleaming glass eye, every twitch of Annie's smile or early wrinkle deepening, it was hard to believe the horrifying thing had even happened.

It would be so much easier to convince herself that this was all Annie would do going forward. So much easier for Sam to just close off the Repair Room as an isolated incident and maintain the illusion that nothing at all was wrong with the Dream House, nor with Annie.

But there was a whole *wing* of doll storage, plus the ballroom and who knew what other secret rooms, and if Annie was like any other child, she'd want to show off *all* her dolls.

The children Sam had watched over in daycare had had favorite toys they'd gone back to time and again because routine was comfortable, routine was familiar, and at a young age, there were a lot fewer diminishing returns with repetition. Whether Annie had the mind of a child or not, though, her sheer number of years would lead to a certain amount of boredom with that repetition.

That's why she had so many toys in her bedroom. That's why she switched them out. That's why she needed so many rooms for so many dolls. Because what she liked didn't change, but she would need variety to maintain that joy, and she could afford variety.

She could play Tea Party in a playhouse with stuffed animals, and she could play House with people whose joints had been dislocated to make them posable. These things weren't conflicting in the slightest.

Just because Annie was playing quietly and sweetly now didn't mean that the Repair Room was an anomaly.

At the same time, Sam was going to wear herself out if she anticipated the worst at every moment. She needed these quiet times to think, and she couldn't think if she panicked.

She couldn't trust that Annie hadn't taken her phone. One of the maids also could have taken it any time after Sam had last checked her messages. She'd never locked her bedroom door. Had she even told Lila she'd arrived, or had she only thought about it? Lila knew she wouldn't hear from Sam for a while. How long before she became concerned? Or would she just think Sam was ghosting her, which she'd probably already thought Sam was doing by leaving?

After uprooting herself from every aspect of her life, would *anyone* notice she was missing or just assume she'd burned every bridge behind her?

Mr. Lange had asked about friends. She'd said she didn't have any, just her work. He'd asked about her family, her home life. She'd all but told him she wanted nothing to do with her family and that Lila would be happy she was gone.

She couldn't just hope and pray someone from the outside would save her. And she couldn't hope and pray someone on the inside would save her, either. The staff were entirely cowed. The toys were injured and bound.

If she could just last long enough to figure out how to get out...

But if Annie went back into the Repair Room and locked Sam in with her, Sam didn't know whether she would make it. She wasn't a nice or good person, but she was better than that. She didn't want to hurt anyone. She *never* wanted to hurt anyone. Couldn't fathom what she'd done and didn't know if she could do it again.

Yet, she *had* done it once. And she needed to somehow last longer than a week. The next time she knew for certain someone would open those gates was when Mr. Lange returned after a month. Until then, she had to find whatever Annie might use to communicate with him or any other part of the outside world. Grocery delivery involved some kind of communication as well, so they would know what to bring each week. She needed to assume Ji-an had already tried to get out, though.

The secret seemed to be finding a line of communication with the outside world and some kind of collaboration with other members of the staff. If *everyone* resisted, if *everyone* broke the rules and risked punishment, maybe they'd have a chance. But that would require surreptitious coordination between household factions deliberately kept separate, and whoever *they* were would probably know. If there even was a *they* beyond Annie and her father, which was *they* enough, given their resources.

If only everything could be stuffed animals and snack cakes, a blissful library, a fireplace in autumn, a rich family that could at least approximate normal. When had people become dolls to Annie? Had they always been, and Mr. Lange just hadn't been able to argue with her in his grief? Or had people always been dolls to the Lange family as a whole? Had the house been reconfigured for Annie's collection, or had it been created for this when it had been built for Mr. Lange's wife?

So many questions, not enough answers, nothing more solid than the house itself, and Annie had much more conviction, even in playing Tea Party and making her own conversation. She barely needed Sam to interject except to express how delicious the cakes were and agree with the stuffed animals' observations about the state of the playhouse neighborhood, which apparently had a Homeowners' Association that the haunted house flouted on every level. Bland, banal things—funny coming from a thirty-something child who lived in an HOA-free neighborhood.

If Sam could find Annie funny anymore. If she'd ever found Annie funny.

When tea was finished and Annie ran out of small talk, she climbed out of the playhouse with Sam.

Before Annie could express her own preference, Sam quickly said, "Shall we go back to the library? You can do all your coloring there, and we can wait for dinner while we watch the sunset through the windows."

Annie smoothed her hands over her ribbon and skirt and considered. Then she grabbed some coloring things from her coloring tables and skipped happily to the library.

Sam knew better than to believe she could distract Annie to the preferred behavior every time, but she wondered if that was the key to surviving this place: being an actual nanny, reinforcing it just as insistently as Annie justified her delusion.

She only needed to make it long enough. Long enough to figure out how to get out.

Coloring until dinner, playroom until bed. Sam would have breathed a sigh of relief, but there would be another day, and another.

"Miss Sam?" Annie said as Sam headed out of the playroom.

"Yes, Annie?"

"I miss Daddy."

I miss your daddy, too. I have a few things to say to him, and I'm pretty sure they involve bankrupting myself in a swear jar. "He'll be home before you know it."

"No. He's gone for such a long time."

Sam sighed at the doorway, then stepped back in toward the bed, where Annie sat up among her stuffed animals—new ones tonight. New conversations, new sensations, new friends. "What do you miss about your dad?"

"I miss how he tells stories about Mommy."

"I wish I could tell you those kinds of stories. But I didn't know your mom. I would have liked to." *To see whether she was as fucked up as the rest of you or whether her dying is the reason everything got fucked up in the first place.*

"Can you sleep in here with me tonight, Miss Sam?" Annie patted her cloud-like covers.

"I can sleep on one of the beanbags, I think, if you'd like me to stay."

"There's plenty of room to sleep in here, where it's warm. You can share one of my friends. It'll be like a sleepover."

"That's your bed, Annie. I'd rather you sleep in your bed and I sleep in my bed."

"I can sleep in yours with you, if you want to sleep in your bed tonight," Annie offered. "I just don't want to be alone."

"You're never alone. Look at all your friends." Sam gestured to all her dolls, to the stuffed animals Annie hugged close.

Annie pouted.

Sam shook out a quilt from the selection in a basket next to the bed and sank down into a beanbag chair with a crunch. "See? Nice and snug. I'm right here, Annie. Now, why don't you close your eyes and try to get some sleep?"

Annie nestled into her much warmer bed with a huff, covering herself entirely with the duvet.

It was difficult for Sam to believe she could sleep, but she was exhausted from holding everything in, like shopping bags up and down both arms all day. Unconsciousness had nearly pulled her under when Annie reemerged from her cocoon, sitting up in bed with a sudden rustle. Sam's eyes snapped open to the disturbance of grass on the savanna in lion territory. Lionesses, after all, did most of the hunting.

"Miss Sam, can you talk to me?"

"Mmm."

"Daddy told me that you live with another girl."

Sam didn't dare hesitate. "Mm-hmm."

"And not like people live together in college. He says you live with her like he lived with Mommy."

"Mm-hmm."

"Is she who you wanted to call?"

"I was supposed to let her know when I got here. That's something good friends do when they go new places with new people. But I think I forgot to let her know. I assume she texted, but I can't find my phone. Do you know who took my phone, Annie?"

"What's her name?"

Sam wasn't sure if she'd shared Lila's name with Mr. Lange. If she had, he might have shared it with Annie. "Lila."

"Is Lila your wife, like Mommy was Daddy's? You don't wear a ring."

"She's my girlfriend. You should get some sleep." *You goddamn fucking brat. Don't you fucking say her name. And don't you tell your daddy to do anything to her.* Sam didn't have to be on good terms with her girlfriend to want her to stay the hell away from this place.

"Do you love her like Daddy loved Mommy?"

Sam sighed. "It's complicated, Annie."

"That's a no."

"That's a complicated."

"Why?"

"It's personal."

"Then tell me as a story."

Sam sighed again, turning over on the beanbag. Annie wasn't going to let it go, and either way, she'd keep Sam from sleeping. "We were going through a rough patch when I took this job. It wasn't either of our faults. We might not be compatible anymore just by virtue of our schedules. That doesn't mean I don't love her, just that it's hard to remember why."

"What made you fall in love with her?" Annie sounded sleepier now.

Sam lay there for a while, staring up at the fairy lights, trying to see Lila in her mind—and trying not to at the same time because it hurt too much. But she wasn't even sure if she missed Lila and wanted to go back to her so much as wanted to be back in the world she'd come from rather than the one she was in. "I don't remember."

"Try."

"She was… She was ordering soup at a restaurant I was at. She was in college. I was working. She had a bag full of books and I was dog tired, but she was really pretty and dropped her muffin from the bakery there on the floor. I bought her a new one. We ate together outside the restaurant because it was a rare kind of nice outside. Then she asked me out."

"Had you been with another girl before?"

"Yes. A whole lot of nothing for a long time, though, except enough to know that I liked girls more than boys. Nothing was better than negative. Lila was better than both. We got closer and closer until she graduated. Then, even though we started living together, we drifted farther and farther apart. Then living together was all we did, and barely that."

Had Sam ever loved her? Did it matter? Neither love nor indifference would save Sam, but maybe indifference would help Lila.

She remembered Lila on that first day, though. Remembered feeling twice as old instead of just a few years. Remembered how silly and tongue-tied Lila had made her, in the worst and best way. Remembered the sun behind Lila and her hair blowing in her face. Remembered how sad Lila had been when she'd dropped the muffin. How significant it had felt when Sam had offered to buy her another one. How the way Sam had phrased it made Lila crack up, then Sam—like a tennis ball (or muffin) passed back and forth between them while the teenager at the cash register stared at them, bemused.

She remembered how it had felt to be asked out when she'd barely felt anything for anybody since high school. She'd gone out with Lila because Lila had made her feel alive inside after all the ways her family had killed the most important and unique parts of her.

It hadn't been their fault, except her mother's for not doing her job. Her sisters hadn't chosen to be born, and an older brother more interested in drums than in making sure his sisters were fed that day probably wouldn't have done a much better job than their mother. But in becoming a mother as soon as she was old enough to realize they didn't really have one, Sam had had to lose herself.

She'd gone through a few hormonal explosions. Things had pressed upon her, against her, inside her, and it had sometimes been terrible and sometimes okay. Sometimes with boys and sometimes with girls, curiosity each time, or just plain old need, and anger that she had to grab young life in starving fistfuls while her siblings never went hungry because of her.

Lila had been different. Lila had been hers. Lila had been something she could hold and who held her back instead of clung. It had felt so nice to want and be wanted rather than need and be needed. To actually make an effort to date because it had been worth it for that smile and her laugh and the way she'd kissed her way from neck to ear. The way she'd squirmed under Sam as Sam had discovered whole new and exciting things about being with a woman because she had the *time* to explore and less self-consciousness about doing it. And when they'd first moved in together, all the shitty things about the apartment hadn't added up yet; it had been right before they'd had to start doing twice as much to fall behind.

When Sam had told her mother that she'd be moving in with Lila, her mom had burst out laughing. *"Well, that's one way to keep from having to change another diaper. I'd munch carpet myself if I didn't like dick so much."* Her mom still thought it was one big joke every time Sam mentioned her girlfriend and would laugh sometimes until she cried.

Sam didn't know if it had ever been love or whether she could have coasted forever on exceptional like with a little lust. But she didn't miss the numbness she'd left. Lila probably didn't, either.

If only Sam hadn't walked straight into something so much worse—where she had to explain Lila in such a way that no one went after her for Sam's sin of believing things might get easier for once in her miserable life.

"Miss Sam?"

"Last question, Annie. Then you need to get your beauty sleep."

"Do you think she called you when you didn't call her?"

Sam tightened her grip on the blanket where Annie couldn't see her. "I don't know."

Sam woke to someone sleeping against her back and immediately knew it wasn't Lila. Lila had sometimes fallen asleep as the big spoon, but she'd never stayed that way and would end up on her own side of the bed sometime while she slept. Also, Sam was sleeping on beans, not a bed.

Annie had tucked herself as close to Sam as clothes would allow and wrapped her arm around Sam's abdomen as though she were a stuffed animal who didn't need to breathe. Annie's fist had left a bruise under Sam's ribs. She was surprised the unpleasant arrangement hadn't woken her up sooner. She must have been really tired, or sleep might have been a much-needed escape.

Sam twitched at realizing she was being spooned by the girl pulling her strings, and Annie tightened her hold.

Sam didn't like waking up in the Dream House again. And she didn't like Annie tucked against her instead of in her own big bed, as though to remind Sam before she even opened her eyes that her indefinite future would consist of asking which would be worse: becoming a monster or becoming a doll.

She certainly knew which one would hurt more.

Sam eased herself from Annie's hold and climbed off the beanbag. She couldn't tell how long Annie had been there, but it felt like slime coated her skin, absorbed through her pores.

Annie woke more slowly and *stretched*, her legs short but slender and strong. To Sam's horror, her clit twitched, a fully physical reaction rather than emotional, and when Annie opened her eyes, there was something there that seemed neither childlike nor cold.

Eleven had been around the time Sam's desires had awoken, little though she'd been able to spare the time to properly indulge or explore through her teenage years. Whether Annie thought so or not, her body was adult and might react as involuntarily as Sam's, newly awoken, reflexes slow.

Now Sam really needed to clean herself off.

"Go back to sleep," Sam said. Morning exposure wasn't so direct on this side of the house, but the sky was lighter, with a hint of golden red on the other side of the turrets. The rainbow clock said Annie still had an hour and a half before she was supposed to get up. "I need to take a shower, since I didn't have one last night. I'll wake you up for breakfast."

"Okay," Annie said blearily. She climbed back into the bed she'd abandoned sometime in the night to sleep behind Sam, as though Annie had known that waking up with her there was precisely the last thing Sam had wanted to do.

No one stopped Sam as she went back to her room, took a shower, and changed. She wished that made her feel better, but she crouched in front of the toilet against a wave of nausea burning through her stomach. Could someone get a bleeding ulcer over the course of only a few days?

The nausea didn't go away, but it subsided.

She didn't know how to dress for a morning of leisurely study and an afternoon of potentially playing with pieces of people, but she didn't think she needed to try to dress appropriately anymore. She chose a pair of sweats and a band t-shirt she'd cut up to suit her.

Ji-an had already set out a thermos cup of coffee on the serving counter thirty minutes before Annie needed to wake up, which meant Sam had effectively established a caffeine schedule.

She headed back to Annie's room, contemplating just letting her sleep forever. But when she peeked in, Annie was already up and getting ready for her morning. She came out in a pink dress that would have been sickeningly sweet if not for the stark black ribbons she wore around her waist and hair— pigtails today, curled into ringlets, her bangs like a doll's wig, starched into such a perfect curl.

"I think it's going to be a beautiful day," she said.

The coffee burned a bigger hole through what Sam had already done to her stomach.

Annie beckoned for her hand. Sam let herself be led.

After lunch, Annie practically dragged her from the parfait back toward the east wing.

"Annie, slow down. You don't want to slip and fall and tear your pretty dress." *Please. Please fall and knock your head on the marble. Have a concussion. Hell, have a coma.*

Annie looked genuinely chagrined and stopped pulling on Sam's hand. "Sorry. I've just been looking forward to introducing you to more of my dolls."

As they entered the east wing, a whine of wet vacs and regular vacuum cleaners emanated from Annie's playroom and bedroom as well as the curved corridor behind her wing. Sam couldn't see any maids, just the housekeeper standing at the corridor entrance like a sentinel, her colorless lips pursed and sucked in like a shrunken head. Sam tried to discern more than stiff spine and disapproval in the housekeeper's expression, but there was nothing. Perhaps the housekeeper just didn't like children—regardless of age—and had no respect for every hapless, short-lived nanny who came through the door.

"Mrs. Fratello," Annie said, noticing Sam notice the housekeeper. "She was with us at our old house and moved with us to the Dream House. She loves working for us. She'd be my nanny if she weren't so old."

"How long has Ji-an been with you?" Sam asked.

Annie shrugged. "Not until after we moved here. Our last chef is over here."

In the cross corridor, Annie opened the first white door on the right.

On the other side was another door, this one plexiglass with holes cored into it—although not so what was inside could breathe, because the room was ventilated.

The glass door was closed tight, no handle to open. Sam assumed the only way to open it was a master keycard. But even if Sam had been able to open the door on her own, she would never have let out the man inside.

The medical box next to the door's edge held an IV bag with the same yellowish material that had 'lubricated' the broken dolls in the Repair Room. The man appeared pretty well drugged, on a light but steady drip rather than a sudden rush.

He slumped splay-legged in the middle of the room, feet forcibly swollen with some kind of injectable, possibly silicone. His shoes had been made to his new specifications, but the alterations were visible through the opening at the top.

He wore ballooning pants that might have at one time fit his waist. He carried a potbelly still, but it hung, pendulous, splat over his thighs, and his bare chest was flattened like a pancake by rainbow suspenders. Vomit flecked his chest hair, his belly, the front of his polka-dotted pants, but he didn't seem to mind.

He was also as erect as a balloon animal underneath.

Sam immediately made the association because the room was full of balloons, inflated by a machine in the corner. The machine blew up a balloon, then tied it off to let it fall to the floor in a cheery garden around the clown's depressed posture. When the room eventually filled with too many balloons, spikes on the walls popped some, leaving room for more. Maids would presumably remove the dead excess.

The room also had a small metal combination toilet and sink in the corner. There was no food flap on the door or anywhere else in the room that Sam could see, like one might expect in a solitary prison cell. With the exception of his block feet, he'd lost massive amounts of weight, but he couldn't have been starved for all the years he'd been locked away, so they gave him food somehow.

As light from the hallway seeped into his dark rainbow-colored world, the orange-tufted clown looked up.

A nasogastric tube was taped to his cheek, which had been split from mouth almost to ear on both sides, then stitched not together but apart so they scarred over unclosed. His rotting teeth were exposed, incisor to molar, in a huge, shit-eating grin not his own.

His eyelids, too, had been split into harlequin scarring. One of the splits hadn't gone according to plan, the eye cloudy with damage and probably blind. More scars created the illusion of crow's feet smile lines.

His undamaged eye was glazed over, barely seeing Sam on the other side until he noticed Annie staring down at him with her hands clasped in front of her, like a good girl staring down at her favorite zoo chimpanzee.

He jerked back in delayed reaction, then blinked, both eyes heavy with gummy tears. He rubbed the gum away. The scarring around his wrists wasn't the same as the damage done to people in the Repair Room. He could stand with more ease, although his feet clearly pained him, as though they'd explode from putting weight on them. But he did it anyway, to the calliope music that played like Muzak in his room.

Then he danced. It wasn't good dancing. Vaudevillian schtick with cinder-block feet didn't lend itself to skill. But it was to a beat, and he made jazz hands and forced a greater smile through his already forced smile. His erection bobbed just like a balloon giraffe's neck.

When his song ended, he stomped—a wince in his squinting eyes and twitching cheeks—to the plexiglass, where he pressed his gloved hands against the door and stared down at Annie with hatred that even his muzziness couldn't conceal. He grasped his cock through the oversized pants held up solely by suspenders and jerked the circus-tent pitch of his erection without finesse or any additional lubrication, besides what steadily entered into the dock in his arm.

Annie gazed up at him with a pleasant smile, unshaken, unshocked. "He overcooked his meat, which was why we preferred his egg custards, but he always had the best balloon animals. He's just as silly now as he was then."

When Sam swallowed, she thought her throat might get stuck that way and never open again. "He's...colorful."

"You should see him with a new coat of paint. He's filthy right now. The maids can only do their best to keep my doll boxes clean until I can get to them again."

"You mean the maids clean up biological waste?"

Annie looked at her strangely. "They just clean the boxes, Miss Sam. But yes, they clean toilets, too."

She stroked the glass in front of the clown. He thrust against the door like he wanted to stab her with his cock instead of fuck her with it. Before he could come, she shut the door.

She skipped to the next door. "After they're repaired, I can make them into anything I want. They're so pretty when they're restored. See?"

When Annie opened the door, a chandelier switched on above a woman Sam thought might be standing on her hands. Music—classical, unobtrusive—spilled into the room with the light. The woman's sequined leotard suggested some kind of dancer. Or gymnast, given that she was doing a handstand.

She wasn't alone. Another dancer or gymnast climbed from a pallet on the ground and joined the other in her jerky yet somehow elegant handstand dance triggered by the music.

Sam reeled back from the glass door so hard that she struck the opposite wall.

Both women showed signs of being in the Repair Room, but their joints had since healed—including where the arms had been attached to the pelvic sockets and the legs had been attached to the shoulder sockets.

They crouched, bowlegged, with their heads between their thighs. The leotards covered their crotches but had been tailored for a diminished ass, given that the thigh muscles had been attached to the shoulder in a mind-bending configuration, with a bulge of buttock over each shoulder blade. If it weren't so goddamn horrifying, maybe Sam would have been fascinated by the artistry and the fact that whatever procedure they'd done had clearly worked. Aside from both women walking upside-down on their legs, they appeared perfectly healthy. In fact, they looked like they'd had years to heal, years to practice, years to walk almost as well as normal in their little box.

Their mouths had been sewn shut into drawn smiles. Their eyes had been removed and replaced with what looked like blue marble glass. Like the clown, nasogastric tubes had been taped to their hollow cheeks, and their IVs connected to bags in the box next to the door.

They paraded and twirled around each other, hands raised in fifth position. When the music changed keys, they danced together, sliding their hands over the leotard, over the narrow crotches that threatened to disappear between their folds.

Annie clapped in time with the music; the women twitched with every clap. Sam covered her mouth and tried desperately not to scream until Annie closed the door again.

Perhaps it was no wonder they went along with Annie's preferred play after being thoroughly 'lubricated' and 'repaired.' Sam wouldn't be surprised if they'd gone completely insane. It would be the only way to survive, if one could call this survival.

Annie could learn many things over the course of a decade or two, but surely she hadn't reached the point of being an expert engineer, seamstress, *and* surgeon. The rich could buy almost everything, but they usually outsourced skill. Boredom made Annie an expert in some things, but only studying in the mornings meant she probably hadn't acquired expertise in the realm of the medically risky and improbable. That seemed more the purview of an actual surgeon—the self-same surgeon on call for Annie, for instance. With an endless supply of subjects and no real repercussions for failure, *someone* could do a lot of damage to those who managed to survive the procedures.

Annie danced in front of the next door to music only she could hear. "Again." She flung open the door so forcefully it hit the door jamb.

Sam stayed against the wall but crept to the side, drawn by her own terrible curiosity like Bluebeard's wife to witness what was beyond the glass.

Two women sat on a swing that moved to new music, something light and springlike in the dark gray cell. The women were dressed to white Lolita nines and connected at the hips as though scissoring. Their ruffled skirts didn't allow Sam to tell if they were attached at the crotch like they looked. However, part of the reason they seemed attached was because they had each lost their right leg and right arm and cinched together perfectly because of it.

One of them roused with the swing and the music; the other didn't.

Annie frowned and knocked sharply on the glass.

The awake girl shook the other, who finally blinked, bleary, as though she'd clawed her way through a mud swamp to reach consciousness. Annie swayed with the swing's rhythm as the two women did their own little dance with their arms and kissed each other lightly between harpsicord verses.

Annie clapped, then closed the door and moved to the next, waving for Sam to follow her again.

"Annie, are there going to be any small dolls on this doll tour?" Sam asked, trying to keep her parfait on the inside and not quaver when she spoke.

"This one is smaller, I think."

The next room was so dimly lit that Sam had to step closer to see through the hallway reflection in the glass.

A carved wooden box crouched in the middle of the room. No toilet or sink; the pipes were still there but closed off. The IV bag was connected to a tube that snaked through a small hole between the box and its lid. On the other side of the box, a pulley crank moved in a circle with help from a bicycle chain triggered by the same mechanism that turned on the light.

A plinky toy-song "Pop Goes the Weasel" played from inside the box. Annie hummed along, then sang, clutching her skirt as she braced for the inevitable yet unpredictable jack-in-the-box conclusion.

Sam half covered her mouth again with an entirely different kind of anticipation. Her imagination filled in the blanks of what was inside that compact box with more and more horrible things—and even worse, understanding that the horrible thing *would* be a person, or had been once.

Annie shrieked in delight, jumping back from the glass into Sam as the box flipped open and Jack popped out, bouncing on the end of a spring. The spring had to be sturdy to support the whole top half of a person.

Sam fought not to vomit in Annie's hair. The man's entire lower half—from pelvis down—had been removed. Just a torso and a round, bald head with a clown cone cap sewn onto the scalp. His mouth had been sewn together in a scar smile, his eyes replaced with large, black buttons. A nasogastric feeding tube threaded into his nose like the others, but he also had a half-full urine bag connected to a catheter and a full colostomy bag.

His heavy head sagged on his neck.

Annie stopped laughing. She knocked on the glass again. This time, the doll inside didn't wake up.

She adjusted the drip rate on the IV box as though she'd done it a thousand times, waited a few more rounds of "Pop Goes the Weasel," then knocked on the glass door, harder this time.

Still nothing.

She stomped her foot, then slipped out her keycard and swiped it below the IV box. She wrinkled her nose as she stepped in. The smell hit Sam a few seconds later: shit and living decay.

Sam covered her nose and crept closer. The place where the surgical steel spiraled into his body was violent red and reaching. Scar tissue covered his lips, but his nails were blue. The colostomy bag had burst somewhere in the box. Loose stools dripped into the deeper dark where he lived.

"Oh no. I don't think I can repair this one anymore." Annie lifted the man's head, felt his cheeks and brow. When he didn't jerk up or try to strangle her to take advantage of her proximity, Sam knew for certain he wasn't long for this world, if he wasn't already dead. The sick odor of gangrene mingled with the already awful smell of diarrhea.

Sam reeled back again, this time to run for Annie's bedroom—more specifically her bathroom.

She wasn't going to make it.

After veering into the solarium, which at least had tile instead of carpet, she fell to her knees and threw up everything she'd managed to eat from breakfast and lunch.

She knelt over her mess, panting, waiting out the sour roil and understanding that if she couldn't thicken her stomach and her skin, she'd find herself on the other side of one of those sliding glass doors—dead or alive.

Sam cleaned up after herself the best she could and tossed the dirty washcloth into Annie's laundry hamper. Then she took one of Annie's apple juice boxes from the mini fridge to get the taste of vomit out of her mouth and attempt to settle her stomach.

She took it with her back to the hallway where Annie still stood in front of the open room. Annie had her arms around Mrs. Fratello as she wept into the matronly woman's stiff chest. Mrs. Fratello patted her shoulder.

"I can't wake him," Annie hiccupped. "Dr. Panabaker can fix him, can't she?" The question devolved into a shrill siren wail that shuddered into another sob.

Mrs. Fratello heard Sam before Annie did and glared over Annie's shoulder. She tapped Annie's back, then gestured to Sam.

Annie's red eyes widened in the epitome of innocence. She ran from Mrs. Fratello's arms to Sam's, hitting her like a dense bag of logs and nearly sending them both crashing to the floor. Mrs. Fratello was a larger, sturdier woman. Sam staggered but managed to keep from falling. Tears literally soaked the front of Sam's t-shirt.

"I called the doctor," Mrs. Fratello said. Sam had been half certain Annie had taken her tongue. Turned out she was simply spare with her conversation. "But the doll looks irrevocably broken. I told her that's what happens when you remove the parts they need to work."

Annie made fists in Sam's shirt and shook her head. "He was such a good jack-in-the-box. So bouncy and happy."

"I'll need to clean the mess." Mrs. Fratello's severe black eyes were hawkish. If the woman was trying to tell her something between the lines, Sam couldn't interpret, and she certainly wasn't psychic. Finally, Mrs. Fratello sighed. "The doctor will be here. If I need to clean more mess, Miss Annie should be elsewhere."

"I see. Should we go to the library, Annie, or would you like to go outside?" *Please. Anywhere but here.*

Mrs. Fratello slipped her hand into the pocket of her black apron. Sam heard a distant buzz, like several phones on vibrate in other rooms.

Annie's head hung, less loose than Jack's. She shuffled dejectedly past Mrs. Fratello and Jack's open room. "I want to go see Darla. I'll take you to Darla."

Chapter 6: TINY DANCER

Annie brought Sam to the next intersection across from the one off Annie's room. To the right, it seemed to stretch out to a small window on the other side of forever, but Sam had walked this side of the house. It didn't go on forever. The rooms were just so small that there were a terrifying number of doors between the intersection and that window.

Annie took Sam left instead of right, to a room similarly sized to the Repair Room, labeled Ballet Barre.

"Did you ever take dance classes, Miss Sam?" Annie said between thick sniffles as she unlocked the door with her keycard. "I did when I was young, before I can remember up to when I was eight. I stopped because other kids were mean, but for a while, I loved doing ballet."

"I never did dance or gymnastics. One of my sisters took modern dance, and I drove her to lessons. She stopped before high school." Sam willed Annie not to turn on the lights after she opened the door, but the lights here were already on.

Classical piano with a string quartet played through unseen speakers—accompaniment that befit the grace of the tiny person dancing in the middle of the room.

In stature, she was only a little shorter than Annie and Sam, but she was bone thin, her knees nearly larger than her thighs. When Sam got a better look at her, she realized the reason for her joints appearing so prominent wasn't just her slight figure but completely healed scar tissue. The smooth pearliness was visible only in certain angles from the light of the single golden chandelier, reflected a million times in all the mirrors on the arched ceiling and walls, burnished on the floor.

Sam was almost afraid of taking a step and cracking one, earning more bad luck than she and everyone except the Langes already had. But if the larger people on ottomans around the center mirrored stage hadn't broken the floors, Sam probably wouldn't damage them. They were an avid audience for the smooth, white-skinned doll dancing for them.

She wore a leotard the same pure milkiness of her skin, which must not have seen sun for as long as her scars had been healing. The paleness only accentuated the shadows of bones jutting against flesh, the concavity of her abdomen beyond even the thrust of her hips, the prominence of every rib, the blades of her scapula and clavicle.

Implants of some kind filled out her chest and buttocks. They were the only softness in her body, uncannily perky, with an uncanny jiggle, all the more obvious because of her unnatural, unhealthy thinness. She, too, had a feeding tube through her nose, but her eyes were her own, albeit with contacts that made them a river-glass green, and her smile was her own, teeth as brilliantly white as the rest of her. Her lips, though, had been painted a deep matte red.

No, *tattooed*, along with her black eyeliner, so that she would always look the same.

She'd been stripped of any hair, which must have taken electrolysis and laser hair treatments over the course of years, in addition to hormones or other medications. That included the hair on her head, without even the hint of follicular shadow beneath, only an indentation at the mandibular hinge and dark eye sockets.

Unlike other dolls, she didn't have an IV dock, although scars old and new in the crook of her elbow suggested she sometimes received something through injection or IV line.

As though she didn't need the extra lubrication anymore.

She'd already been dancing when Annie and Sam entered, perhaps for the audience watching her as unblinkingly as any collection of dolls. She was like some music-box ballerina, a broken doll still going through her motions, endlessly wound so that she never, ever stopped. She was skinny as a rail, but when she raised herself up en pointe or changed arm position or bent backward, she displayed not just bone but fibrous, tight, harshly sculpted muscle. Her whole body seemed in an endless state of contraction.

With all the elements that made her so strange and doll-like, Sam couldn't pin down her age, except she had to be late twenties or early thirties just by virtue of her scars. She wasn't like Annie, who was clearly adult, if de-aged slightly by an abundant lack of stressors. This woman had been altered into agelessness—the perfect plaything.

Annie released Sam's hand and ran toward the dancing doll. The tears streaking her cheeks and staining the top of her pink dress were forgotten as she reached out for the doll. "Darla!"

The dancer shifted in her routine to embrace Annie with the somehow elegant jerkiness one might expect from a living doll. Despite her cold palette and silhouette, the embrace was warm, with a comfortable hum. Then she went right back to dancing, this time with Annie, who suffered in comparison to the woman who practiced all day, every day. Annie had some grace, some style, some muscle memory, but none of the same grace. She only did it for fun. For the doll, it was all she did. All she was.

A cushioned cot had been tucked in the corner, near another toilet and sink. The dancer wasn't tethered like the others. She was kept in a room of honor, surrounded by silent admirers who watched her every move. Sam wondered whether her audience slept on the ottomans or if they were brought here from other rooms in the mornings.

Sam crept closer. She'd been so entranced and unsettled by Darla that she hadn't really noticed the audience—mostly men, some young and some old, still as mannequins.

Because that's what they were, in the sense that they were covered with some kind of shiny resin. Sam touched one of their arms. Smooth, sanded hard. Some of the gallery of frozen admirers sat upright. Others leaned back, braced on their hands. A few lounged on their backs or sides. Some of them blinked, now that Sam had the time to watch for it. Sam rounded one of the ottomans to an audience member in a half-open shirt and rumpled trousers too big for his legs. He wasn't blinking. She'd assumed the ones who weren't blinking were actual mannequins, but upon closer inspection, she realized the reason he wasn't blinking was because his eyeballs had sunken back in the sockets, dried like prunes.

Because he was dead. And had been for a while.

A combination of steady dry air and the resin had preserved the rest of him almost perfectly, but the dried eyeballs, too, had been sprayed with a light layer of resin, to preserve the desiccation.

Sam wrenched back.

The dead man continued watching the skeletal ballet performance, appearing so entranced that he couldn't close his eyes. So entranced, in fact, that he was hard beneath the loose folds of his shirt and pants. Once Sam noticed, she couldn't unnotice, especially since it seemed to be a Dream House theme. His wasn't the only prominent erection there.

Unlike Darla, the living mannequins had IV tubes that led surreptitiously into the ottomans, which explained some of the erections. No nasogastric tubes, so Sam assumed they received nutrients some other way, perhaps from something set lower and less conspicuously into their bodies.

The dead mannequins, however, didn't have a drug-related explanation for the particularly large tents and bulges in their clothes. They had to have been preserved that way or made hard somehow after death.

Annie pushed Darla toward Sam—or rather, toward the mannequin man with the forever erection.

Darla stretched her leg up, her toes an elegant point above her head, then leapt onto the ottoman, landing on her knees on either side of his thighs.

Sam jumped in surprise—not that Darla was there, but how. Darla reached for her with a sinuous beckon of fingers that caught on Sam's cut sleeve, but Sam backed away. Darla's smile was so much more unnerving up close.

Sam's clit also twitched again, without will or reason, and she didn't like what it said about her own curiosity, that it knew no reason or morality.

Darla's bright red and white smile softened before she turned her attention from Sam to the mummified mannequin beneath her. The erratic grace didn't end; it was just applied to a different dance than ballet.

Darla moved her hips over the mannequin's lap, her grace sinuous, the jerkiness translating as needy. She unbuttoned the mannequin's shirt, then pressed down on the front of his loose trousers to define the erection with exaggerated shock.

Unlike the despair of so many of the dolls when they met Sam's eyes—if they could see at all—Darla looked straight at Sam. Or maybe she looked at Annie through the mirrors behind Sam and it just felt like eye contact.

Darla quickened the rhythm of her hips over the mannequin's lap, pressing the front of her leotard against the unrelenting, unmoving stiffness the way one would a firm dildo. Living for so long with all these mirrors, performing for an audience, perhaps new eyes were a rarity to savor, because although she could, she barely blinked. Light, breathy moans—almost sighs, but unmistakably sexual—escaped her parted lips.

She was making Sam a part of this, like Annie, but unlike Annie, Darla didn't look or act like a child. She acted like a professional ballerina doll, and professional ballerinas had once been offered to patrons to take advantage of their lithe grace, strength, flexibility, and obedience.

That's what this performance felt like, as though it was for Sam's benefit on Annie's behalf. And part of her reacted favorably, low, heavy, heated, confused, pulsing with blood flow.

The rest of Sam was more and more horrified in a different way than the Repair Room as Darla pushed aside her leotard to reveal a perfectly hairless pussy, feverish red against the pale rest of her, and glistening as she raised herself up to rub more directly on the dead dick, dampening the trouser material.

Then Darla opened the trousers. What was inside looked just like a living cock, rendered into hard plastic, and she crooned as though it were a vibrator rubbing over the little clitoris peeking engorged from the front of her labia. She had no mons—not enough body fat—and very little labia, but what was there was visibly aroused, slickening the already smooth, shining cock enhanced by whatever procedure had preserved it.

Sam retreated again when Darla lifted her hips and took the large cock into her little pink pussy. Her head fell back, creating an almost impossible line with her skinny, hairless, alien body.

She fucked herself mercilessly on a cock so thick against her thinness that it should have hurt, but none of the sounds she made were of pain, whether it hurt or not. She was a consummate performer, an en-pointe ballerina who knew a little something about the beauty of pain. Whatever she was on, it was as much of an aphrodisiac as what made the men erect so quickly.

Annie's smile fell away, her lips slack as she stared between her favorite doll fucking a preserved corpse and her new nanny watching. She pressed one fist against her chest above the wide bow around her waist, then brought the other hand to her skirt, to the dip between her legs. She touched herself, cheeks red, making her own little sounds like the cooing of mourning doves—as though she didn't even know what she felt except that it was good.

"Annie..." The word came out barely a whisper. Sam coughed to find her strength, still shaky from vomiting and from whatever *this* was—which felt bigger than a little girl playing with dolls.

"Isn't she wonderful?" Annie said. "She's my best. My favorite. I've had her a long time, and she does everything right. *Oh.*"

Darla was so enthusiastic that the dead mannequin fell back on the ottoman, his legs arched stiffly in the air. That just made him look like he was really into what Darla was doing, like he was about to curl his toes while she posted back against him, wild, animal, desperate, until she shivered, her abdominal muscles and thighs quivering, her moans low and grating through her throat.

When she lifted herself off, the erection was slick, her cum fluids connected to the head by a thin thread, as though to prove to Sam that it was real. And Sam knew that *smell*, didn't think they could fake that fleshly sweetness, nor the sweat beading over Darla's forehead and down her back.

Darla put the dead mannequin back into place and rubbed her cheek over his face and chest like a cat as she rebuttoned his clothes and arranged him in some semblance of order. Then she returned to the center of the carousel of mirrors and proceeded to dance again as though she hadn't stopped for sex at all.

Annie kept touching herself, curling her fingers to grind against her pubic bone, but not with any kind of urgency—the way some people twirled their hair or scratched at a phantom itch. She allowed Darla to dance over to her and draw her hand away, then curtsy and kiss her fingers, with a dart of tongue that made Annie bite her lip.

They danced in innocent circles together like a child and her doll, with Darla on her toes and Annie on the balls of her feet in mimicry. Sometimes, Darla bent to kiss Annie on the cheek. When Annie turned her face, she kissed her on the lips— still utterly innocent and childlike.

Sam drank down the rest of her apple juice and tried to look away from the twisted scene. The reflections wouldn't let her. They were everywhere.

"Miss Sam, Miss Sam, look at me. Look at me."

Annie sat facing forward in another mannequin's lap—this one alive. She moved her hips in uncomfortable similarity to what Darla was now doing to another mannequin, this one more clearly dead than the previous.

He lay on his back, his eyes sunken closed, his mouth open in a cry of what looked like pain, but his even larger erection suggested otherwise. This time Darla rode the mouth. Since there was no tongue, she ground against his firm lips and chin instead, then arched with terrible flexibility back to sink her mouth around the cock, deep enough to bulge her slender swan throat.

"Can I do that, Miss Sam? Can I do that?" Annie asked, her voice higher as she ground against the cock behind her and her fingers in front of her.

Sam couldn't stand her body's sickening confusion at the even sicker things happening in front of her—lovely, graceful, elegant, awful, disgusting, desecrating. She determinedly stared at the floor, at the reflection of herself from her shoes up, as she strode to the room entrance.

"Do what you want, Annie."

The door hadn't closed all the way. Sam had to believe that was either on purpose or because Annie had been so distraught by her dead or dying jack-in-the-box that she hadn't made sure it locked behind them.

"Deeper! Deeper! Can you do it deeper? Oh, that's wonderful."

Annie clapped in delight. Then she grunted slightly in the same rhythm as Darla choking and gagging on a dead man's cock. Sam yanked open the door and ran back into the hall.

I can't do this. Fuck, I can't do this. Her tears were dried up, but she hit herself in the forehead with the heels of her hands, trying to strike what she'd seen—and what she hadn't—from her mind's eye.

At the sound of conversation down the cross corridor, Sam crept to the corner of the intersection.

An automatic wheelchair sat empty in the hallway. Mrs. Fratello stood over a white-coated woman on her knees in the jack-in-the-box room.

Sam's shoes creaked slightly as she stepped around the corner. Mrs. Fratello directed her pointed glare back at Sam, with a sharp shake of her head to tell Sam to stay back. But she didn't indicate for her to leave, so Sam remained, trying to determine what the doctor was doing. From what Sam could see from her bad angle, Jack had been raised up on his spring so the doctor could check where the metal entered him, leaving a perpetually open wound for infection to invade.

The doctor sat back on her heels and shook her head. "She's going to have to find another Jack. This one is gone. We might as well help him along before unscrewing him. Help me back up."

Mrs. Fratello hooked her arm under the doctor's shoulder and dead-lifted her, which was necessary because most of the doctor's feet had been removed. The scarring was minimal. She would be more than capable of handling her own aftercare.

She wondered if Annie or the doctor had wielded the bone saw through its first cut.

As Mrs. Fratello lowered the doctor back into her wheelchair, the doctor gripped the arms, revealing that she'd also lost both ring and little fingers.

Leaving her with only the fingers she needed to hold a syringe and scalpel.

She was a wan, tired woman who might once have seemed formidable, with strong jaw line and broad cheekbones. The light in her eyes was more vibrant than Mrs. Fratello's, but her skin was the same dull matte, her hair lifeless and greasy, as though she'd stopped taking care of herself beyond what basic necessities kept her alive and healthy. Relatively healthy, given the brittle fingernails on the fingers she still had.

She kept her limp hair in an uninspired bob. Her skin was pale from lack of sun rather than genetics, and her lips were almost the same color as her skin. She was otherwise a solid woman, where structure hadn't been damaged, and her wheelchair was top of the line, with ergonomic cushions that gave her a sense of dignity in her posture and electronic controls that gave her smoother, more variant mobility.

Nothing but the best for the Dream House doctor.

Dr. Panabaker noticed Sam when she looked up, but she deliberately turned her back as she drew herself to the IV box. She switched the drip rate to its highest level, from a green light on the monitor into yellow, then into warning red.

"When he's finished, take him to the barn," Dr. Panabaker said to Mrs. Fratello. Then she headed in the opposite direction from Sam while four maids strode up the sides of the hall out of her way, their shoulders hunched and heads still down so far that Sam couldn't see their faces.

"Wait!" Sam tried to go after her, but the maids closed ranks and didn't move out of Sam's way.

"The doctor is very busy," Mrs. Fratello said. "She speaks only with me, Ji-an, and Miss Annie, unless Miss Annie has an emergency."

"What's she so busy doing, other than helping Annie torture and kill people?" Sam snapped.

"I don't see how you're doing any better," Mrs. Fratello said coldly. "The doctor ensures feeding tubes are functioning and injection sites aren't infected. She does what she can with what she's given. She's very busy. And you have a job to do."

"I need to talk to her," Sam said. "When can I talk to her? Where can I talk to her? *Please.*"

"I'm busy, too. Go watch over Annie."

"Annie's doing things I don't want to watch."

"It's your *job* to watch," Mrs. Fratello said. "It's the doctor's job to fix. It's the chef's job to feed. And it's my job to clean. The job never ends. Step aside, girl. You're in the way."

Sam withdrew, but not before one of the maids raised her head. Sam nearly screamed from the jagged, stitch-like, scarred-shut mouth so close to her when least expected. There was a small hole in the center of what remained of the maid's mouth—big enough for a straw.

That explained the blenders.

Although Sam probably stared longer than was polite, the maid also had a job to do, and unlike Sam, she couldn't talk back.

Sam absolutely would not return to the Ballet Barre. She slid down the wall across from the barre room and covered her ears when the maids started unscrewing Jack from his surgical-steel spring.

All too soon, Annie emerged from the barre room, relaxed but otherwise unchanged, unstained, unrumpled. "Why did you leave? Darla wasn't finished."

"Does Darla ever finish?" Sam asked, not getting up from the carpeted floor.

"She needs to be rewound every hour or so, and of course, she sleeps at night, like all my dolls in the dark." Annie pulled on Sam's arm. "Why are you mad at me? I thought you'd like Darla. You prefer girl dolls, don't you?"

Sam looked over at Mrs. Fratello and her cadre of solemn, silent maids all in black, ghosts at a perpetual funeral. They didn't acknowledge Annie, and Mrs. Fratello was focused on the former Jack.

Then Sam looked back at Annie, searching for the answer to a question she didn't know how to ask a child who was also an adult who was also a teenager who was also a toddler, in turns—an innocent sadist.

Finally, Sam pushed herself standing. Then she crossed her arms and lifted her chin, adopting her sternest expression. Good for all ages. "The things you showed me were things you're supposed to do by yourself, Annie. You're not supposed to include me in those things. And the kinds of people I prefer in my private life are *private*. They aren't relevant here."

Annie seemed taken aback, with quivering lip, although her wide eyes remained dry.

"It's not wrong to touch yourself, but that's something you do when you're alone. I don't need or want to be a part of it. Do I make myself clear?" Sam asked.

"N-no one ever told me it was something I shouldn't do," Annie said, stammering for the first time since Sam had known her. Maybe because it was the first time since Sam had arrived that she'd really told Annie *no*. "Not one of them. They all watched, because that's what nannies are supposed to do. Daddy would tell you that you shouldn't have left me alone."

"I wasn't hired to watch you. I was hired to watch *over* you. There's a difference. One means your daddy might as well have hired a parrot. The other means I teach you when your play is something we do together and when it's something you should do by yourself. If other nannies haven't taught you that masturbating in front of other people is inappropriate and rude, that sounds like their mistake. It's even more inappropriate to try to make me a part of it, because I don't like it. Now, am I clear?"

Nascent lines deepened from the ugly contortion of Annie's expression. She wasn't just bewildered. She was angry. But Sam had dealt with angry children before, as well as angry adults bigger than she was.

"I want to go back to the barre room," Annie said. "And I want you to play with me in there."

"I'll play with you, Annie. I can even play with Darla. But if you're going to touch yourself or if you try to make Darla touch me, I'm going to walk away again."

"I'll lock the door."

"Doesn't stop me from walking away," Sam said. "Just from walking out. Now, do you want to do private things in the barre room?"

Annie ground her teeth in frustration.

"If you can't respect my boundaries, I think we need to step away from the dolls entirely and focus on coloring for the rest of the day. Would you maybe like a midday snack from the kitchen?"

Annie stomped her foot. "I want to play in the barre room, and you need to be there."

"Annie, you can either go to the library with me and I'll get you some blueberries and cream, or I'll take you back to your room, where you can spend the rest of the afternoon. You have plenty of dolls in there to play with and can do your private things without me. You can play with Darla another time, but you've already overplayed with some of your toys, which is why Mrs. Fratello is having to clean up." Sam nodded toward the jack-in-the-box room. "What'll it be, Annie? Berries and cream or quiet contemplation alone?"

She held out her hand, willing this to work.

Annie narrowed her eyes. But she let Sam lead her out of the east wing and toward the quiet of the library.

Sam even put a record on while she went to the kitchen. Annie ate all her blueberries and cream and quietly seethed the rest of the day, coloring every picture in shades of black.

Chapter 7: PLAYING DOCTOR

Annie asked Sam to stay with her overnight again.

Sam said she'd come back when she finished getting ready to go to sleep. Annie pouted, but Sam assumed she'd either sleep through Sam returning or stay awake until Sam returned. Either way, Sam would have to come back. She dreaded putting herself back in the position to wake up with Annie behind her, especially with Annie sulking and more likely to act out.

Annie was a child in the body of a grown woman. She was used to making the executive decisions in her father's absence, and she was an able-bodied adult who didn't really need Sam as anything but a parent she didn't actually want. Sam didn't know if the traditional path of establishing boundaries and giving a child choices and clear consequences would work on Annie when Sam had no concrete authority over the rest of the household. How the rest of their time would go depended on whether Annie decided a nanny was someone to defer to.

Sam headed toward the east wing corridors, listening for whispering feet and starched aprons or the soft whir of an electric wheelchair. To manage a collection of people this extensive, surely they had to work late into the evening and begin early in the morning.

The rooms were all well insulated—presumably so Annie wouldn't have to hear them scream unless she wanted to—but an almost inaudible vibration guided Sam from the east wing back into the main house, where the vibration became the more familiar sound of the electric wheelchair in the echoing foyer.

Sam ran on tiptoe to the grand staircase and peeked around.

Dr. Panabaker was heading for the ballroom, although there was no way she could get down there the way Annie had shown Sam—not if she still wanted to be mobile by the bottom of the stairs.

The doctor veered toward a piece of abstract art that was probably worth a small house. There, she opened a nearly invisible control panel that slid the wooden panel aside to reveal a single-person elevator. When she pressed the button to go down, the elevator opened immediately.

Dr. Panabaker backed her chair into the elevator, which closed behind her, and so did the wooden panel.

Sam ran over before she lost sight of the mechanism. Then she waited what she hoped was about five minutes and pushed the up button.

The elevator took a minute to reach ground floor again, but when it opened, it was empty. Sam stepped inside. The buttons inside gave three options: Ballroom, Entrance, and Tower.

Sam chose Tower.

The elevator took her up what felt like the equivalent of three or four floors. Hard to tell, because the elevator was state of the art and so smooth and fast that it was almost like not moving at all.

The elevator opened into a room bigger than small and smaller than big, roughly the size of a spacious studio apartment. It was nicely furnished with a full-size bed and a kitchen on one side, but the other half looked like a doctor's office, with a vinyl dentist chair and a stainless steel surgery table under dormant pendant lights.

Because it was a tower with a turret, the primary part of the room was circular. Nothing properly fit flush against the walls, but they were segmented with industrial mesh shelves, metal file cabinets and lockers, and several laboratory refrigerators that hummed across from the kitchen.

A large desk had been set up in front of the only window. It was the one warm place in the room, with a red Persian-style rug underneath. No chair.

Near the bed in the secondary part of the room, which was not bound to the same cylindrical structure, an opaque plastic curtain surrounded a toilet and shower area. Next to the curtain was a rolling shower chair.

Sam switched on the lights one by one. The pendant lights were blinding, coldly clinical against the steel and vinyl. The lamplight was kinder, and she almost switched off the pendants. Then she got a better look at what the doctor stored on her shelves.

She didn't display them with the same loving reverence as Annie showed off her dolls—her actual ones, anyway. No neon lights. No bright colors. Nevertheless, shelves and shelves of human body parts.

Feet—two of which might have been her own. Eyes like pickled eggs. Hands. Tongues. Organs, hearts to intestines. Even a few heads. None of the more arcane designs had been immortalized here like the plasticized mannequins, but there was no medical reason to keep them, floating in formaldehyde, except as some kind of trophy.

"What if I were to show up uninvited in your room and snoop around while you weren't there?"

Sam faced the elevator as Dr. Panabaker exited it. "I don't have anything to hide."

"I'm not hiding it, either, you might notice. Get out."

"I need to talk with you."

"I don't talk to nannies."

"Because we're lower than you?"

"Because none of you last long as nannies." Not unkindly. Not kindly. Matter-of-fact, with the resignation of the long suffering. "The better I know you, the harder it is to cut. But that won't change that I'll have to cut."

"I didn't come here to beg for mercy or a phone," Sam said. "You're in a goddamn tower. You're just as much a prisoner as the rest of us. You don't have mercy to give and even if you have a phone to communicate with Mr. Lange, you're probably just as scared as everyone else about giving it to me."

Dr. Panabaker scoffed, her smile humorless. "Well, that makes you smarter than about half the nannies who make it this far."

"I just want to ask some questions. Mr. Lange didn't explain enough, and I don't know…how I'm going to break this cycle. I just don't know what I'm supposed to *do*."

Tears that had dried up sprang anew. The doctor may not have been completely sane anymore, but she was a more stable presence in Annie's life than her shiftless father and possibly more likely to talk than Mrs. Fratello.

"You do what Annie says," Dr. Panabaker said. "That's all any of us do."

"Why? Why the fuck is everyone just going along with it, encouraging her, helping her?"

"Why are *you* helping her?" Dr. Panabaker asked gently.

"I'm just trying not to be turned into a doll."

Dr. Panabaker opened her hands in a 'there you go' gesture.

"But if we all stopped—"

With shrill laughter more like suppressed screams, Dr. Panabaker continued into the room past Sam. "Do you really think Annie's the only one running this show? Oh, she's queen bee. What she says goes. But there are other people involved to make sure we all keep in line, and if overthrowing oppressors by sheer numbers and everything to gain led to employment revolution, we'd see a lot more of it, wouldn't we? Annie's not following any kind of Better Business Bureau. There's something—and usually some*one*—over each of us. They pick martyrs and saints on purpose."

"I'm not a martyr or a saint," Sam said. "I'm not even a good person."

"They're not mutually inclusive." Dr. Panabaker went straight for the wet bar at the end of her kitchen. She poured herself half a tumbler of absinthe, which would have seemed excessive under any other circumstances. She offered to pour another, but Sam declined. "And you're good enough if Annie's dolls upset you."

"You don't have to be a good person to be upset by Annie's dolls."

"Good *enough*. Some of us can't even say that anymore." She took a deep swallow of the absinthe. Sam hoped she'd eaten something beforehand. "I read your résumé. You're a giver. Annie's a taker. It's just what she is, and she's good at it. They find good givers, and they've perfected the taking to a science."

"They, they, they… There's that *they* again. Who's *they*?"

Dr. Panabaker shrugged. "Harold Lange is one of them. I know that much. And whoever brings people in when he's away on business. You can't see it from the corridors, but there are screens in the walls of every room so the dolls can watch other dolls. They're encouraged to snitch. They get better food and better drugs if they catch someone doing something they shouldn't, and watching punishments is so much more satisfying than watching someone get out when you can't."

"Wait, there are cameras watching all the dolls?"

"And in here, watching and listening to us now. Probably in your bedroom and shower, too. That's just how it is. So telling Annie to do her self-exploration in private doesn't really work, and she knows it. She doesn't understand private."

Sam struggled with where to start first. Even when she'd been hopeful, edging on happy, she'd been part of someone's game. They'd seen her naked. They'd watched Annie crawling into the beanbag with her. Watched them sleeping. Watched her help Annie rape two broken dolls. Watched Annie and Darla in the barre room.

Of course. That's why Darla kept dancing even when Annie wasn't there. She did it for whomever watched, because she was a doll who danced when she was wound, whether she wanted to or not.

Sam looked for somewhere to sit, but there was only the bed, and that was too personal. She stepped back to lean against the surgical table, although that wasn't the ideal option, either.

"What *does* Annie understand?" she asked slowly. "She's such an inconsistent child. Does she understand what she's doing to people, actual people, and just pretending they're dolls? Or does she really think they're dolls?"

"I'm a surgeon, not a psychiatrist. Then again, I used to be a cardiothoracic surgeon with all my fingers and two full feet, not a six-fingered orthopedic surgeon with a standing wheelchair, so..." Dr. Panabaker gulped down another swallow of absinthe. "It's hard to tell what goes on in Annie's head, if it's contrived, a case of Peter Pan syndrome, untreated trauma regression, brain damage, dementia, or whether Harold just didn't want his little girl to grow up too much like his dead wife. Girl or woman, she's petulant and spoiled and always gets what she wants, whether she gets it for herself or someone else gets it for her. I heard you deny her, but I suspect it was twenty-five years too late."

"Yeah. I don't think that will go unpunished," Sam said softly. "But maybe neither should she."

"And what do you recommend? A spanking? She might enjoy that. A switch? A gun? The loss of all but necessary digits?" Dr. Panabaker raised her hands as though they were heavy as enhanced clown feet.

"Did you— Or did she?"

"Oh, she's an accomplished amateur surgeon. Easier to develop those skills when life-or-death stakes don't matter," Dr. Panabaker said. "She started on her own, with me cleaning up after her, which is what we all do in the end. I tried to teach her on the already dead so she wouldn't make as many of them. When I started telling her more and more that what she wanted was impossible, she removed my fingers with a butcher knife, no morphine. She stitched them up herself, too. She was already an exceptional seamstress. And with enough study, practice, and willingness to discard the errors, she started making what was impossible possible—to a point. I learned to work within her designs. But when I tried to use my time on the other side of the wall to get help, she made me remove half of my own feet, then followed my direction when I was too overcome by the drugs she gave me to make it easier. Most of the major surgery you see in the dolls are all her now. I oversee healing and make any necessary repairs behind her."

"But Ji-an and Mrs. Fratello, neither of them are hurt," Sam said.

"Ji-an's mostly recovered by now. Mrs. Fratello has been with Annie since the beginning. She was Annie's first nanny. She's completely cowed, completely loyal. I've worked under the assumption that Annie did things to her before I came on as doctor. I don't know what, but with everything I've seen, even without the engineering and costuming and theater, Annie has always been capable of cruelty."

"Is she cruel to be cruel or does she really not know better?"

"Does it matter?"

"To a courtroom."

"She's never going to see the inside of a courtroom. Ask her dolls if it matters. Ask me." Dr. Panabaker finished her absinthe, then poured herself another. Alcohol poisoning didn't appear to factor into her decision-making. "Would you like to see what she did to me?"

She drove to her desk and switched on the three large, curved monitors. On two of them was a series of rotating screens, most in night vision.

"Every camera livestreams to me and records twenty-four-seven so I can better assess my patients. As a result, they have hours and hours of footage to hold over my head, just like they have a few minutes to hold over you. Right now, you're scared. You have some grace. But soon, helping her is a choice, and if Annie goes down, so do you, and so do we all. We are all her drones, complicit in her hive."

Most of the small rooms held two people, probably to keep them from going too mad in the dark alone. The girls from the swing were on their pallet now and kissing more sincerely, slow and sultry and crying and comforting. Two halves became whole in the dark.

With more women than men, if there was a man in a shared room, they were with a woman. Some of the men and women were fucking each other, but some of the cameras clearly showed the woman either passed out, utterly passive, or resisting. The drugs had a very specific effect on men, and darkness and torture would have worn down reluctance, mores, the tenuous barriers of civilization.

Sam clenched her jaw to the point of pain, dug grooves into her palms even with her shorter nails. There was nothing civil here. This was human ugliness, as contagious as any infection. She was angrier at Annie, though, than the men, because *she* was the one to wear away their will, their resistance, their very humanity, leaving behind only creatures of sexual depravity and performance.

Did they know, like Darla, that they were being watched? Were they rewarded for rape as well as gossip?

"The key is to not look at anything except what you're looking for." Dr. Panabaker was finally showing the effects of the absinthe, squinting and moving her mouse more slowly to keep from overshooting. She ignored the live images and opened an old folder of videos labeled with her name.

The views were from two angles. If sound was an option, Dr. Panabaker didn't offer it.

Annie grabbed a butcher knife from the kitchen, then indicated for Dr. Panabaker to put her hand on the butcher block island. Annie pointed the knife at Dr. Panabaker's face, then her hand. Dr. Panabaker's mouth moved in a stream of pleading and multisyllabic words. Annie appeared to concede by putting the blade only on the last two fingers.

Then she cut through like slicing difficult carrots.

Dr. Panabaker screamed, collapsing to her knees, but Annie brought the knife back to her face until the doctor put her other hand on the chopping block.

Sam winced with each slice, but she couldn't look away, either. This was the reality she would have to face every single day. She might not make it out of here alive. She'd almost certainly not make it with all her parts.

It didn't feel real. Especially up here in the tower, where everything was clean, cold, clinical, perfumed with astringent and lemon. Maybe that's why they put the doctor up here—in the trenches during the day, removed from the filth at night.

"She even memorialized them for me." Dr. Panabaker held up what Sam had assumed was just another acrylic paperweight. Inside, four fingers dissolved to bone had been suspended like relics of a saint. But Dr. Panabaker was no more a saint than Sam was.

"Is this all she has on you? These videos?"

"Isn't that enough? I'm a collaborator. I'm scared as hell of a little girl in a little woman's body, but by my accountant's reckoning—conveniently the same accountant who manages Harold's affairs—I run a thriving private surgery center. I keep careful account of all my 'patients.' I bill them. Harold pays cash on their behalf. When I absolutely must go out into the world, I wear prosthetics, and someone follows my every move. When the continuance of my practice is threatened by my physical state, Harold greases palms."

"So he's the one pulling the strings—"

Dr. Panabaker laughed, snorting, then giggling like a girl and struggling to stop. "Only because Annie tells him what strings to pull. He's spineless in everything but what he does for her. And he doesn't come home often. These month-long business trips are a regular thing. Hard to say which he mourns more: his little girl from when she was still a little girl or the wife that he lost, because Annie looks so much like her mother. Maybe that's why he doesn't deny her, have her evaluated, possibly committed, or at least cared for by a nurse who ignores her delusions. But are they?" Dr. Panabaker took a swig from the refreshed tumbler. "Are they delusions when she makes them reality? She would be called an enchantress in another time, but I don't believe in such things. So she is simply

Miss Annie, the princess. But not in the tower. Oh no. That's for her own personal mad doctor, the apothecarist for her alchemy."

Dr. Panabaker was drifting, drooping over her desk, watching Annie cradle her hand, watching Annie sew her up.

"How do I stay alive?" Sam said. "How do I stay a nanny instead of a doll?"

"Don't you see? Don't you understand? You're not a nanny. You're a playmate. And if you don't play, you're a plaything. It's only a matter of time. That's why I wish Harold wouldn't tell me the names of every nanny, maid, and cook he brings in. But I'm the keeper of such things. It's for my extensive records, as you can see. Eventually, I'm going to have to create an invoice for you, Samantha. I'm sorry."

Sam slapped her.

Dr. Panabaker jerked back in her chair.

"I told you I wasn't good," Sam said. "And yes, I'm young and new and maybe naïve, full of hope and sunny optimism even in the face of the little girl with a little curl right in the middle of her forehead. Now, you *will* tell me what I need to do."

"I don't *know.*" Dr. Panabaker struck her hands on the desk to punctuate her helplessness. "I survive by doing what she says. Mrs. Fratello survives by doing what she says. Ji-an survives by staying out of her way and insisting Annie stay out of the kitchen in return. It's one of the only boundaries she's managed to follow, and that's because she never got it into her mind to bake or cook. Yet. I dread the day she does—and what she decides to do with the wealth of meat at her disposal, just out of curiosity. You want to survive? Do what she says. That's it. If you don't like what she says, you'll eventually not have a choice. She'll make you do what she wants. And I make that easier for her."

"What's in those IV bags? What's the lubrication?"

Dr. Panabaker laughed, this time without the shriller edge. "Is that what she's calling it now? It used to be dolly juice. I can't make a specialized composition for each doll, but I have several variations on the formula: different drip rates depending on size of subject, different chemicals for men and women. Most of the dolls have some form of diazepam, sildenafil, scopolamine, and morphine…all inventoried through my highly successful practice, of course. For a layperson, that's Valium, Viagra, suggestibility serum, and medical-grade heroin.

"When they've been successfully integrated into their new personas and roles, they don't need the scopolamine anymore. I switch it out for MDMA—ecstasy—which only reinforces their euphoria when they do what Annie wants. And there are other variants for other things she needs, other ingredients to counteract the contraindications… It's a highly lubricated operation around here. She's given me so many dolls to experiment with, to perfect each compound, then made me play with them using my own compounds against me. They saved videos of me shooting up with morphine while I was healing from my injuries. Drugs make it easier. Heroin, especially. Or even just a heavy stone. The kitchen staff grows a patch of cannabis around here for pain management, particularly for the maids. Because if they can drink, they can smoke."

Dr. Panabaker giggled madly, losing control of her funny bone. "I can help you numb yourself to what she's doing, if you want. I've got a whole damn pharmacy. Or I can just hand you a scalpel and oversee you while you slit your wrists. Then you disappear into the barn. You left weeks ago, no forwarding address, no idea where she might have disappeared to, Officer."

She laughed until tears streamed from her red eyes.

She'd utterly given up. And maybe she had good reason, but she was actually safer than anyone else in the Dream House. Annie needed a surgeon more than she needed a nanny.

Yet, the mad doctor had no more wisdom to offer except to hurt other people before Annie could hurt her.

"Has anyone ever tried to kill her?" Sam asked. "You, of all people, have the means. It would even be merciful."

"Oh, Samantha—"

"Sam."

"Forgive Annie, for she knows not what she does. She wouldn't even be responsible for her own sins. At least a year too young, by her own reckoning." Dr. Panabaker wiped the tears from her face. "I tried once. I almost got her while she was sleeping. But someone saw me coming. She knows where I keep the drugs, and she's the only other one who knows where I keep my keys. She forced scopolamine into my veins, with sodium pentothal for good measure, made me talk for hours, then injected me with a paralytic and set her dolls on me for another few hours. Didn't give me back my chair until she thought I'd been in time-out long enough. I can't help you on this."

"God, you're fucking useless." Sam pushed herself away from the desk, leaving Dr. Panabaker to marinate in aniseed. "This has to end."

"She's thirty-six. She's got a good forty years left to go, if she's really committed."

"You should have committed her. All of you should have."

"You think you've seen everything. You think you know her worst. You've been *spared*, Sam."

"Fuck you. If you had any more spine than her father, you'd help me."

"Do you know how many nannies I've worked on?" Dr. Panabaker said blearily, choking a little on something when she swallowed. "Do you know how many names I've forgotten? I'll forget yours, too."

"This is about more than me."

"Say you do it. Say you stop Annie, kill her, lock her in a closet, whatever. What then? We're still locked in here, and they'd know. If they didn't come in here and mow us all down with AK-47s before burning everything to the fucking ground, all they'd have to do is cut off power and supplies. We'd run out of drugs before we ran out of food. What do you think would happen if over a hundred people completely dependent upon the drugs I give them suddenly didn't receive it? Would withdrawals get them, or would the pain of being fucking *sawn in half with a fucking coil up your ass like a goddamn jack-in-the-box* kill them first? I wonder."

Sam strode to the elevator.

"Did you even think of the dolls?" Dr. Panabaker asked. "Did you stop to think that they're not suited for any place but this? Even if the source of physical pain is long gone, they'd have to deal with the absolute fucking clarity of what's happened to them, what they've become. I'm the poster child for it not being the end of the world to lose a piece of yourself, but imagine walking out into the world like the Upside-Down Twins, see how fucking far you go."

"So she shouldn't be stopped because of what she's already done?" Sam snapped, opening the elevator door. "Look, I can't change who she hurt, but I can maybe change who gets hurt in the future. And since you won't, it might as well be me."

"Tell me again about how you're not a martyr."

Sam slapped the elevator button down. "Oh, believe me, I don't plan on dying."

Back in the dark of the foyer, she couldn't maintain her bravado, especially now that Dr. Panabaker had confirmed cameras were watching at any time, any angle. Paranoia made ghosts of every shadow. Sam ran faster and faster up the stairs to her bedroom.

Before she even turned on the light in her room, the foul smell hit her, like a backed-up toilet.

A pile of shit in the middle of her bedsheets.

Juvenile retribution to ensure Sam wouldn't be able to sneak into her own bed during the night. Punishment for saying no. Punishment for saying that she'd come back instead of staying. Punishment for not coming back fast enough.

It wasn't the worst thing Annie could have done.

Sam cleaned up as best as she could, but the sheets and protective mattress cover all had to be removed. Sam bundled them up and put them in the bathroom tub to dry, with the fan on to dispel some of the stink.

She eschewed a shower and left a note on the door for the maids to take the sheets out of the bathtub, although she didn't know how often they came to clean after her. Then she changed into comfier clothes and brushed her teeth—almost as good as a shower. But every time she closed her eyes, all she could see were Annie's terrible dolls: the dead and the dancing, the degenerate, the debased, the desperate, the sexually resigned and the sexually deranged.

She needed to find a phone.

If they—*they* again—were smart, they destroyed victims' phones, including Sam's. But if they needed them for some reason, maybe to use the contact list... There was a possibility they hid them somewhere. The problem, of course, was that the house was huge, with lots of little rooms and closets and cabinets, not to mention secret rooms behind panels and under floors. If they had a safe just for active phones, they could hide them literally anywhere.

But Annie herself had to have a phone, too, for her dad to call her and vice versa, either to connect or collude. Dr. Panabaker had a computer, and Sam was pretty sure it had internet access if she was expected to interact with the outside world to seem like a legitimate business. There was only the matter of the password. Maybe the doctor wrote the information down somewhere, but Sam couldn't depend on that. On a phone, though, she should be able to call emergency without signing in. If it was a landline, even better.

Fire would risk too many of the dolls—if they even cared at this point. Last resort. The kitchen also had knives, which might have been why she wasn't allowed back there.

Sam spat out her toothpaste, which had started to sting her mouth, then braced her hands on the counter and stared at herself in the mirror. Unthinkable that the sight had remained unchanged in the last few days. Unthinkable that she'd only been here a few days. Unthinkable that she'd expected to be here for six months to years and thought she was being overpaid.

A paltry thousand dollars in advance for someone who Mr. Lange had anticipated would become a doll before he had to pay her another red cent—and most people he hired wouldn't have even asked for that. Slavery almost across the board saved a lot of money for secret passages.

Sam wondered how many other houses were just like this. If there was a God, this would be the only one. Then again, if there were a God, this one wouldn't have been so goddamned successful, would it?

What if all the houses in this secluded forest were just as depraved? What if that's what they'd all bought in for?

Maybe they were fine, good neighbors enjoying their solitude, no way to hear what was going on. Maybe they would even be shocked and appalled and ultimately helpful. But Sam couldn't trust them. If this forest was a haven for one monster, it could shelter others.

Even if they weren't as bad, this was Texas. They could shoot her on sight for no reason other than the fact she was on their property without permission.

Sam slapped her cheek. Then the other. Then each again.

She needed to focus. She needed to concentrate on *getting out* before she started assuming everyone was evil.

Except everyone was capable, weren't they? Even if they needed a gun to their head to do it. She heard Jesse's groans in her mind, reminding her of early attempts with boyfriends that had left her sloppy and sweaty and gross as he'd asked if she'd come when he'd done literally nothing but poke her for less than two minutes.

But she'd been the one pushing Jesse's hips away from her and his cock into someone else who hadn't wanted it there. She'd done that because she hadn't wanted to be the one on the other side of his groans.

She was quite capable of being a monster.

Sam picked up a change of clothes for the morning and opened the window slightly to continue letting the room air out. Then she braced herself for sleeping in the monster's den and what she might wake up to.

Chapter 8: VOICE BOXES

Sam had anticipated waking up with Annie next to her, so she'd grabbed a pillow and blanket and climbed onto the bed, hoping Annie wouldn't shit where she slept. She didn't make it all the way up to the marshmallow mountain of pillows but slept at the foot of the bed instead.

She woke to Annie in front of her, inscrutable as she stroked the path of Sam's lank black hair to the top of her chest. On the very edge of inappropriate. Sam didn't doubt that was on purpose.

"Good morning, Annie."

"Good morning, Miss Sam."

"You pooped in my bed last night, Annie."

Annie didn't blink, unashamed. "I was mad."

"You're old enough to know that you shouldn't poop anywhere but the toilet. Do I have to find diapers for you?"

Annie wrinkled her nose, almost smiling. The smile faded when she realized Sam wasn't kidding.

"No chocolate milk today," Sam said. "Chocolate milk is for good girls, and good girls know better than to get scatological when they're upset. You need to use your words." She sat up out of reach of Annie's hands and looked down at the somewhat bewildered upset rising in Annie's adult face. "Do you want to use your words with me now?"

"You're not being fair."

"'Fair' is my middle name. You understand the concept of cause and effect, action and consequence, because you gave me an ultimatum. I'll play with you, Annie, but I'm your nanny, not your friend. You pooped in my bed; therefore, you get no chocolate milk today. That's an appropriate response to the inconvenience you caused me, but since I wasn't going to sleep in that bed anyway, it's an even bigger inconvenience to your maids, who will have to launder the sheets. And I think they have enough to do, don't you?" Sam patted Annie's hip, then unwrapped herself from her blanket and crawled off the bed. "Go ahead and sleep through the rest of your morning before the alarm. I need to take a shower in your bathroom, because my bedding is presently in mine. I'll see you in a little while."

"I'm still going to have my chocolate milk tonight," Annie said.

"No, you're not."

"I can't drink my white milk without it."

"Things are going to change around here. And you might be a bit uncomfortable now and then. But I think it'll be better for you, and for your dolls, if you learn that just because you can do anything doesn't necessarily mean you should do everything. I've been lenient because I'm new. You've taken advantage of that. No more. Now, get some sleep. We'll go to breakfast and lessons after I take a shower."

"I want to come." Annie clambered to the edge of the bed.

"Your alarm goes off in an hour. You don't have to sleep. You can play with your dolls or read, if you like. But you stay in that bed until the alarm."

"Or what?" Annie frowned, holding one of the posts.

"Or we don't play after lunch. Your lessons have been entirely unstructured, but I can expand them into something more formal."

"I always play after lunch," Annie said.

"And I probably can't stop you," Sam said mildly. "But *I* would be in the library, fashioning a curriculum. If you want me to play dolls with you—gently—you'll do as you should and stay in bed. It's your choice, Annie."

Sam entered Annie's bathroom and closed the door. There was no lock, but as far as Sam was aware, Annie didn't enter.

She used Annie's toiletries, which all smelled fruity—not Sam's aromatic palette of choice. She looked around to see if she could find a spy cam, although Sam didn't think Mr. Lange would have put one where his daughter would be caught naked. After all, Annie had kept her dress on while she'd humped the man's lap and masturbated, and her little girl clothes were actually quite modest, considering the way she played House. Annie didn't make a spectacle of herself the way she made a spectacle of her dolls.

Sam would honestly rather shower in Annie's bathroom going forward if that was the case, aggressive berry scents notwithstanding. She smelled like a pavlova.

When Sam left the bathroom, Annie was in bed playing with her stuffed animals. She glared daggers while Sam crossed the room, but she'd done as she was supposed to. Sam didn't think it was going to keep being this easy—shitting in someone else's bed was a stone's throw away from flinging that poo at someone—but it was still a good sign.

In the dining room, someone had put Sam's coffee on a mug warmer so it wouldn't go cold because she was late.

"Thank you," she called into the kitchen. "I'd like to make an amendment to dinner, please."

"What do you need?" Ji-an asked, distracted.

"Annie will not be having chocolate milk."

There was a noticeable pause in the bustle of the kitchen. "Did Annie authorize this?"

"Annie knows why she will not be having chocolate milk, yes."

"That wasn't the question."

"Annie is being punished for something she did to me. So she will not be having chocolate milk tonight. And if she retaliates, I will instruct that there will be no dessert. Okay?"

The pause became prolonged.

"That is a bad idea," Ji-an said.

"Undoubtedly. But Mr. Lange put me in charge of Annie. I decide if she has her little treats, not her. Am I clear?"

"Dinner will be adjusted. I hope you know what you're doing."

"Not in the slightest."

Sam poured her coffee into the thermos next to it and sipped it on her way back to Annie's room.

Annie's alarm had already gone off, and she'd kept the radio on while she was in her bathroom and closet. Sam waited in a beanbag chair. Annie came out in different kind of dress today, as frilly and pink as her nightgown, with a lacy bib collar and a thinner pink ribbon around her waist to match the ones in her hair—pigtails again instead of braids. Bright white patent leather Mary Janes tapped on the tile as she headed down into the solarium toward the bedroom door while determinedly ignoring Sam.

Annie sulked all through breakfast and lessons. Sam considered bracing herself for something far worse than shit in her bed, but she had no idea what to brace for—a tantrum or a creative amputation. Should she stick a butter knife up her sleeve, or did she need to prepare to spank Annie? Sam would never spank another human being who didn't ask her to—and that had only been one time—but Annie seemed a prime candidate for corporal punishment, given her tendency for corporal play. At the very least, it could instill the slightest bit of empathy.

As Sam brought their plates to the serving hatch after their light lunch, Annie stood next to her chair, clicking her heels together and clenching her teeth.

"Now, what would you like to play today, Annie?" Sam asked. "We can play outside. It's a beautiful day, and I've only been outside once. There are some lovely climbing trees out front. Or you could show me some of your smaller doll collections that you promised. Or your antique doll collection. I was really looking forward to those. Like a room in a haunted house."

Annie hesitated, forgetting to clench her teeth. The hard edge to her eyes smoothed out but didn't quite soften. "Do you like haunted houses?"

"Depends on the house."

"What do you like about them?"

"I like when they're not real."

"I can show you my Monster High dolls. They have their own room."

Annie led her by the hand back into the east wing, past the Repair Room and cross corridor, past the curved corridor that cradled Annie's bedroom. That bald curve made Sam more and more nervous every time, like the line of dark from a closet that wasn't supposed to be open. But she wasn't going to explore it on her own. She had enough to deal with in the places she'd already been.

Annie stopped in front of one of the small rooms on the right. Almost immediately, Sam sighed in relief because there wasn't a sliding door on the other side. No card reader, no IV bag in a glass box.

Annie switched on the lights: ghoulish, radioactive green against black-painted walls.

Now Sam could see why Annie had given the Monster High dolls their own room. She'd constructed her own three-dimensional façade against the opposite wall and curving onto the adjacent, in the style of a haunted-mansion-slash-castle. Neon lightning bolted from cotton clouds in time with the thunderstorm track that had turned on with the lights, along with electronic-styled classical songs often used in scary soundtracks.

In spite of absolutely everything, Sam couldn't help the smile that spread, genuine and delighted, across her face. "Did you do all this, Annie?"

Annie nodded, a little shy.

To the side was a table to display the Monster High Deadluxe High School and Catacombs Castle. Some of the dolls had been arranged there with the playsets' furniture and accessories. The rest had been arranged in the dollhouse Annie had created herself, and although the Monster High dollhouses were impressive, they paled in comparison to Annie's, from wallpapered and carpeted plywood to little cobwebbed sconces.

It really was a shame that someone so wonderfully creative had to be such a monster—like H.H. Holmes.

Why is this not enough for you, Annie? Why can't you just do this?

"It took me two months to make this dollhouse just right. On Halloween, Mrs. Fratello sets up a television in here. I turn off the music and just watch spooky movies with the storm sounds. If you like this, you'll like the old-fashioned doll rooms, too."

Annie took Sam's hand again and drew her back into the corridor, quieting the storm before she closed the door.

The next room had once been three rooms. The doors were still there, but the walls had been knocked out for Annie to put all her antique and antique-style dolls together, a sea of baby and little girl faces. They wore everything from christening dresses to grown women's period gowns.

The three rooms had been arranged into three separate living spaces of grand antiques, with even a three-seated conversation chair. The switching on of low-lit shaded lamps and glass lanterns with false flames was accompanied by a soft soundtrack of whispers that crept with spider legs along the back of Sam's neck. The flickering light made the dolls' glass eyes seem alive, following Annie's and Sam's progress through the room like portraiture.

"The rugs are bought, but I restored most of the furniture, at least well enough for dolls to sit on," Annie said. "I don't enjoy building things that aren't dolls or dollhouses, but working on these taught me skills I needed for making my own dollhouses how I want them."

At the other end of the room was a white four-poster twin bed with a lacy canopy, like over a bassinet. More dolls with chubby faces and white lace dresses crowded on the covers. Some faces were chipped of paint or porcelain, but they were by and large clean and bright, and their clothes had been carefully laundered like new.

"Would you like to play with some of these dolls, Annie? I'm almost afraid to touch them, but I'd be open to play with the Monster High dolls with you."

Annie picked up one of the baby dolls with a lacy cap and long baptismal gown from the bed. It gazed up at her with wide, innocent eyes—painted rather than glass. "Why so quiet, little baby boy? Do you need to be fed? Changed? I can't tell what you need if you're not crying. Come on, baby boy. I'll find you a voice."

She cradled the baby with the tenderness required for such an old, delicate antique and rocked it all the way to the third door. Sam's deepening anxiety had nothing to do with the abrupt end of whispers as Annie turned out the light on her way out, nearly leaving Sam in complete darkness. She ran to the door before it closed.

Annie chucked the doll under its chin and baby-talked to it as she continued down the hall, asking if it was hungry, *hungry-wungry*, telling it to *cry, cry, cry*, and making crying sounds herself with eerie mimicry.

It plucked a nerve as uncomfortable as the funny bone, a pressure point in Sam's mind that made her want to do *anything* to make the crying stop, or else another child would start crying or yelling or one of her mom's boyfriends would yell—or hit Sam or whoever was crying. And her mom had never done anything, because she'd be passed out or distracted by her phone or the television or who the fuck knew. Sam had long stopped excusing her mother. She'd learned to seethe and soothe at the same time.

Just as Annie could sound like a fifteen-year-old or a five-year-old, she could also make herself sound like an upset five-week-old—that grating, gritty sound of toothless mouth and need that knew no *later* and needed to be sated *now*. As much as Sam hated the part of her that hopped to, it hopped to and had nowhere to hop, just a bucketful of fear to accompany the anxiety.

Sam took several deep breaths to calm herself, because she suspected that the good little girl side of Annie was not long for this day. She followed, though, because Annie hadn't yet stepped over the line.

"I think we need to repair someone's voice box," Annie said, entering a room to her left.

It was soundproofed, with nothing but foam insulation on the walls. A sound and recording board had been arranged on a counter, with an anaconda of wires leading beyond the wall. Next to the sound board sat a plastic tub of small, white plastic voice boxes—the kind that played a phrase or two and could be sewn into a toy. Relatively low-tech in comparison to the control boards.

Annie handed the baby to Sam, who took it and automatically started rocking and swaying, which made Annie grin as she turned toward the board. Sam didn't make herself stop the conditioned behavior. She needed to show how she would commit to playing with Annie when she was being reasonable.

"Let's see. We have some of the classics here." Annie pushed the first few buttons on the sound board. The first was the typical sample of a baby crying that could be heard in a million movies. The second was another baby cry.

Sam rocked and swayed harder.

The third was a plaintive *mama*, what an old baby doll would say when tipped over.

"I think we can do better." Annie hit each button down each row like a child in a skyscraper elevator.

The speakers in the room played lullabies like "Twinkle, Twinkle, Little Star," "Rockabye Baby," and "Itsy-Bitsy Spider," then said 'I love you' in the voice of men, women, and children, even in a few other languages.

The foam insulation swallowed the sound like sponge absorbed water.

By the fourth row, the typical human sounds gave way to animal: a wolf howl, a wolf pack howling together, a loon hooting, coyotes whooping, a cat meowing, a scared cat meowing and hissing, a dog barking happily, a dog barking viciously, the sound of flesh ripping.

Then screams. At first, they could have been from an animal—fox, peacock, mountain lion—but then there was no mistaking the human element, as though they were on the edge of a *no*. Then they included *no* amid the terrified or pained screams. But they were still just public domain samples. Sam had heard them before in music and movies.

By the sixth row, the screams became far too specific.

"Please stop! Please stop! I'll do anything."

"That hurts. That hurts. Oh, God, God, fuck, that…"

"What are you doing with that? What are you doing? What are you doing?"

"Stay away from me! Don't touch me!"

"Stop, please, for the love of God, stop!"

Unmoving, Sam held the doll like a dead baby in her cold arms.

"I think those might give the wrong impression for such a sweet little baby. Maybe one of these," Annie said.

On to the eighth row of ten.

"Oh, it's so big."

"That's not supposed to go there."

"Oh yes, yes, oh, oh, oh fuck, oh fuck…"

"So hot, God, baby, so tight."

"Harder. Yes, yes, fuck me harder, oh yeah, oh, oh…"

"Annie, remember when we talked about things that should stay personal and private?" Sam said. "If you're going to—"

"That's definitely not the right impression," Annie said. "Let's skip to the end."

Tenth row.

"I'll play with you, Annie."

"Wait, there are cameras?"

"I'm not a martyr, and I'm not a saint."

Sam's voice. Sam's voice from when she was with Annie. Sam's voice from when she was with Dr. Panabaker.

"Why are you helping her?"

"Has anyone ever tried to kill Annie?"

Sam tightened her arms around the baby doll to keep from dropping it. The face would definitely shatter, and she wasn't sure what Annie would do to *her* face if she damaged one of the antique dolls.

Annie turned around to hop up onto the counter, where she swung her pure Mary Janes under her swishy skirt. "Why do you want to kill me, Miss Sam?"

Sam tried to swallow. It took some effort. "I don't want to kill you, Annie."

"Want to try again?" Annie said.

"I asked the doctor whether anyone had ever tried. I don't want to kill you, Annie. I don't want *anyone* to die. I watched Dr. Panabaker kill your jack-in-the-box because he was already well on his way. And your favorite doll, Darla, is one thin heart muscle away from death."

"Miss Sam…" Annie pushed off the counter and approached where Sam stood in the doorway with the baby. She stared straight into Sam's eyes. "They're dolls. They're not real. If I want to smash my doll's face in, even though he's a baby, I can do that, because he's mine."

Annie snatched the baby doll from Sam's arms and flung it to the ground. The face opened like a teacup and shattered outward, dangerous flower petals caught in the carpet.

"See? It's just a damn doll. You were the one holding it like you could soothe its cries. I was pretending to cry for it. So who, of the two of us, can't seem to tell the difference?"

With the soundproofed room closing in on her, Sam stepped back into the corridor. "The antique dolls, the Bratz and Barbies, the Monster High, the stuffed animals—hell, even the taxidermy—those are dolls. The ones with flesh and blood who talk back at you, they're people you decided were dolls. They can experience pain, which is why you drug them. And they can die, which is why you need a new jack-in-the-box. You shouldn't have them in the first place, but if you're going to have them, you need to take much better care of your things."

Annie ran her tongue along her teeth behind her lips. "Why? Dolls are dolls. They just have to do what I make them do, what they were designed to do, and they won't hurt. It's easy."

"It's simple, but it's not easy. And you're doing such irresponsible things because—"

"Because Daddy never told me *no* as a child?"

"Among other things, I'm sure," Sam said softly. No point denying it; Annie had already heard what she thought.

Annie reached behind Sam and opened another door.

This one had a glass door and IV bag on the other side.

An armless woman scarified in a scale pattern knelt gape-mouthed, dislocated mandible swinging when she jerked around toward the open door, the light. In front of her, a man leaned against the wall, gripped in shackles, although he hadn't been last night when Sam had seen him on the doctor's screens with the girl on their pallet, in as unwelcome a situation as now.

His cock had been enhanced with inorganic fillers to bolster his girth and length to unnatural proportions, but another shackle at the base acted as a cock ring to hold it up and keep it properly erect and blood-filled. He arched, keen with need that had to be painful if he was like this all the time, given vasodilators *and* prevented from coming.

The shackles kept him at bay, but after what she'd already seen, Sam knew they'd let him go that night, when he'd be able to do whatever he wanted to the girl. Sam dearly hoped he'd be able to muster some restraint without someone doing it for him. She didn't have much hope.

Neither did the girl. When Annie pointed the woman forward, she closed her eyes against her fear and loathing, shuffled forward on her knees, then worked her loose lips around the thicker cock to take it in. She couldn't use much of her mouth without painful spasms, but the dislocated jaw encouraged her to take more anyway. The man's hips jerked him in even deeper, punching the back of her throat as his eyes rolled back.

"Speak," Annie said through the air holes.

The woman squeezed her eyes shut against tears but made no sound beyond a wet gag. Both the woman's and man's throats had an identical, nearly invisible vertical scar over the center.

"Speak," Annie said again, more forcefully. Both man and woman flinched.

The woman pressed her shoulder, where a heart-shaped disc raised the skin, against the man's thigh. The sound sample she triggered was muffled through skin and glass, but loud enough it could still be heard. Sam couldn't know if these were their original voices, but whoever spoke for the recording was clearly afraid.

"I'm hungry. Wah-wah. Feed me. Wah-wah."

Then, jaw tightening, the man pressed his palm, which had a heart of its own. *"Here comes the bullet train. Choo-choo."*

The woman: *"Mmm, mmm. Yummy in my tummy."*

"Eat it all up for Daddy."

"I'm such a good girl. I clean all *my plate."*

Then the recordings recycled, but the man and woman kept pressing while the man thrust into her mouth and Annie watched, her fingers curled through the breathing holes.

Sam struggled for strength in her abdomen to breathe, to speak, given that the whole thing seemed like a threat against what she'd said and was saying to Annie. "These aren't dolls. These are people. People who experience pain. They are experiencing pain now because you're treating them like dolls. You need to understand—"

"*You* seem to be the only one who doesn't understand," Annie snapped. "You don't get to decide what I do. You don't get to tell me what is and isn't a doll. You're not in charge here. You're just the nanny."

"I *am* in charge of you," Sam shot back, proud for keeping her voice level with all the grunting and gagging in the background from voiceless pleasure and pain. "When your father isn't here, I'm the parent. When your father is here but isn't in the room, I'm the parent. I like your doll collections, Annie. I think they're neat. I think they're beautiful. I think you're really skilled at a lot of things. And if you want to destroy your *dolls*, I'm not going to stand in your way. But these are *people*. If you're going to hurt people, I'm not going to be a part of it. Now, I'm going outside. I might walk the hedge maze. I might dangle my legs in the pool. I might climb some trees. I want you to come with me. You haven't earned playing with people dolls if this is what you do to them."

She held out her hand to Annie.

Annie slapped Sam's hand away.

Sam held it out again, and Annie slapped it away again.

"Annie, I'm not going to be a part of this. Things *are* going to change around here."

Annie slapped Sam's face. It was like a thunderclap in Sam's head, stunning her for a few seconds, enough for Annie to slap her again, striking down and catching Sam's teeth against her inner cheek.

Sam grabbed both of Annie's wrists when she raised the other hand to slap the other side of Sam's face. Sam shook, but not from pain or shock or fear. She had to tighten every last fiber of willpower to keep from striking Annie back.

On the one hand, Annie was in desperate need of someone to literally fight back against her. But Sam wasn't quite a victim. At worst, she was in Annie's little dugout of minions whose status could change at any time. It wasn't Sam's place to hit her; as her nanny, it was, in fact, her job not to.

If Annie was a child—albeit a precocious and mean one in an adult body—Sam needed to treat her like a child. That meant not lashing out like Annie was. She'd been caregiver to enough children and adults by now that she knew to control the impulse to retaliate, because giving in would only reinforce the violence.

Everything told her to lay Annie out on the floor in response, as she'd wanted to do to some of her siblings and some of her needier or brattier clients. However, although she squeezed Annie's wrists to keep Annie from hitting her again, she locked her temper inside with her disgust.

"Annie, you're too old for hitting like a toddler," Sam said as calmly as she could through a jaw that screamed to clench. "I'm going outside, whether you want to join me or not, because you're also too big to drag along with me. But I won't be playing with you. If you don't like how I do things, you can call your dad. He can come fire me in person, since he was the one who hired me."

Yes, go call Daddy. Then maybe I can figure out where you keep a fucking phone—or confirm that you have one at all.

Annie stamped her foot as Sam walked away.

But by the time Sam had almost reached the dining room, she heard Annie's Mary Janes on the hall marble—walking not running—then following her onto the cement tile of the porch. It really was a nice day outside, as long as Sam didn't think about all the people trapped in tiny windowless rooms and left to their own drug-fueled devices. There weren't a lot of nice days in Texas. Had to enjoy them when they came.

Sam did everything she said she was going to do. She walked the small hedge maze, which was more like a meditation labyrinth with lower hedges. She kicked off her shoes, pulled up her sweatpants, and dangled her feet in the cold pool, making ripples on the flat, clear surface. Then she felt like a kid again as she monkeyed over tree branches almost as big around as she was.

And the entire time, Annie joined her like a stubborn thirteen-year-old forced into the family trip but refusing to enjoy it. While Sam walked the hedge maze, Annie pouted from the porch, sulking on one of the deck chairs. While Sam dangled her feet in the pool, Annie removed her Mary Janes and frilly lace and pearl bead socks and dangled hers on the other side, mirroring Sam's little kicks but not returning Sam's effort at a smile or conversation. While Sam climbed a tree in the front of the house, Annie climbed another one, then sat on the branch and fumed in Sam's direction.

Sam knew better than to assume she'd won anything. On the contrary, Annie was probably planning her next revenge. Or maybe Annie was just contemplating what kind of doll would suit her. Either way, Sam had to act as though Annie were a perfectly reasonable eleven-year-old—as reasonable as they could be—albeit one that had been spoiled rotten.

Rotten. Her exterior was shiny Red Delicious skin, but her insides were full of worms, mushy oxidized sugar, and mold. If she were an apple, there would be no fixing her.

And maybe there simply wasn't.

Rotten. Sometimes Sam felt like something was rotten in her, too, and had been for a while. As though necrotizing flesh wore away to leave her a stench-filled hollow, poisonous as a black-mold basement, condemned as the house it held up. Water damage took time, but before you knew it, it was pervasive, invasive, insidious, and there was no recourse but to cut it out and start again. She was ugly inside, a giver only because she'd had to be and didn't know how to be anything else.

Diapers her mother hadn't wanted to change. Potty-training. Keeping scared kids quiet after nightmares when her mom or her mom's boyfriend wanted to sleep. Bailing her older brother out after DUIs. Bailing her younger sister out after a DUI and a possession charge. Cleaning the pigsty of a house, then cleaning the neater pigsty of an apartment, just wanting one day that smelled *clean* and not like cockroaches, cigarettes, heavily preserved snack cakes, shit, and gasoline—all festering inside of her.

Day by day, a fungus-caked fingernail scratched at the wrinkly gray matter in her brain pan, making her duller and duller, drinking her soul sip by sip, if she even had a soul.

She was horrified by the Dream House, yet here she was, smelling flowers and the surrounding cedar, in dappled sunlight with a cool breeze unsettling her hair, rough bark under her palms. Not quite free, but freer than those in misery whether Annie played with them or not. She was taking time they didn't have because *she* might have time.

Perhaps it was uncharacteristically naïve of Sam to assume she was the first to try this tactic of treating Annie like she would any other child. As far as Sam saw it, she had only one choice: go along with Annie or change Annie's behavior like the responsible parent Annie had probably never had. She *couldn't* go along with what Annie did, even if she seemed willing to let it keep happening out of her sight.

She'd never been good at putting the oxygen mask on herself first. After a while, she'd stopped being so good at putting the oxygen mask on anyone who wasn't clamoring for it. And she hadn't been able to breathe. She still couldn't breathe. The fresh air was filled with an invisible, odorless gas slowly killing or mutating everything that inhaled it. Her cells—and her soul, if she still had one—were starving.

But she had to take her time, climbing trees.

"Ready for dinner?" Sam called across the yard to where Annie sat.

Annie climbed down when Sam climbed down. Halfway back to the French doors from the porch, Annie held out her hand to take Sam's rather than strike her. She didn't even squeeze too tightly when Sam accepted. Then, before they entered, Annie stood still for Sam to brush away stray dirt and bark from her dress.

Ji-an came out with Annie's tray first, as she always did. There was no chocolate milk next to the white milk.

Annie glared at her. "I can't drink my white milk if I don't have chocolate milk."

"Your white milk comes with a straw. You can put the straw to the back of your mouth and swallow really fast. That's how I used to have to drink it. But you don't get chocolate milk today, and no dessert for either of us," she added to Ji-an.

"I *want* my chocolate milk and chocolate cake. I always have chocolate milk with white milk, and I always have chocolate cake on Friday," Annie insisted. "Ji-an, give me my things."

"Your nanny was very clear," Ji-an said. "No chocolate milk, no dessert."

"You don't answer to her," Annie said, enunciating very clearly. If she could spit fire through her eyeballs, Ji-an would have been flambéed. "You answer to me."

"Miss Annie, your nanny is just trying to take care of you," Ji-an said in her characteristic clipped, no-nonsense tone. "If she doesn't tell me to hold the chocolate milk again, you'll have it tomorrow. It won't hurt you to not have it today. It is not an integral part of your balanced diet. Good evening."

Ji-an headed back to the swinging door.

Annie picked up her fork in her fist. "So help me, Ji-an…"

Sam cut through her green chile and sour cream enchiladas. "Are you really going to go scorched earth over chocolate milk, Annie? Really?"

Ji-an took advantage of Sam's distraction and let the door swing closed behind her.

"Where's your sense of proportion? It's just one night, just chocolate milk and dessert. You still have a wonderful meal, and you have snack things in your room that I can't keep from you. Why is this where you think you need to draw the line? Let Ji-an be. She's just doing her job."

"Her job is to serve me," Annie said.

"And she has."

"Her job is to serve me what I want."

"Her job is to serve you nutritionally valuable meals and the occasional treat. But we don't get treats when we've done things we know we shouldn't. That's just part of life. I understand it might not be a part of life you're familiar with, but even if I don't teach it to you now, you'll learn that eventually. Might as well get ahead of it before it bites you in the butt."

Because there was no way the Dream House would be able to continue on indefinitely. Annie would eventually hit a point in her aging when she wouldn't be able to keep people in line, either because she was frailer or people simply took her little-girl mind and behavior less seriously. Every new person coming in would be less and less likely to play along.

At the very least, Mr. Lange would eventually die. Annie would inherit the Dream House and would probably have a trust in her name. Maybe he'd even allow her to be in charge of it. But at this point, Mr. Lange was the face the outside world saw. She'd either have to take over that side of it herself or find someone she could intimidate into doing it for her, and they might be less inclined to take threats from a woman seriously, much less one who thought she was eleven years old.

It would be better for everyone, including Annie, if the Dream House as a dollhouse wound down sooner rather than later. Annie would probably end up in a facility, where she belonged, where she would encounter an abundance of *no* and derision for her authority, even if she bought her way into the best room with the best drugs in the best institution in the country.

Maybe then, the dolls would be saved—as much as they could be saved.

Anything other than things staying exactly as they were.

"Now, eat your dinner. Or don't eat your dinner. Throw the plate to the floor like you did your baby doll. Makes no difference to me. But after playing today, *I'm* hungry, so I assume you're hungry, too."

Annie reached for Sam's plate, but Sam anticipated the move and grabbed her plate away, then stood and took her glass of water down to the other end of the table.

"Eat your dinner, Annie," Sam said, "or you can go to your room to play there."

"I want to play with my dolls. You didn't let me play with my dolls."

"You have dolls in your bedroom."

Annie threw her white milk glass on the floor, where it shattered even more spectacularly than the baby doll, because the glass broke in more pieces and splattered milk along with it.

Sam blinked through the loud noise but otherwise didn't feed the tantrum. Ji-an started through the swinging door, but Sam held up her hand. "She'll finish her dinner or leave the table. Then you can deal with the mess. Thank you, Ji-an. You keep doing whatever you were doing."

Ji-an, who hadn't been the slightest bit impressed with Sam at the beginning, gave her a measuring glance, then backed into the kitchen again.

"My socks are wet," Annie said.

"Whose fault is that?" Sam continued eating her meal.

Annie shrieked. But that was all she did. She didn't want to step into the mess of the milk, even though she had milk on her shoes and socks already, and Sam could attest that sulking alone could be exhausting. Sam had had entire screaming arguments with her mother or siblings in her head without saying a single word, but they'd left her utterly drained every time.

She couldn't remember the last time she'd been angry with Lila. That had never been their problem. Their relationship had gone cold, not hot.

Annie sawed so hard at the soft enchiladas that the knife squeak-scraped on the porcelain. Sam didn't do anything but wince again. It would be more unpleasant to Annie, who was nearer to it, which was why she calmed her sawing to a more civilized purpose and ate what was on her plate. No milk, white or chocolate, so she had nothing to wash it down with. Yet, she managed. Because she was hungry.

Sam and Annie had a quiet but tense dinner.

When Sam was done, she waited, her fists under her chin, for Annie to finish. Then she stood. "Would you like help over the milk, or do you need to do it yourself?"

"I think I need to climb on the table."

"That's fine. Take off your socks and shoes. I'll hold them. It's not ladylike to climb on top of the table while wearing a skirt, but it's your table and no one else is here. Besides, I'm not particularly ladylike, either."

Annie removed her shoes, then her socks. Sam tucked the socks into the shoes. Neither were terribly soaked, but socks wet to any degree were uncomfortable; the shoes would wipe down. If Annie's legs had been wet, she must have dried herself off with her skirt, which was already dirty from climbing. Nothing wrong with a little girl in dirty clothes if she was doing good girl things, as far as Sam was concerned.

Then Annie climbed onto her chair and crawled over the table until she reached where milk hadn't spattered. Sam helped her back to the ground.

"Do you want me to join you in the library or your room?" Sam asked.

"My room. I want to play with my teddy bears. I want you to play with me."

"I can play with teddy bears. Is it going to be a tea party?"

"No. I like to cuddle with my bears."

Chapter 9: TEDDY BEAR NIGHTMARE

Sam let Annie lead this time and took her shoes and socks to the closet to toss the socks in the hamper, then rinse her shoes off in the bathroom sink. Annie changed out of her dirty dress into a simpler one: no ribbons, no lace, so much less stylized that it was harder to pretend she was a little girl, except for the pigtails. Only the proportion of skirt to bodice made it seem girlish. Her shoes, too, were more casual, matte Mary Janes with a duller rubber sole.

Annie skipped lightly to her snack bar and found herself a snack cake to nibble on. It probably paled in comparison to freshly baked chocolate cake from Ji-an's kitchen, but it would satiate a sweet tooth. Sam tidied a little, although the room didn't need much help.

When Annie had finished her snack cake, she turned back to Sam with her hands behind her back, the very picture of contrition.

Sam didn't trust it for a second. The evening was still young.

"Would you like to see my teddy bear collection, Miss Sam?"

"That depends, Annie," Sam said slowly. "Would we have to go out into the halls to see them?"

"Oh, no. We can stay here in the bedroom. I keep my best teddy bears hidden, but when I hit this button"—Annie backed toward one of the shelves and tapped a panel next to one of the Bratz display boxes—"they all appear for me to choose from."

"Fuck, no." It came out a whisper, a whimper, and Sam didn't even mean to say it. But she didn't have to see the teddy bears yet to know something was going to be terribly and horrifyingly wrong.

All the shelves displaying actual dolls swung on platforms and flipped around, revealing glass boxes about half the size of the doll rooms, too short for anyone to stand without bending all the way over.

Each teddy bear sat on their respective floor, slumped, weighed down more by their confined, sedentary lifestyles and resultant size than by any chains. They were all much more well fed than most of their counterparts, with broad chests, curved shoulders, ponderous bellies hanging over thick thighs. All of them had their own mouths, which made them easier to feed and made it easier for them to eat, and because they were all left to their own solitary, eating would be one of the only things they could do.

Also, unlike the other dolls, they weren't connected to an IV drip, but many of them were already getting hard by the time the platforms stopped turning. Only one of them didn't, and that was because she was a woman, with heavy breasts to join her large, comforting stomach.

All the teddy bears were naked, to a point. Sam would never have thought it was possible to literally attach a costume to someone's skin, but Annie seemed to have figured out a way by sewing ragged costume edges to medical mesh lace, then suturing sliced skin to the mesh. Thick scarring consumed the mesh almost to the edge of the fake fur attached to their arms, chests, legs, like a teddy bear costume that they'd burst out of. The fur was the kind one might find on an actual teddy bear rather than any real bear or even something soft like a rabbit.

They wore the suits like skins, no apparent reaction, no itch, no blood, no pus, no recent attempts to remove the mesh. Unbound.

Free now to move around and even run—though that might strain the mesh—yet they slouched in place and stared with dull interest up from where they sat, satisfied and sleepy.

Annie skipped up to one with dark brown fur on either side of his matted chest chair. His teddy bear hood covered his head, woven into his hair and carefully tended beard. He flushed a deep red over his face and chest as Annie approached him, and he took her hand and let her guide him to his feet, which were padded like teddy bear pajamas. The bedroom was always kept cool. Their rooms had to be kept extra chilly so the teddy bears wouldn't overheat, even with the way the fur gaped over their chests and bellies, open over chubby genitals and instead sewn in to frame the thighs.

The back of the teddy bear costume had a little flap, which explained how the bears shit in their cells. But they were clean. A little sweaty, but clean. Their fur was brushed, their hair washed, their scars carefully tended. The one Annie led down from his platform moved a little gingerly when his suit pulled at the scars, but he followed without resistance, even though he had a mouth to speak and scream at her. Even though he was at least twice her size, probably closer to three times. He just looked down at her with golden retriever devotion and followed without leash or command.

As bad a feeling as she had with the other broken people, Sam got an even worse feeling from these—these lazy, dozy, soft teddy bears who could run but didn't, who could fight but didn't, who could swarm Annie but didn't. They just watched and idly scratched or stroked over fur or skin as Annie led her chosen bear to her bed to join with the rest of the stuffed animals she had arranged in the nest.

"I know it's early to go to bed, Miss Sam, but I'm awfully tired." Annie yawned and stretched her arms and legs, which lifted her skirt.

The teddy bear stared at the stretch of thigh with a kind of empty intensity, as though that was what he was expected to do rather than what he would have done of his own accord.

"I think I just want to play in bed tonight. Come here with us." Annie beckoned Sam with thin, delicate fingers tipped with pink nail polish. "Bruno is so soft and warm to cuddle."

"Annie, I don't think I could have been any clearer," Sam said slowly, backing through the neighborhood of playhouses toward the bedroom door. "I know you're testing your boundaries, but I was pretty clear about mine. I won't do this with you. I won't help you hurt your dolls."

"Do they look hurt, Miss Sam?" Annie leaned against the teddy bear, who wrapped his arm around her. She stroked over his chest fur, his chest hair, not distinguishing between bear and man. The man, however, responded, his already chubby cock reddening and thickening over the thick thigh fur, and quickly. No IV, but probably still on some kind of cocktail. For Darla, Annie had called it a 'winding.'

"They look well trained, but learned helplessness isn't love, Annie, and the scars are enough of a story for me."

"It's just part of the creative process," Annie said, "and they're so much more content for it. Aren't you, sweet boy?"

She trailed her fingers down to his soft belly, then hugged him around his middle to rest her head on it. The teddy bear flopped back onto the bed to sit with her, and she tucked herself against him, stroking his belly and humming contentedly. "See? Placid and sweet as anything. They're my happy bears. You want me to get something from the toy box, Bruno? Would that make you even happier?"

Annie climbed down from the bed while Bruno sat where Sam had slept, his legs curved into arrows on either side of his heavy trunk, but his erection continued to thicken, stretch, as Annie danced over to a wooden toy chest next to her bed.

The compartments inside were full of nothing but sex toys.

While Annie dug through the chest, Sam ran to the bedroom door.

Locked.

Sam turned the dead bolt locked and unlocked, but the door still wouldn't open. The knob wouldn't even turn under the cold sweat on her palms.

"When the teddy bear compounds are all open, the doors to their rooms and mine automatically lock," Annie said mildly as she climbed onto the bed with her bear, a six-inch purple cock attached to a strap-on harness she'd buckled over her dress, splitting her skirt to hang to the sides. She set a small lube container next to her.

Bruno was all the more avid now. The redness on his chest spread down past the edge of the bear fur and deepened in his cock, which now smeared pre-ejaculate against the bottom of his belly. He didn't touch himself, though, just tightened his bear paws in the comforter and licked his lips over and over, so hungry he drooled into his beard.

"It was needed more in the beginning. They had numbers and size, but I had my own tricks. When I have them all out like this, I don't want to leave anyway." Annie wrapped her arms around Bruno's neck and rubbed her cheek on his bear ear. He still didn't move his arms.

Of course he didn't move his arms. He was a teddy bear. He was a teddy bear until she wanted him to be more, like when he walked with her, like when he couldn't stop his cock from twitching as she stroked along the edge of the fur, brushing his nipple and tickling through the hair there as well.

"If you needed precautions to keep them from escaping, then you hurt them to achieve this loyalty," Sam said. "Let me out."

"Oh, I didn't hurt them."

Annie lowered herself to her elbows on the bed and brought her mouth to the tip of his erection. She kissed him, like kissing a teddy bear nose. He bucked slightly and grunted, tightening his pawed fists on the duvet. Then she parted her lips, so slowly, and slipped the head into her mouth in a wet caress that turned his wordless grunt into a loud, unrestrained groan. She sucked on him like a lollipop, all tongue, savoring the sweet.

Sam looked determinedly away through the solarium windows toward the fading sunset on the porch. The light in Annie's bedroom made it seem like the only part of the world left, a glass-clad apocalypse.

She couldn't unhear the wet and wetter sounds of Annie's mouth and Bruno's unfiltered and still wordless pleasure.

"He's a real bear, this one," Annie finally said. Sam still didn't look back, but it sounded like she might be wiping her mouth. "It took a while, but we found out what worked, didn't we, Bruno? He likes it when I take him in the ass, and when he's turned on enough, it doesn't matter what the mouth is attached to. He knows I'll give him what he needs. I'm good to all my bears. They're gentle, Miss Sam. They don't bite, unless you tell them to. Eyes closed, it can feel just like what your girlfriend does to you."

"My girlfriend doesn't—" Sam shook her head and squeezed her eyes shut. "I'm not talking about my girlfriend with you, Annie. I'm not playing with your bears. And tomorrow, we're going to have a talk about lessons. I'm sure you have an ethics book in that library of yours."

"You still don't seem to understand, Miss Sam, how this is going to go."

Sam tried to smash the door open, but she already knew that wasn't going to work. The doors in the east wing hallways, including her own bedroom, were construction grade and probably could be broken with enough force and adrenaline. But the rest of the house was custom construction. Annie's bedroom door wasn't moving for anything except an axe.

Sam ran back down into the solarium to get as far away from the teddy bear platforms as she could while Annie stroked Bruno with long, slow pulls. The others watched, limp-limbed and hypnotized.

The bedroom door may have been locked, but Annie wouldn't lock herself out of her bathroom. Sam hurried toward the open bathroom door. If she had to sleep in the goddamn tub…

"Cole, stop her."

The bear woman was closer, but a big, tall man with black bear fur clambered to his feet with some difficulty but undeniable speed. Once he was up, momentum worked in his favor as he stumbled forward, strong under his fat, straining the scar stitching as he ran toward Sam.

Sam screamed as he swiped at her. For a moment, she thought she'd make it. Then the man's big arms closed around her top half, lifted her from the long steps leading up to the bathroom, and flung her against the solarium windows.

She thought the glass would shatter, but it had been paned for hailstorms. Instead, something inside of her shattered, or at least cracked, or maybe that was just the shock going through her. Either way, when she fell to the carpeted floor, she couldn't move.

The bigger bear hooked her under her arms. When nothing internally screamed as he lifted her from the ground, she figured she hadn't broken anything more than a hairline fracture. She still couldn't do anything other than barely breathe through her stunned body, which hurt and throbbed everywhere like a newly stubbed toe.

Cole dragged her up to the canopied bed, where Bruno was on his back, sucking with relish on the flavored lube coating Annie's strap-on. Annie sprawled in the opposite direction over the mountain of his body, with all the luxuriant laziness of reclining on a bear-skin rug, to suck much more slowly and torturously over Bruno's cock. The taut flex in his bent legs suggested he would have preferred a more insistent rhythm.

As Sam slowly regained control of herself, she struggled against Cole's hold on her and the press of his large erection probing at her back.

Finally, Bruno couldn't help it. He whimpered around the dildo and curled his toes in the bear footsies, grasping his legs to keep from bucking up into Annie's mouth. She hummed a lullaby between swallowing, too slow to keep cum from dripping back down his cock and balls. When she lifted off from his cock, she deliberately licked to clean him, then closed her mouth over him again to suck—hard. Bruno whined, muffle-shouted, and couldn't help bucking now. Annie clutched his knees and rode his belly and thighs, giggling.

Then she eased her dildo out of his mouth and crawled back around, her cheek sliding over his chest, his beard, before reaching his open, panting mouth, his tongue thick and wet behind his teeth, because he knew what was coming. When Annie opened her mouth, what cum she hadn't swallowed spilled onto his questing tongue.

She petted his beard, his cheeks, his furry hooded head, while he panted and smiled dopily up at her approval. Then she rose on her knees and looked at Sam, stroking her spit- and lube-slick dildo.

"You want a taste, Miss Sam? It's like strawberry soda."

Sam stared at her, panting for entirely different reasons than Bruno. She couldn't breathe, she was so afraid.

Annie climbed off the bed to approach Sam. The dildo sticking out from its harness should have looked ridiculous, comical, especially over her young dress. Instead, Sam's panic sluiced burning ice through her veins, over her nerves. She couldn't tell her body to move right. When she tried to yank her arms in, she elbowed out at Cole anyway.

He just wrapped his arms tighter around her, needful and silent.

"Sometimes when I let them out, we go on walks through the house, out in the yard, and yes, sometimes we climb trees. I can't put them in the pool, because their fur gets so heavy, but we do play together. Play and take tea and sleep. They're so hot when winter comes and the house gets so cold even without the air conditioning. Three-bear nights. The one holding you likes girls, women. He can keep me warm for hours. If I can teach a gay man to crave me, what do you think I could teach you, Miss Sam—with enough time and the right lubrication? Cole-ar Bear, kneel down, won't you? Make her kneel with you."

When he brought her down, his legs flanked hers. Annie was right—he was warm, he was hot, he was burning against her, worse for his desire and for her fear, but as Annie continued to approach, Cole became so much less frightening to Sam than the smiling woman with ringleted pigtails and little cherries embroidered on her dress.

"Stay away from me. Get away from me," Sam managed to hiss, like a frightened rattlesnake. She tried to burrow into the man behind her, but he was too solid, and she jerked her hips away from where he unintentionally tried to burrow into her.

"Play with us. Play with *me.* We'll have fun, then snuggle like puppies in my bed. You're already sleeping with me, Miss Sam. And so are they. They don't have to touch you, but they're so soft, so sweet. You can wear the strap-on for Bruno, or for Margaret, if that's your preference. You can even wear it with me. I've played with plenty of girl dolls, including a few who maybe didn't know certain things about themselves yet. But do you know you'd be my first lesbian?"

"Get the *fuck* away from me." Sam spat, globbing saliva onto Annie's dress. "Let me go, goddamn it. Let me fucking go. Stop—"

Annie grabbed her by the hair and twisted her hand to force Sam's head back against the fur on the man's shoulders, then gathered what spit hadn't absorbed into her dress. Sam thought Annie would force the fingers in Sam's mouth—which would have led to losing a few digits in a messier slice than Dr. Panabaker's. But Annie slipped her fingers into Cole's mouth instead.

His grunts so near Sam's ear repulsed her, as did the wet slide of his tongue over Annie's fingers. Like an animal. None of them talked. Could they even talk anymore? Had they forgotten everything but sitting and waiting for attention? Everything but Annie?

Then, holding Sam still, she brought the smooth velvet tip of the dildo to Sam's mouth.

Sam clenched her teeth and mashed her lips together.

Annie removed her fingers from Cole's mouth and struck the same tender place she'd already hit Sam. It jostled her skull, clicked her teeth open, and Annie shoved the dildo into Sam's mouth. Not deep, but she kept Sam from pulling back, and Sam gagged from having something on her tongue that she wanted *off* her tongue.

Annie withdrew after only a few seconds and released Sam's hair, stepping back with a smug grin. "Surely you've done something like that before."

Sam spat again, this time onto the floor to get the taste of unwanted cock, strawberry lube, and Bruno's saliva out of her mouth. Fear was shifting in her from ice to fire. She'd rip out her arms before she stopped fighting the larger teddy bear's hold over her. Tears, hot and stinging, sprinkled the carpet around them as she jerked her head from side to side in her effort, as though she had a raincloud over her.

Cole hugged her like she was the teddy bear and buried his face against her neck, sniffing at her as though her sour fear and exertion sweat were perfume she'd put on for him. His hips jerked with biological imperative. If he did anything to her, she didn't think it would be out of malice, but that wouldn't be any less of a violation—no less than what Annie did to her.

Sam stilled, calmed, slowed her breathing even as her heart raced, which made her head swim and tilt as though the world turned without her. "Get off me." This time she didn't yell, didn't grate her throat. "Let me go."

Annie tilted her head, still smiling like a little girl, all the way to her eyes—unrestrained and a little mad.

"I've had sex with men before, Annie. But when I have sex with women and we bring out the toys, I'm the one with the strap-on. Let me go."

"Promise you won't run?"

Sam nodded.

"You'll play with us now?"

She nodded again.

Annie indicated for Cole to loosen his hold on Sam. He seemed reluctant, with a low moan into her neck, but he opened his arms for Sam to climb to her feet at the foot of Annie's bed.

Annie combed her fingers through Sam's hair, putting her back to rights there, although she could do nothing for Sam's rumpled clothes. "You have such pretty hair. Thick, black, healthy. After we're finished playing, I'll brush it until you fall asleep. Oh, Miss Sam, we'll have so much fun. Finally."

She stood on her toes to kiss Sam—chaste in the sense that she was closed-mouthed—but Sam grimaced and turned her head to break the kiss.

"You realize your father can see everything you're doing," Sam said evenly.

"Of course he can. He's probably watching right now. That's what he does. That's what he's always done. Oh, don't look like that. All he ever did was watch, even after Mommy died. Watched me in my little dresses. Watched me out of my little dresses."

Annie curtsied to the sound system, which didn't have a red light or anything else to indicate a camera, but she seemed certain.

"Once I recognized how he watched me, all I had to do was catch him doing it, then catch him doing what he did afterward, when he thought he was alone. Then he let me do whatever I wanted, because I kept letting him watch, and I let him see so much more. *Then* I started letting him play with my dolls. A shot of spiked bourbon and a fluffy Lolita skirt, and he buys me another mockingbird and diamond ring." Annie stroked Sam's hair with both hands, gentler now—not combing, just touching. "Everyone's mine in the end. Is it time to go to bed, Miss Sam?"

Sam jerked her arm back and punched Annie in the face.

Bruno jolted up on the bed to catch Annie as she hit the footboard and started sliding down. Cole bellowed—again, without words—and grabbed Sam by her arms, his big paws tightening so hard that Sam's knees buckled against the pressure. He yanked her back from the bed while Annie recovered from the blow.

Sam prayed she'd punched nose cartilage into Annie's brain, but no such luck. She seemed disoriented, but she was gradually able to look around and find Sam struggling in Cole's arms again. Blood trickled from her nostrils.

Annie wiped the back of her hand over the drip. All she succeeded in doing was to smear it while a new trickle slithered out. "You're going to be in so much trouble, Miss Sam."

Then Sam was laughing, though nothing was funny. Annie lowered her hand, bewildered and suspicious.

When Sam could stop giggling, she finally said, "Stop it, Annie. Just stop. And call off your goon."

"You haven't given me good reason to, Miss Sam."

"*Stop* it, Annie. I figured it out. I get why everything feels all wrong. I'm sure I'm not the only one who bought into it. But that's the trick, isn't it?"

Annie wiped her face, a little more successfully this time. "What trick?"

Sam wrenched against Cole until Annie indicated with her hands that he should loosen his hold, but not release her completely. At least Sam wasn't distracted by those meat hooks beneath the bear paws digging new bruises into her biceps. She managed to find her feet again. The taller she got, the less she laughed, until she wasn't smiling, just baring her teeth.

"You're not Miss Havisham reliving your past. You're not Norma Desmond reliving your glory days. You're not Elizabeth Moss from *Girl, Interrupted* acting like a child to be liked."

Annie shook her arm from Bruno once she could stand on her own. She gazed down at Sam like a bishop to a penitent.

"You're not developmentally delayed or delusional. That's what you want people to think. Maybe the heaps of sugar you pour on help even your victims swallow what you do to them. But you're not a child, Annie. You're my age, give or take a few years."

Annie blinked, recoiling.

"You're not a child, and you *know* it. You're just a monster. You do these things not because you don't know better and can't tell fantasy from reality. You do them because you want to."

Annie looked shocked for a while. Too long. Then she half smiled, lowered her head, and covered her mouth to whisper, "What did it?"

"Honestly? Everything. It's so easy, though, to believe something just because it's told to us as truth by someone who should have the facts—like your father. There were so many reasons not to believe it, but because everyone else did… You begin with a foregone conclusion, then bend over backward to make things fit. But it was wrong from the start, not least because you couldn't figure out what fucking age you wanted to be."

"Mmm, hitting and swearing. Nice to meet you, real Miss Sam."

"Oh, you knew the real Sam before. That's how I am with children. This is how I am with adults when I don't have to take their bullshit anymore. What really did it, what cut the cord suspending my disbelief? I can believe in a sexually curious young girl in a woman's body. But your prodigious sex toy collection shifts you from sexually curious to sexually adventurous, and if you think I can't recognize an experienced woman…"

Annie raised her chin in understanding. "I see. It's a shame, because I really wanted you to play with me, Sam. I wasn't lying about never having someone like you before. I can't decide if Daddy chose you more for me or him. Well, Daddy, I hope you're watching. No, I wasn't lying about that, either. He's probably watching us right now, door locked, blinds closed, pants halfway down his legs, hand a frantic blur."

She wrapped her own hand around her dildo and jerked it mercilessly, grunting like a man on the edge of an orgasm. After all this time hearing her use a little girl voice—which must have become second nature to her, because she'd continued using it—the grunt low in her register was a harsh contrast that turned Sam's stomach all over again. And caused another clit twitch, which just made Sam want to punch Annie harder.

"He'll abuse himself until he bleeds as long as I'm wearing this strap-on. All these years, Daddy, watching me, imagining I'm your little girl, imagining I'm your wife, imagining I'm both at the same time. The things he wants to do… He's broken more dolls than I have, pretending they're me. He knows better than to try and take this for himself."

Annie ran her hands over her body, from the harness up to her breasts, then caressed her neck and flipped her pigtails.

"What I do for him untouched is far more interesting than what he could do to me in just one night. Because then he'd lose the Dream House. He doesn't have the guts, the heart, or the brain to build or maintain a dollhouse. I'm the reason for what keeps him up at night and distracts you during the day. He's not on a business trip." Annie snorted. "He just needs to get away from me. Afraid of what he'll do to me. Afraid of what I'll do to him. But he still makes a tidy profit from every last frame my program sends him."

"Snuff films," Sam said. "Rape tapes."

Annie shrugged. "If you like. He finds other people, people like him—with money, with power. He shows them the tamer videos to hook them. He keeps showing them more and more,

more esoteric, more perverted. That makes them trust him, makes them complicit, conspiratorial. Then he brings them here for his annual Christmas and May Day parties. We have more blackmail material than we know what to do with. On top of Daddy's money, thousands and thousands of dollars come in every month from people who would kill for us to keep what we know from the press. Not quite mutually assured destruction. They only have their word about what we do, while Daddy and I have hard proof—so to speak—of what they've done," Annie added, deceptively offhand. "And when it comes to Daddy, he's in more danger than me. He's a bad man. I'm insane."

"You're not insane. You know exactly what you're doing. You know your dolls aren't dolls. You know you're hurting people, and you know it's wrong."

Annie toyed with the tip of the dildo with her pink fingernails. "If it comes down to it, I'm traumatized by Daddy's appetites, raised with them, inspired by them. Then traumatized by my mother's death. I can't stand the thought of him touching me, can't stand the reality of Mommy dying. So I seek refuge in the age before I knew these things." She tilted her head to bounce her ringlet pigtails. "I retain a whole dishonesty of lawyers to hire a baker's dozen of psychiatrists who will testify to that effect."

"I don't know if you're traumatized or not, but it doesn't fucking matter. Traumatized people might develop a few self-destructive and other-destructive habits, but you taught yourself sewing, engineering, and medicine and learned brainwashing and torture techniques on the fly to break people into dolls."

Sam stopped trying to escape Cole. Instead, stomach acid rising to her throat, she reached behind her to stroke over the man's cock. She wasn't so far removed from compulsive heterosexuality that she didn't remember how. Sam couldn't fight him. The only option left she could think of was to catch the fly with sweeter honey than Annie offered, in a language he understood.

"You might have a fucking personality disorder," she continued, "but *legally*, especially by Texas standards, I hope everyone in this godforsaken place gets to watch you die by lethal injection gone wrong."

Annie could plainly see that Sam was jerking Cole off, because she matched rhythm on her dildo, licked her lips when Sam clenched her teeth again, as though Annie knew how it made Sam react against her will.

Annie had been doing this for almost two decades—to countless hired help, to her own father. She'd convinced at least six dolls to be more than just prisoners but willing sex slaves who didn't or couldn't talk. She knew exactly what the fuck she was doing.

Sam forced herself to rest her head back against Cole's chest and looked up at him. "I don't know if you can hear or understand me. Maybe she took your eardrums. Maybe she paralyzed your vocal cords. Maybe she electroshocked or drugged you into a fermented mushy version of yourself. But if you're still in there and can think about anything other than your dick, have you been listening? She's not a little girl. She's a grown woman, completely aware of everything she's done to destroy you. You don't have to listen to her. Her bones break more easily than yours."

When Sam looked up into his dark eyes, she thought there was a spark of intelligence there. But his pupils were so large that he was clearly drugged in addition to being aroused, and he glanced furtively at Annie, unable to help himself.

"Sam, it's really no use. Just the sound of my voice is enough to control him. You may have fascinating hands, but if I told him to come, he would. Cole, my sweet boy, why don't you make a mess on Miss Sam's lovely back?"

Cole shuddered, and his breath quickened, intensified, as he rubbed himself against Sam between the hole of her fingers. Sam flinched, eyes closed, as the first shot of semen struck her shirt, warm through the fabric. When he moaned, it wasn't even like a man but like a bear with his foot caught in a bear trap.

"Nice try," Annie whispered in Sam's ear before kissing her cheek. "Oh, you're such a good boy, Cole-ar Bear. You're going to like this part. Bruno, could you help Cole hold Miss Sam? I know she's not quite to your taste, but with all her practice, I'm betting her tongue is to die for. You'd like that, wouldn't you, sweet boy? You like a nice hot mouth to fill."

"Annie, please don't do this." Sam hated begging someone in ribbons and ringlets, but endorphins had done nothing to loosen Cole's hold on her, and now Bruno lumbered over, his cock already restirring.

"You don't even know what I'm going to do, silly. Would you teddies like another cocktail? I'll get you another cocktail for being such good boys." Annie went to the toy box again and pulled out a purple-pink walkie-talkie like the one she kept in her nightstand and had been left in Sam's nightstand. She switched it on and spoke into the receiver. "Lance, you can come in when you're ready."

She set the walkie back in its place, then opened a compartment in the toy box lid, where there were labeled options of injectables in small and large doses. She sang a little song as she selected three small doses.

Sam struggled harder at the idea of being drugged into doing something she didn't want, but Annie left one dose on the bed and stepped down with two doses for her bears, straight into their necks.

Bruno's eyelids fluttered. He smiled as the drug cocktail hit his system and reawakened his erection even faster. Cole leaned his head to the side to offer his neck, nuzzled Annie's hand before she withdrew the delicate needle. She brushed the bristle of his closer, more shaped facial hair, then bent over Sam's head to kiss him, which he responded to as though he were starving, like Bruno had. They had all the food they could want but such limited attention, driven mad in solitary, desperate for affection only Annie could provide.

"Have you ever met a cock you liked?" Annie muttered against Cole's lips.

She pressed the syringe needle to Sam's forehead. No more drugs inside, but the metal could still do damage, if just in its sting.

"Until this place, I've been utterly indifferent," Sam said, compelled to honesty, but with no less tension in her jaw.

"They liked my pussy more than I liked their cock. Once I started dating women, I realized at least part of that was just their lack of effort. But it's not about what's dangling between someone's legs. It's who people are that matters, and I prefer women, present company excluded."

"Are you sure about that? I've caught you looking, Miss Sam. Very naughty."

Sam brought her face closer to Annie's, pressing the needle into her skin. "Why is it naughty, Annie, if you're my age? Besides, don't flatter yourself. I just figured you out. That's all I was trying to do."

"Mm-hmm."

Annie plucked the needle back out of Sam's forehead and stroked her hair back from the sweat on her temples before heading back to the bed, where she threw the used needles into a small trash can. Bruno sidled in to nestle against Cole and Sam. Upset as she was, she was definitely overheating from such warm men and thick fur against her.

Annie lifted the other syringe from her bed and twirled it between her fingers. "I wasn't planning on making this easier for you, Miss Sam, but you're probably going to get a taste of this cocktail eventually, one way or another. So I'm asking you now, while you're embraced by large men with soft lust built into their big teddy bear bodies: Do you want me to lubricate your way through this difficult lesson I now need to teach you? *I'm* certainly interested in how it hits. It affects everyone differently, men and women. Numbs the pain, makes you much more compliant. This particular dose has a dash of GHB to go with it. If you forget everything, I'll always have the video, to watch you watch what you did for me. Would you like a treat, Miss Sam?"

"No," she said quickly. She tried to sidle away from the teddy bear erections and their more and more amorous nuzzling, but in their arms, she had nowhere to go.

"Are you sure? Are you absolutely *sure* you want to be completely awake and aware of what's about to happen?"

"Please, Annie, don't do this. You don't have to do this. You have so much, so many things, so many talents. Why do you need to ruin people's lives, too?"

"Oh, Miss Sam. I just like playing with my things. Fine. Sane and sober, at least for now. Look at that—a visitor."

Sam couldn't turn around in Cole's hold. She could only hear the bedroom door open.

"It locks from the *inside* during lockdown. Now we have two more to play with, because they're not going anywhere until the teddy bears go back into their dens. I'm sure you're looking forward to it, Lance. You like Miss Sam, don't you? Well, she has a *girlfriend*, so this ought to fuel your fantasies for weeks to come. Don't worry, Miss Sam, Lance doesn't play. But he helps with the heavy lifting, don't you? That gives him access, and I know he sometimes goes back to the barn to beat one out. You're going to pull your penis off one day, Lance."

The groundskeeper who'd threatened to shoot Sam didn't say anything—out of embarrassment or shame, or maybe because he simply didn't talk to Annie when she goaded like this. But in addition to a steadier heavy footstep, Sam heard stumbling, shuffling, like he led in someone drunk. More likely drugged.

She didn't need to see to already guess who the visitor was.

"Annie, don't. Annie, don't, please. We're not together anymore. I left her to work here. She has nothing to do with anything. Please don't hurt her. Please don't do this." If Sam had thought she was all out of tears, she was proven wrong, although she determinedly didn't look back, turned away when Lance's shadow shuffling with the guest entered her periphery. "It's not too late to stop this. Please."

"Sam?"

Grimacing, tight-lipped, Sam squeezed her eyes shut at Lila's lilty confusion, but not enough to keep the tears inside.

"Daddy found her after he hired you and asked me if I wanted to make a new doll just for you." From the toy box, Annie picked a massaging wand—the kind never used for massage—and a firm foam pad designed to raise hips and curved to ride. "Once you started scheming, I knew I had to have her. She's pretty, Miss Sam. I can understand why you wanted to play with her. I just don't know how you could let her go."

"You fucking bitch." Sam yanked against the teddy bears' hold, because the last thing she wanted when her girlfriend was in danger was men pawing at her, but they didn't stop, only rubbed themselves closer. "Don't hurt her. Don't you dare hurt her."

"This isn't a room for that, Miss Sam. We don't repair people in here, unless they like it, like Jonathan over there." Annie nodded toward a white-furred, milk-skinned, freckled ginger licking his paw to slick the fur. "His skin is like paper. He bruises so beautifully."

"Don't fucking *touch* her!"

Sam tried using Cole's legs as a launch pad. Just from Cole's surprise at the move, she almost wrenched free.

Annie snapped, and the teddy bears adjusted their hold. Cole almost sat *on* her legs, and not at an angle she could kick up to get him where it would still hurt. He mouthed and licked at her neck—not quite a kiss, although it seemed like he intended comfort—while Bruno covered her mouth to muffle her shouts and gathered her hair to breathe it in.

"Hello, Lila. Yes, Sam is here. Sam is here." Annie stepped down to meet Lila while still wearing the ridiculous strap-on over her cherry skirt.

"I don't feel so good." Lila stared up blearily at Annie as though she couldn't focus. "Don't drink, but I don't feel so good."

"That would be the nitrous oxide you're coming off of." Annie petted Lila's disheveled ponytail, then eased the rubber band out of her hair. While on the same level, Annie had to look up at her. Lila was about a head taller, with a long, kind face. She'd been abducted in her and Sam's home uniform of hoodie and pajama pants, so she wasn't at her best, beyond her scrubbed-clean face. "Come over here, Miss Lila. I have a nice soft bed for you. Don't worry. Nothing bad is going to happen. Nothing bad at all."

Annie helped Lance lead Lila to the foot of the bed. "Come on up here, crawl right here. Yes, that's good. The world stops tilting quite so much on a good bed, doesn't it?"

Lying on her belly, Lila rested her head on the duvet cloud. Annie adjusted Lila's hips until her mound pressed to the foam, the wand strategically taped right below.

"Sam?" Lila called, although she didn't open her eyes. "They told me you were sick and needed a visit. Are you…in the bed? Oh, I think I'm going to throw up."

Annie climbed next to Lila on the bed. Then she picked up the syringe and removed the cap with her teeth. "Don't worry, Lila. You'll feel better soon. So much better."

Sam tried to tell Lila to look out, but nothing coherent made it past Bruno's paw, and when she tried to bite him, all she got was a mouthful of stuffed animal fur.

Annie slid the needle into Lila's neck. Lila didn't even flinch. Annie replaced the syringe cap and tossed it in the general direction of the trash can. Then she rubbed Lila's back through the sweatshirt, with one hand first, then two as Lila hummed in contentment. Any tension from nausea released.

"Mmm, that feels nice."

"It does, doesn't it?" Annie pitched her voice lower, no more little girl, just the woman she was. Even with her pigtails and dress, it was so much harder to see that little girl anymore.

She climbed over Lila's thighs, the dildo still jutting out from her dress, innocuous yet threatening—like a baby copperhead. The new position let her poise herself over Lila and rub not just her back but her shoulders and neck, even scalp, in a more intentional massage.

"Mmm, Sam?"

"I'm right here, baby," Annie purred.

Sam screamed behind the paw.

Lila didn't even search for the sound, though she turned her face around, toward the light, giving Sam the perfect image of Lila smiling as Annie deepened the massage and rubbed the dildo through the crease of her ass. Sam didn't know how accurate Annie's mimicry of her voice was, but it seemed close enough in Lila's altered state, because she raised her hips up to meet her.

"I thought you didn't want to be with me anymore. Been a while since we did this."

"Sex or toys?"

"Both." Too drugged to ask why Sam wouldn't already know the answer.

"I don't know how you could think I'd ever leave you. Not when you're so sweet. So pretty. Such a beautiful girl. There's my beautiful girl."

Sam would never say those things. Maybe she should have, but she didn't. She was quiet during sex, usually with more than enough to occupy her mouth. But Lila smiled again, more than compliant as Annie pushed her sweatshirt up her back, then over her head. She wasn't wearing a bra. When she held herself up from the bed, her bare breasts were unflinchingly visible.

Cole groaned against Sam's neck, lifting the back of her shirt like Annie had done to Lila. He rubbed his fully renewed erection against her back, then lower, to match Annie's rhythm.

While Cole kept himself and Sam kneeling, Bruno stood, which put his thick cock right at mouth level. He bumped the head against her lips as though confused why they weren't open for him, but Sam kept them mashed tightly closed.

Bruno struck her face with his paw—not as hard as Annie had hit her, but it startled Sam enough for Bruno to stick his cock in her mouth, like Annie had forced the dildo.

Once Sam came back to herself, though, she bit down as hard as she could with something so big holding her mouth open.

Bruno yelped and backpedaled, whining like a dog as his red face smeared with tears. There were definite dents below the ridge of the cockhead, and those dents bled.

"What the fuck are you doing?" Lance snapped quietly. He stood near the bed nook—stood in more than one way, either from the little moans Lila was making or from watching the teddy bears with Sam. Didn't matter why. He was literally the least of her worries right now.

"Are you fucking kidding me? Lila—"

Cole stifled her with his paw, even as he started pushing her pants down her thighs like a fumbling teenager.

"She's got your girlfriend," Lance whispered. "What do you think she's going to do if you fight?"

Sam looked back at the bed, where Annie had worked Lila's pajama pants off. She stroked her dildo as she pointed it higher or lower.

Eenie, meenie, miney, moe.

Sam pleaded with Annie through her eyes.

Annie beckoned for Bruno to return to Sam. He inched toward her—literally once bitten, twice shy. But when Cole removed his hand from her mouth and Bruno pressed his lightly bleeding cock back to her lips, Sam shudder-cried but let him slip it in, heavy, damp, thick, and hot. He didn't seem to want to fuck her throat, just twitch over her tongue, his expression bliss.

Now that her head was still, Cole pawed his way down the front of her shirt, then between her legs. She was still in her underwear, like Lila, but Cole was gentle but insistent, pressing at least close to the right places.

She whimpered around Bruno's cock, wriggling like a serpent who didn't want to be handled, but Annie licked her lips and rubbed the back of Lila's thighs, then inward, working her way to the foam pad. She raised an eyebrow at Sam.

Crying in earnest now, Sam forced herself still again. Only then did Annie switch on the wand. Just the lowest setting, but Lila twitched under Annie and moaned, curling her fingers deliciously in the duvet and gathering it closer as Annie massaged the wand head against her clit, which Cole matched on Sam as Annie found Lila's rhythm in the little grinds of her hips downward.

"Oh my God… That feels so good, babe," Lila slurred, her eyes wide and unseeing. "Remind me why we haven't been doing this?"

"I can't imagine," Annie whispered in her ear before kissing her neck, then peeling Lila's underwear down, leaving her naked and thrusting with low, luxurious moans against the wand.

Sam whined again as Cole pushed her underwear down and brought his cock between her legs. Annie poured a generous amount of the lubricant next to her onto the dildo, stroking herself more for Sam's benefit. Then she held the bottle out to Lance, who brought it to Cole. Cole couldn't use his furry paws, so Lance had to pour it like chocolate sauce onto the erection.

Although Sam gazed up at him, trying to plead with someone more sympathetic, his gaze kept dropping to the cock in her mouth, the saliva dripping down her chin, Cole rubbing far more effectively now over her folds and clit and pressing into the nerves over her pubic bone.

She wasn't turned on in the slightest, alarm lights spiraling red in her brain, but her body responded on a purely physical level to the stimulation and Lila's moans—all too familiar, with years of associated memories in the dark and the light, in their own bed or the car or memorably in a Schlotzsky's bathroom. That was where her mind decided to go when Annie turned the massage wand vibration up one more level, then slipped her dildo into Lila's pussy, smooth as anything.

"Sam…" Lila gasped, then bit her arm and came, riding the vibrations.

Cole brought the head of his cock to Sam's entrance and pushed.

Unlike Lila, Sam had only a little natural lubrication from Cole touching her, which he continued to do. The lube Lance had applied did more of the work, but it had still been over a decade since Sam had had anything inside her like this.

Reflexive clenching couldn't keep him out. He was slow, even tender as he did that little mouthing-kiss on her neck and deepened his strokes over her clit, but it was so unpleasant that her body reacted with pain—a blunt stabbing in slow motion.

And she couldn't stop it, nothing she could do as he took her, fucked her.

She couldn't resist, had to force herself to freeze so she wouldn't fight, because Annie was inside Lila, and right now, Lila thought Annie was Sam. Lila didn't know what was happening, and she felt good, which was better than anything she'd feel if she knew otherwise.

Annie thrusted slowly through the aftershocks of Lila's orgasm, searching for just the right angle, stroking up and down her back and thighs as Lila came down. But Annie locked her gaze on Sam as she rode. The press of the dildo base on her clit was an accompaniment for the teddy bears fucking Sam. Lila was an afterthought, a mere accessory to Sam's punishment.

Nails digging into her palms, Sam forced herself not to bite as Bruno bucked his hips, pushing his cock to the back of her mouth in response to the intensifying throb in the vein pressed against her tongue.

Now she was the one with tears and snot and saliva crusting on her face. No blood—not yet.

Annie fucked Lila, and Lila loved it, sometimes saying Sam's name but eventually settling into a dazed dream-like state. Annie murmured in her low voice how wet Lila was, how she wanted to touch herself, how she wanted to suck her fingers. Lila was in such a suggestible state that she did everything Annie told her to do, agreed with everything Annie said, eventually pushing her hips back to meet the dildo and pulse her clit against the wand head. When Annie found the place inside that made her cry out, sob, Annie hit it relentlessly—never looking away from Sam the whole time.

Sam wanted so much to close her eyes, but Lila deserved more than Sam hiding from the devastation she'd caused. She choked, gagged, couldn't breathe because Bruno filled her mouth and snot filled her sinuses. Cole fucking her got a little less painful because Annie fucking Lila acted as a distraction, but it remained profoundly uncomfortable as he struck her cervix—more nudge than punch until his hips started pushing in with their own pressing need and his mouthing-kisses had more bite.

"Oh, Sam, *oh*, right there, right there, don't stop, don't stop, oh fuck, I'm going to come again, *fuck*."

Lila bit the duvet this time as she pressed herself down on the vibrations and squeezed down on the dildo so tight that Annie could only move the dildo up and down and pressed her hips forward to keep Lila from pushing her out.

"Ooh, what's inside my head?" Lila threaded her fingers through her hair. "I'm so dizzy. But that was the best we've ever had, isn't it?"

Annie raised an eyebrow at Sam and pulsed her hips again to make Lila cry out and shudder with another clench. "You're right. The best, babe."

Sam retched as Bruno suddenly pushed past the back of her throat. She threw up hot, sour, stinging dinner over his cock as it throbbed and jerked over her tongue. Bruno groaned like the bear he was from the bilious flood that joined his cum to spill over him and drip down her chin and onto the floor. She couldn't spare a moment of control to keep from crying. She was just trying not to drown in vomit and semen.

She sputtered, struggled, which must have seemed like eagerness to Cole's cock, because he latched to her shoulder with his teeth and buried himself in her pussy, coming inside her, the way he must have come inside Annie a hundred times.

Annie was all over her, under her skin, down her throat, in her pussy, dripping out of her, killing her, because she couldn't *breathe.*

Finally, Bruno pulled himself out of her mouth with another groan. One last thin pulse from his cock flecked her cheek. Sam gasped between silent sobs, trying so hard not to make a sound, to keep Lila happy and completely clueless to what had happened to her, and to what had happened to Sam while it had happened to her.

"Do you want me to—" Lila tried to turn over, but Annie spread her fingers between Lila's shoulders to keep her down as she slid her cock slowly out of Lila's pussy, so that Sam could see how it glistened.

Sam coughed, retched again.

Lila turned toward the sound. Squinted, tilted her head as though the world was tilting on her instead. "Sam? Is that— But—"

She twisted around, away from the vibrator and the foam pad, sinking into the duvet as she tried to reconcile what she thought had happened and what she saw above her—a different shade of brunette, different shade of skin, different smile. Sam would never be caught dead in pigtails or ribbons, nor would she wear a dress for anything other than a funeral.

"Who are you? Who are you and what are you— Oh my God, get off me, get off, get *off*." She batted up at Annie, who giggled as she blocked herself against the weak, inaccurate blows from limbs that didn't want to listen to Lila's commands.

"Stop it, please. Just stop." Sam didn't have any power left, not with the acid in her mouth and a cock still thick inside her, though softening, as semen dribbled down her thigh.

Annie wrestled Lila back onto the bed, naked and vulnerable and more and more confused. "I'm not Sam, but Sam's the reason you're here. And she's the one who decides how hospitable your stay is."

"What the fuck—"

"Sweetie, stop fighting. There's really no use. Lance, blue cap, please." But Annie wasn't urgent in the slightest as she pressed Lila down into the duvet, as though to suffocate her in pastels.

Lance hurried to the toy box and retrieved a different small-dose syringe. He removed the cap and handed it to Annie, who had to let go of one of Lila's arms. Lila slapped at Annie's face, but there was no power behind it. Annie brought the new syringe to Lila's neck and depressed the plunger.

Within seconds, Lila couldn't hold her arms up anymore. She stared at the canopy, murmuring unintelligibly. She twisted a few times, her final struggles, before going still.

Annie plucked the syringe out and held it up for Sam's benefit. "She'll ride the numb for the rest of the night. Lance, clean up the mess Miss Sam made on the floor while she cleans herself up. Supplies are under the sink in the bathroom. Then go find somewhere else to lie down and jerk off. I don't want you here."

Lance hurried into the bathroom to retrieve a tub of basic cleaning supplies while Cole lowered Sam to the floor. She crawled off his cock with a terrible squelch that had her heaving again. On her hands and knees, clothes stained and askew, she tried to climb up to the bed, but Annie clicked her tongue, and Cole grabbed her ankle to pull her back.

Sam screamed—not because Cole scared her but because she couldn't hold in the pain, fury, or misery another second, and Lila was unconscious anyway.

Annie undid the harness, pulled it down her legs, then discarded it to the side to deal with later. Her dress had a little moisture and damp here and there; otherwise, she seemed the least affected by everything that had happened.

"You don't get into this bed until after you've taken off your filthy clothes and washed yourself off, Miss Sam. I can stand jizz in a bed, but absolutely no throw-up. Usually, I'd make you clean up your own mess, too, but Lance doesn't have much other use here."

"You absolute bitch." Sam couldn't climb any farther. She was so furious she could barely function, so furious she could throw up again—projectile vomit right in Annie's face like Linda Blair. Because it was easier to be angry than think about what Annie had done to Lila, to her.

"Sometimes," Annie said, unperturbed. "You can wear something of mine. We're about the same size. Does Cole have to carry you in there?" She waved Sam toward the bathroom.

Sam stared at the weave of carpet, the fibers oversharp, as though they'd grate her corneas just by her looking at them. But she managed to find her elbows and knees again, then her hands to push herself to her feet. She pulled up her underwear and pants and let her shirt fall back over her hips. Cole didn't release her until she headed toward the bathroom.

All the teddy bears left were either idly stroking themselves or had already come and lay on their platform for a sticky sleep, since they hadn't been chosen like the others.

Lance gave her wide berth on the way to clean up behind her.

After she entered the bathroom, she closed the door. No lock. Even if there were, Annie would have the key.

She pulled off her vomit- and spunk-covered shirt and threw it in the trash. She did the same to her pants and underwear.

She felt hollowed out, her rotten places clawed out by big fingers. Like if she poked her own fingers down her throat, they would sink in and spill yellow, seedy bile all over the floor.

Naked, she splashed water on her face at the double vanity and gave a cursory pass to wipe the vomit and semen away. Then, as though in a trance, she went into the shower and washed everything off, scrubbing her skin pink until she thought of Bruno's easy flush and stopped.

Chapter 10: SLEEPOVER

Sam found the least youthful clothes in Annie's dresser drawers, something in purple rather than pink.

They really were similar sizes, although their angles and proportions were different. Sam's legs were longer to the length of her torso, so the shorts seemed shorter than they would have on Annie, but the tank top covered everything relevant, although it was a thin material that made no effort to conceal the press of her nipples. They were pajamas; they weren't supposed to.

She nearly threw up a little again as she pulled on a pair of Annie's underwear—an inoffensive blue, but still not hers. Nothing in the dressers smelled like hers. She and Lila had shared hoodies and t-shirts, but she hadn't minded carrying that smell with her, until their scents had practically merged.

Sam didn't want to merge scents with Annie, but the rest of her things were upstairs or in the trash, and she was stuck here for as long as Annie wanted to play with teddy bears.

She emerged from the closet into a room with only fairy lights on. Some of the bears were already asleep, a few snoring.

Cole and Bruno had been more or less tidied after their own respective messes. Bruno was under the covers, passed out on the pillows. Cole slept half on the covers and half under, cuddling a stuffed kitten and Lila, who was clothed once again so she wouldn't get cold. Lance had dragged a beanbag down to the solarium between the gingerbread house and the Victorian, and if he'd masturbated, he was finished. Sam couldn't tell if he was awake, but he wasn't moving.

She wanted to be mad at him for obeying when he didn't have to, for getting aroused when he shouldn't, but she'd have to get angrier at herself for the same thing.

She didn't have any room in her small body for anything but hatred for Annie, who sat cross-legged in the middle of her bed, all toys put away and waste tossed. She'd changed into pajamas while Sam was in the shower: a short white dress with bloomers.

Sam's legs shook as though she'd been cycling for miles, but when Annie crooked her fingers to beckon her to the bed, Sam came over to stand at the foot.

"Look at us, sharing pajamas. Just like a sleepover. I should make hot cocoa. Would you like some hot cocoa, Miss Sam? I know you must have brushed your teeth, but you repeated your dinner, so you might be hungry again." She crawled to the edge of the bed and climbed off. "I'm going to make mint chocolate cocoa with mini marshmallows."

Sam wanted to yank Lila out of Cole's arms. She was less repelled by men than Sam, but she hadn't agreed to any of this, didn't deserve to be forced to cuddle with a man she didn't know and who might do something to her in her sleep that she wouldn't remember. But Sam didn't think he would unless Annie told him he could, and Annie wasn't punishing Lila. Yet.

Just stay asleep, Liles. Don't wake up. Sam wished the same for herself, but she didn't think she'd be so lucky.

Annie came back with insulated cups of peppermint hot cocoa and mini marshmallows, as promised. Sam was still terribly nauseous and couldn't eat anything substantial, but hot cocoa wasn't substantial, and the mint could help. Then

Annie climbed back in bed and tugged on Sam's tank top to convince her to join all of them.

"What are you doing, Annie?"

"We're having a sleepover party. Can't you see?"

"Annie. You and I are the only ones awake. You don't have to pretend with me anymore."

Annie contemplated Sam, still smiling brightly. Then she handed Sam her mug, crawled to her nightstand, took out a remote, and hit a few buttons.

When she crawled back, the smile had softened and hardened at the same time. She slowly tugged on her ribbons to undo them, then removed the rubber bands from her pigtails until her hair hung below her shoulders. Even in the girlish white pajamas and bloomers, she didn't seem so young anymore.

"Sometimes they like to watch me sleep. Sometimes Daddy watches me sleep, too." Even though she called him 'Daddy,' her little girl voice was gone. Nor was she mimicking Sam again. Just her own lower register, creaky from disuse. "I turned off the cameras. We're alone. I have a strategically placed syringe, and I can wake the teddy bears in a matter of moments. Cole has been instructed to strangle your girlfriend like a baby bunny if you do anything to me."

"She's not my girlfriend," Sam said, without inflection or emotion. "I was ghosting her with this job."

"It's not official until you have the courage to say the words, Sam." Not Miss Sam. Even the trappings of the illusion were gone. "And less than a week isn't long enough to ghost anyone. Besides, she clearly still matters to you."

"That's because I'm a human being."

Annie took her mug back and sipped from her cocoa, wincing when it was still too hot. "Come sit with me, Sam."

"Fuck you."

"I said the cameras weren't recording, not that the rules have changed. We're still having that sleepover."

"How long are you going to keep playing little girl?" Sam asked. Maintaining a level mug while she climbed onto the bed was easier said than done.

Annie shrugged. "As long as I can. People are more forgiving of a woman who wants to be a little girl than they are of men who want to be little boys. Everyone knows the name of it for men, but women are supposed to want to be young forever."

"I don't think that means prepubescent."

"No? Last I checked, the ideal was a child's body with big boobs." She looked down at herself with a self-deprecating grin. "I don't quite fit either anymore. But this isn't about their ideal. It never was. I don't play Lolita for *them*."

"Why on earth is *that* the delusion you decided to latch onto?" Sam gestured to the child's playroom. "Embracing the predatory madam you already are would still achieve your goals. You could have your dollhouse without pretending you really think they're dolls. Little girl clothes, coloring books, playing with actual dolls when you're clearly desperate for more demanding intellectual exercise, based on everything you do to support the delusion... I mean, fuck, the costumes, engineering? Learning how to do fucking surgery? Why on earth would you infantilize yourself when that's clearly not what you want?"

It was strange what not trying to be eleven years old could do to a smile—depth of knowledge, subterfuge, and careful consideration no child could ever imitate. When Annie looked like this, it was difficult to believe she could ever pull off young or innocent.

"You think I don't want the clothes? I made them for myself. You think I don't want the dolls? I bought or asked for every single one, and I enjoy playing with them. Coloring books? Soothing. Everything I do in the Dream House is because I want to."

"But why would you want any of this? Every child dreams of when they'll finally grow up," Sam said. "I don't remember yearning to be an adult the same way that my sisters and brother did, but I looked forward to when I could leave home and do whatever I wanted."

"And how'd that end up for you?" Annie sipped her cocoa again, this time savoring it at just the right temperature.

As Sam drank from her own, it did make her stomach feel a little better—false comfort. "It fucking sucks. But if I want to have Indian takeout or frozen pizza, I can, as long as I can afford it. I can change jobs when I want to—or at least I could. When I'm not working, I can sleep until ten. The problems I'm having with being an adult these days aren't actually about being an adult. They're about being poor."

"Are they, though?" Annie said. "I enjoyed being a little girl when I was one. I didn't have to worry about anything. Not Daddy when he went on his work trips or when he peered around the corner at me in my bedroom. Not Mom when she was having her affairs with groundskeepers and handymen, nor when she got sick. Those were Daddy's problems. He did everything he could to keep her problems from upsetting me, because I was young and shouldn't have to deal with those things. Your mother was unfair to you. You shouldn't have had to become what she wasn't. It wasn't your time."

"No shit, Sherlock. But *should* don't cut wood."

Annie wrinkled her nose. "Did a therapist give you that one?"

"Fuck off."

"I like this Sam."

"I prefer neither Annie. I guess we don't always get what we want."

"All I know is that as I got older, I thought my world would get bigger, but it didn't. We moved to the Dream House, but it was made for Mom, not me. I was given more and more tutors and trainers to fill my time before and after school so I could improve my odds and options for college. Sure, Daddy's rich, but he's quietly rich, and neither he nor Mom started out that way. I looked into the future they had in mind for me, Sam, and didn't see freedom. First, you have your parents telling you what to do. Then you have supervisors and managers. Then you have shareholders. And if you ever become the boss, what will you have sacrificed just to be the first and last word? Besides, no one would ever believe I did it on my own. To them, I would always be Daddy's little girl who needed to dance on his toes to make herself taller."

"Poor thing," Sam said dryly.

"I'm not asking for pity. I had no pity for myself. I felt stifled, sometimes angry, but never sorry for myself. It's just an observation about how the world works. Money isn't your problem, Sam. Your money problems are part of the design. It keeps you feeding from someone else's hand without question. It makes you small and hungry. You think adulthood gives you options. You think you have control. But you've just traded parents for bosses who care much less about you, and there's no one there when something goes wrong. Sure, you had Lila, but you barely had her, didn't you? You couldn't lean on someone who needed to lean on you. So you leaned away."

When Sam drank more of her cocoa, it was harder to swallow.

"You're not supposed to be satisfied. You're supposed to scrape, kneel, beg, obey, scratch for every last inch that they pull out from under you. It's *harder* when you're poor, but the clamoring just changes pitch among the wealthy. I realized what kids and adults realize too late: Being a kid has its issues, but so does being an adult, and being an adult has its benefits, but so does being a kid. I simply didn't want to be an adult. So I became a little girl again."

Annie playfully shook her head, unsettling her ringlets.

"Denying my age is farce, I know. I have gray hair. I have suggestions of wrinkles when I smile. I have breasts and hips, and I have fucking needs that have only grown more intense. But I still decided I wanted to grow up to be a little girl. And no one stopped me. They called it delusion, trauma, illness. They humored me, encouraged me, *coddled* me, which was all I needed them to do—believe that I believed it. Daddy wanted me to stay his little girl, so he didn't fight too hard. He gets what he wants, his little girl and dead wife in one package. When what I did became more and more elaborate, he justified it with the earnestness of a disciple. Everyone did. Because it's easier to believe in a little girl with a little curl on her forehead playing with dolls than a woman in a short dress with a knack for manipulation and feeding unconventional appetites."

"Unconventional appetites is liking to be spanked. It's horse play and adult babies. It's wanting your wife to call you Daddy and not mean it like you do," Sam said. "You're not feeding unconventional appetites. The fact you're doing it to calliope music doesn't make it any less evil."

"You think I'm evil?" Annie smiled, thoroughly amused.

"I used to think evil was those little prickly seed things that get stuck on your socks, in person form. They pale in comparison to you. Men cornered the market on what you're doing, but you're a fucking warlord in the fucking heart of Texas. They should put your picture on evil's Wikipedia page. You shame the devil."

Annie laughed, a hint of little girl in her delight, as though Sam had been reading her a bedtime story. Some of the teddy bears stirred, but if Annie woke them, they fell back to sleep without trouble. "I love it. I shame the devil."

"Do you even realize just how awful of a person you are? You never leave your dollhouse. You don't know what the real world is like. You don't know what my life was like. You don't know what normal is."

"I haven't always been locked behind bars by my own volition," Annie said. "I went to public schools, Sam, because my parents went to public schools. At least until the bullying for the way I dressed for the job I wanted got so bad and my responses so commensurate that Daddy pulled me out and switched to nannies and tutors. Even after that, I went out all the time for enrichment, travel. But the more I made the Dream House my own, the less I wanted to leave. I haven't left in five years. I doubt the world has changed much since last I visited."

Sam finished her cocoa about the same time that Annie did. She took the mug when Annie offered it and climbed off the bed to put them next to the toy box for now—the way she might have with any other adult, not because she was the help. "So how do you feel about it? Being evil."

"I don't much care what you think about my morals or ethics. I take great pride and pleasure in what I've managed to accomplish. No one's going to stop me, least of all you, and those who might have the power to do it have too much skin in my game. For every few I lose, I have a teddy bear or music-box ballerina. You can't say you've ever enjoyed your work this much."

"Most of us work because we need to pay rent and because our passions don't pay, simple as that," Sam said. "Being able to do what you love, either because someone else is supporting you or because it pays—both of which is true for you—is tremendous privilege on its own. Add in the price tag of what you do, and you have *no* idea what it's like in the real world. You think you're such hot shit, with your ten-years-younger face and easy sleep, but you're just a psychopath with a fuck ton of money and no responsibilities. You're still a spoiled brat, just older."

"I am a spoiled brat." Annie rested her elbows on her knees without effort, which Sam couldn't do with the same ease. "And you may not like it, but I do. I can't help that I was born into a fucked-up rich family I could take advantage of, any more than you could help being born into a fucked-up family that took advantage of you. And here I am, just another boss for you to appease. Now, I can't change what I've already done to you—nor would I want to. I'm not going to insult your revelation by pretending contrition. But there's a way you can transcend what brought you here, what I made you do, made happen to you. I showed it to you the first day I introduced you to the real dollhouse."

She rocked forward onto her forearms and adjusted her legs under her to crawl closer to Sam. Sam leaned away, fought not to scurry back and fall off the bed entirely. She had to face Annie sooner or later. At least here and now, no one else was watching. Annie hadn't wanted them watching, either.

She settled so close that her legs overlapped with Sam's on the duvet. She twirled her finger in Sam's lank, drying hair. "I had to punish insubordination tonight, but I reward ingenuity, too. I think you have potential, Sam. I think I'd enjoy playing with you, although I'm still trying to figure out how best to fix you. But more importantly, I think you could learn to enjoy playing with me."

"You're fucking joking."

"Everyone needs our money, comes to work for us hoping things will be easier, but you've got so much anger and resentment, and not just because you're scared of what I can do to you. You're tired of subsuming yourself under others' needs. What if I let you do things you only ever imagined you could do? What if, instead of watching me fuck your girlfriend or my bears fucking you, you could fuck any man you chose until he bled through both ends? What if I found your worst boss and let you dislocate every one of his ball-socket joints, then make him dance and sing before putting his own head up his ass? What if you were the girl dolls' succor, the one angel in the hell I put them through?"

Sam just stared. She was vaguely aware that nothing was happening on her outside, but she desperately tried to get control of herself on the inside, thrown completely off axis, threatening to spin wild off into nothing.

"Haven't you ever wanted to just scream and kick and bite and hit? Haven't you ever wanted to visit one of those rage rooms and break things? Slam your siblings' heads into the wall to make them do what you tell them to do? I think you have, Sam. You're five muscle knots in a trench coat. For the last twenty years, I've had no use for nannies, but especially for the last five, I *have* wanted a playmate. A man would be too easy, and if I bring a man into my dollhouse on my level, he'll eventually make a doll of me."

"Like you did to me," Sam said.

"Oh, sweetie, no. I punished you like a person, not a doll. You think you know what it's like to be played with because a few of my dolls played with you. No, no, no, no. You can't understand yet. But if you don't want to play with me, I'll make you understand. Believe me."

Sam believed her.

"I think if we can strip back whatever made you go from surrogate mother to daycare to senior care to night-shift gas station attendant just so you wouldn't have to care anymore, you might actually find some joy exerting your will. I'll teach you how to make dolls crawl from you to the farthest corner and shit themselves at the sight of you, and I'll teach you how to make them feed from your hand."

Sam leaned close enough to kiss her, even tilted her head when Annie did, which was the punchline of the whole joke. Then she said, as clearly as humanly possible, "No."

Annie didn't move away from their almost-kiss, which meant Sam couldn't, either. Like the staring game, with overlapped breath hot between them. "Some people do everything I want them to do in hopes an opportunity arises, but if it does, it arises way too late for them to do anything. By then, all they know is doing what I want them to do. Others resist from the start. You didn't. Even now, you're going along to get along. You're not a rebel. You just wish you were."

"Aren't you afraid that if you help me become like you, you'll be making your own enemy, just like if I were a man?" Sam said.

"It helps that you're my size." Annie finally settled back, rolling her shoulders to suggest it hurt to stay in that position rather than that she'd blinked first. "I really do think we'd have more fun playing together than competing. Like I said, I've played with women before, but never with a woman who already knows what she likes from another woman. I can learn more of that from you. And you could learn from me just how deep the well of your own desires can go. You'll surprise yourself. You'll disgust yourself. But you'll come out the other side with something that's been missing from your life: passion."

Sam recoiled, which was more of a blink than what Annie had done. She coughed again, trying to tell the cocoa to stay down.

"Not just that kind. Can you imagine actually being excited again? Eager to go to sleep at night so you'll be that much closer to the next morning, when you're eager again to get out of bed? There's something to be said for childlike enthusiasm, the way they love what they love before they're taught it's wrong. I think we can make each other better, and I think if you give yourself a chance, you'll come to see things my way. When Daddy is in no more state to continue running the business, I'll need someone who can be the adult to my child, one who won't buckle under masculine bluster and grandstanding. God, Sam, I could make you so much stronger, more powerful, because you'd have the time, the opportunity, the money, everything you've ever wanted and didn't even know you needed."

When Annie took her hand, it didn't feel like a child taking her nanny's hand anymore. It was staggering how many details Annie had perfected to sell the delusion to other people without having it herself.

"You can sleep in every day, eat chocolate cake whenever you want, make grown men beg you not to destroy their lives like a game of Jenga. They'll crawl on their knees to you in the middle of their fancy offices for the chance to slip into your cunt, and you'll be able to tell them no, then force them to sit on a spike for your amusement." Annie giggled. "It's great."

"So my choices are become a doll or turn evil," Sam said.

"That's not quite all. You see, if you become a doll, Lila becomes a doll. I haven't decided if it would be worse to never see each other again or to assign you to the same cell. If you choose to play with me, though, Lila doesn't get hurt. She'll stay in Time-Out, unaware but unbroken. You'll let her out yourself when you're ready. She'll be so drugged to the gills, she won't remember most of anything that happened. She might need a few courses of rehab for that opioid addiction, but at least she'll be out of the dollhouse. Or you'll make her a doll yourself, because you want to keep her."

"You fucking bitch."

"First lesson: Know your subjects' weaknesses. You already let yourself be fucked by two men and bore it as quietly as you could. What else will you do for her?"

"You fucking *bitch*." Sam was shaking again, like she was cold, but she wasn't cold. She couldn't help it, even though it made her look weak, because it showed what the teddy bears had done terrified her, how even more deeply Annie terrified her. The teddy bears were just proxies, like the strap-on. Annie had really been the one fucking Sam while she'd fucked Lila. And she could do it again—with the same men, other men, a whole room of men, machines she built from scratch…

"Kiss me, Samantha. Kiss me like you love me. I know you can. Just pretend I'm her. Pretend I told you to kiss her like you need to save her life." She leaned forward again, brushing her lips against Sam's. Then she spread her mouth in a smile too broad and toothsome.

Sam shoved her back. "What's the fucking point of this? You don't love anything except yourself and your things—as things. You don't love me. You're not straight. You're not gay. You're not anything, except a sadist."

"If I'm nothing but a sadist, then you know what the point of this is." Annie leaned back on the bed, her breasts pressing against the thin cloth and her darker nipples visible through the white fabric. She slowly parted her legs to invite Sam between them. "You need to prove that you're with me. Every day, you need to convince me that you're mine as a person, unless you'd rather be mine as a doll. Now, come here, Sam, or else I'll think you don't want to make it out of this with all your limbs intact. No one's watching. No one will see what you do—except Lance, but who gives a fuck about him?"

She laid back and beckoned with her fingers.

Sam crawled over her and pressed her lips against Annie's—not the closed-mouth peck of before or the facial smash Annie made some of her girls do.

Annie might not have expected Sam to sink into the kiss so quickly, tasting her, bringing her body down over Annie's. She made a noise of pleased surprise, then laughed into the kiss— not a little girl laugh high in her head but low, almost in her chest as Sam settled next to her on the bed, sliding her arms around Annie's back, their mostly bare legs tangling together.

Sam shook even more, a bodyful vibration, tears sprung into tired eyes, but she kept pushing her feelings down under action, told herself she wanted this, she liked this, this wasn't

Annie at all but some random hook-up now that she was informally separated from Lila—who was just a few feet away, within reach if Sam really tried.

She detached from her own body. Annie brought her thigh up flush between hers, and Sam rocked her hips to rub against it. Annie's laughter shifted into a soft moan as they tasted the remnants of chocolate and peppermint on each other's tongues, as Annie slipped her hands under Sam's shirt and cupped her breasts, bothering the peaks with her thumbs, slowly shifting their positions until Annie was almost on top.

She hadn't come the whole time she'd fucked Lila and watched the teddy bears fuck Sam—at least she hadn't given any indication that she had. Some people were like that. But she ground against Sam's thigh as though she hadn't, as though she'd been aching all this time and just *waiting* for when she could make Sam do this for her, just *waiting* to taste Sam's submission to a power greater than her own.

Sam's nipples were hard against Annie's palms and playful fingers, and they each dampened the others' thighs. Sam thought she was going to faint or be sick again or both. But still she kissed Annie the way she'd wanted to be kissed for over a year—if she could have found the energy to feel anything at all. Now she wished she still didn't feel anything, but neither God nor Annie would be so kind.

She was floating and turned on and repulsed, and Annie was whining, grinding harder and harder. She grabbed Sam's hand and brought it between her legs to press and rub with more focused attention until Annie shuddered as violently as Sam and cried out, open-mouthed, as they kissed.

"Mmm, good girl," Annie murmured into her mouth, still rocking over her fingers. "I've been wanting that for *days.*"

Sam pushed her onto her back, pushed Annie's hands out from under her shirt but kissed her harder, deeper, until Annie wrapped her legs around Sam's hips and hummed happily. Sam pressed Annie into the duvet, prayed the down feathers would swallow her up, suffocate her.

"I hate you," Sam murmured into her mouth.

Annie rolled them back over and bit Sam's lower lip, sucked with relish. "You won't for long. Give me a year. You'll be much more sanguine, in this bed and out."

Sam writhed beneath her, hating herself the whole time but also angry enough to commit. She tried to remember her last orgasm with Lila and mimicked the same motions and sounds as Annie kissed down to her neck. She couldn't resist a shudder when Annie found the place where Cole had kissed a bruise to the skin and left bitemarks through his climax.

Then she shoved Annie off to fall into the cushion of her duvet.

"But will it be real or will I just be faking so you won't hurt Lila?" Sam snarled.

Annie stretched luxuriously. "Don't you understand? It doesn't matter. It doesn't matter what you feel. It matters what you do. After long enough, what you do determines how you feel more than what you feel shapes what you do. If I make you do enough damage, how long before you start justifying it, making them dolls in your own mind, to protect your sanity? How long before a fake orgasm turns real? Do you really think I won't break you, Sam?"

Claustrophobia among all the people in the bed, the huge duvet, the stuffed animals, and the canopy curtains pressed down on Sam from every side. No escape.

Annie crawled to the nightstand again to push more buttons on the remote. "We're back, Daddy, in case you were worried." And back, too, was the little girl voice and deceptive innocence in her expression as she clambered back to the foot of the bed. "Lay down, Miss Sam. It's time to sleep. Can't have a sleepover without sleep. Do you want a teddy bear of your own? Lila looks so comfortable. We can invite another to keep us warm. Or do you want Karma Darling to sleep with? The frog." She held up the stuffed animal in question.

Sam lowered herself to the duvet, legs tucked in almost fetal and tightly closed. "Let's just go to sleep, Annie."

Annie pounced on the duvet in front of Sam and bounced her way into mirroring Sam's position. "Good night, Miss Sam. I think tomorrow's going to be a beautiful day."

Sam couldn't sleep for the longest time in the rainbow fairy lights of the room, through teddy bear snores and heavy breathing from across the room where Lance slept in an awkward position.

Annie seemed to have no trouble, though as she submerged, she inched closer and closer to Sam until she could press her mouth to Sam's chest if she chose.

Sam was afraid to move, afraid to unsettle her, for the sweetness—feigned or deliberate—to shift into more murderous intent. Annie was right there. Sam could close her hands over her throat, stifle her with a stuffed animal, asphyxiate her before the night was over.

And maybe her father would see. Maybe he'd kill Lila just for spite or integrate her into the dollhouse anyway.

Fuck you, Annie. I don't know when or how, but I'm going to burn this whole house to the ground.

Chapter 11: PLAYGROUND

Sam woke to rain pattering on the solarium windows—and an empty bed.

She sat up, disoriented after everything had seemed so crowded last night.

The teddy bear platforms had been replaced once more by the shelves of prized dolls. Lance had vacated his beanbag chair. And Lila was gone.

Everything was as though nothing had happened the previous night, but Sam's vagina still felt...off, like microtears and internal bruising. And she was wearing Annie's clothes.

The rain was soft, with a few waves of wind to shift the patter to pelt, but it was still a calming sound, no lightning or thunder to disturb the peace. There shouldn't have been any peace after what had happened, when there was a place like this in the world.

But of course, time moved implacably forward. There would even be people waking from the best night of their life, while other people would go on to have the best day of their life. Terrible and wonderful could exist together, sometimes even in the same person.

Sam couldn't remember wonderful. But the rain was nice.

She crawled like a caterpillar to the edge of the bed and eased off. Yes, she felt stretched, her muscles ached from fighting back against Cole and Bruno, her jaw hurt from being forced open, and her throat hurt from being pummeled. After screaming and crying and struggling not to do either, her eyes were swollen, her sinuses congested, and she was tired, as though she'd only slept the shallowest dreams. Not that she could remember any of them.

Her hands shook a little when she held them up, and her legs were tight and loose at the same time, like well-cooked noodles, but she managed to find her feet as she padded down into the gentle light of the solarium.

Annie's clock said it was fifteen to 9:00. If Annie was still sticking with her usual schedule, she'd be near or in the dining room.

Sam looked for any sign of where Lila had been taken, but she doubted Lila had been in any state to leave breadcrumbs. If she had, it likely would have been noticed and cleaned away by now.

When she stepped out of Annie's room, the house was quiet, other than the rain against the empty hall's windows.

In the library, Annie was coloring, her purple dress emblazoned with sunflowers. Sam's coffee was in the service hatch. Everything was back to how it had been, and in a way, Annie was right: Sam wanted to take one of the dining room chairs and throw it through the glass windows or across the dining room table to disrupt the runner and candlesticks, scratch the wood. She wanted to destroy something, or she wanted something to be changed, transformed by being destroyed.

Sam ran barefoot across the marble and up the stairs to her room. The beshitted sheets and comforter had been removed from the bathroom, the window closed, and everything cleaned, without the hint of scent left behind. Again, as though it hadn't happened.

She yanked off Annie's clothes and stood naked in her bedroom, searching for signs. She could feel but couldn't see the marks on her shoulder, and there were some shadows on her arms, but Cole had mostly bound her with his bear hug. She thought she found a few more bruises on her legs, tender spots without visible darkening, but it was difficult to tell.

Someone was probably watching, but she didn't give a shit if someone jerked off to her checking for post-assault injuries, like checking for ticks after a long walk in the woods. That they were terrible people was academic. She wasn't going to change their behavior by trying not to get caught naked. She had to proceed with her life as though they weren't there, or else she wouldn't be able to proceed at all.

Finally, she dug through her clothes, which she hadn't even had time to take out of her suitcase; that's how quickly things had gone off the rails.

In sweatpants and another modified band t-shirt, she headed back down to the dining room—a little late. Ji-an had already set out breakfast. Sam mostly picked at it, but Annie was voracious, leaving behind just a few smears of sunny-side-up eggs and maple syrup.

Sam carried Annie's empty plate and her mostly full plate to the service hatch, then leaned in. "Ji-an?"

"Yes, Miss Sam?"

"Annie will not be having chocolate milk or dessert tonight, either. Nor will I. Thank you."

There was a shuffling sound on the kitchen side. Then Ji-an poked her head under the sliding door. "Are you sure?"

She knows. Somehow she knows. Sam's cheeks and ears heated out of embarrassment, out of shame, but she nodded without checking back with Annie.

"Very well." Ji-an pulled down the hatch door quickly, right before Annie reached Sam.

Annie kicked her in the calves with hard saddle shoes. "What do you think you're doing?"

"Following through. I'm not depriving you of sugar and chocolate because you raped me and Lila, Annie, but because you deliberately crossed the boundaries I set because you were mad at me for setting them," Sam said, exaggerating her nanny-speak as much as Annie exaggerated her child-speak. "When you're grown up, you can decide to have a whole cake for dinner and tater tots for dessert. But as long as you're a child, I get to decide what the consequences are for breaking rules. I also get to decide what the rules are, and I think mine are pretty reasonable. If you have a problem with that…" Sam leaned forward just enough to put their eye levels even. Then she muttered low enough that no one else would hear, "Grow up."

Annie stamped her foot again, but Sam could tell from the writhing and clenching twitches of her face that she was furious her point hadn't been made last night. "That's not what we agreed to."

"It's what your dad and I agreed to. If he wants to alter my contract, he can come here himself, and we can discuss it like two grown adults. Until then, I'm your nanny and you're an eleven-year-old child. Now, it's such a lovely gloomy day. Are you going to ruin it with frowny-pouting?"

Although Annie was used to being treated like a child by everyone else, it appeared to rankle her that Sam did, too—perhaps because last night she'd finally been able to drop the façade. Twenty years was a long time to play little girl.

Poor fucking thing.

Annie thought she'd chosen to be a child, but she'd only chosen to be childish. She'd discovered being an adult wasn't everything she'd ever wanted, so she'd mined the aspects of childhood and adulthood that she liked and discarded the rest. It wasn't that she'd shunned a life of responsibility. She just wanted to avoid consequences, and she thought being a child would excuse her from them. But if she were really just a child, she could be controlled. Annie would not be controlled; Sam already knew she'd suffer retaliation.

Hell, she could just tell Annie she was trying to make her conceit more believable. If she really wanted Sam to be the adult, then Sam had to be the adult.

"Now, I can tell you're eager to get to the main event, Annie," Sam said, more placatory. "I think we can waive lessons today."

Annie hesitated a beat. Then she plastered a smile on her face again and clapped her hands, stirring tantrum forgotten. "Really? Oh, Miss Sam, let's go."

"If…"

Annie stopped at the cased opening to the library. "If what?"

"We can skip lessons if you show me where you're keeping Lila. I don't have to talk with her, and she doesn't have to see me. I just want to know she's okay."

Annie rolled her eyes. "All of you are like this at the beginning. She's fine. When she woke up this morning on the drip, she said she doesn't remember a thing before being taken from her apartment. She might not even remember that in a few days."

"I want to see her. Then we can do whatever you want, Annie."

"I like the sound of the second part. Fine. I'll show you the Time-Out Room. You can visit her all you want. You can even talk to her. But memory will slip through her lubricated fingers like water. Most just look in to make sure they're not in any pain. And they never are. The worst she'll suffer is a black eye because she walked into a wall trying to follow the White Rabbit."

Annie led her to the foyer once more, to the opposite side of the ballroom entrance and Dr. Panabaker's elevator. She lifted a frameless canvas off where it hung on the wall. A frame would have made it too heavy for her to move away from the large two-way mirror on the other side.

Through the looking glass was a Wonderland-themed tea room filled with stuffed white rabbits—taxidermy as well as toys. The people were dressed in ill-fitting costumes: pinafores, damask vests and skirts, red collars, Mad Hatter top hats. Annie presumably didn't do the good custom work until they became dolls. The panel walls inside were also covered with mirrors of varying sizes and frames. The two-way mirror would appear like just another. Some of the mirrors were funhouse-distorted, adding more disorientation for the people in the room. Some were as young as teenagers, some as old as

Sam's clients at the senior center. A few of them wandered, but when they did, the rabbits and reflections seemed to startle and frighten them.

Two maids sat in corners on opposite sides of the room. Plastic tubs next to their chairs held cleaning supplies and small medical kits. Someone emerged from the bathroom to the right—Lila, stumbling as though drunk, holding her head. One of the maids took her arm and gently led her back to her seat, where they attached her IV again. Everyone's IVs originated like jellyfish tentacles from beneath the table and led to docks in their arms. Most of the hostages, if they weren't staring at nothing, stared instead at something to the right of the two-way mirror. Background noise suggested it was a television playing *Law & Order.*

Sam pressed a hand to the mirror, not giving a fuck about prints. Lila looked so little like herself, as though who she was had been sucked out of her like moisture from a mummy, leaving only a barely aware husk. Deader inside than she and Lila had already become in their own ways—a kind of dead Sam wished she could go back to, rather than the new kind of dead that hurt in all the wrong places

"Let's go, Miss Sam. They're not entertaining for very long." Annie slipped her hand under Sam's on the mirror. Sam allowed Annie to lead her away from the room. Annie didn't bother putting the painting back up. She left that task for someone else. "Since it's raining, we can't play outside like we did the other day when you refused to play with me, then punished me."

"I told you what I was willing to do, and you didn't listen. You disobeyed. Then I told you I couldn't stop you playing with your toys on your own, and you *decided* to come out with me. If you're so desperate for a playmate, maybe you should be nicer to them."

"Oh, I've been nice, Miss Sam. I've been so nice. But you keep taking things from me."

"I keep taking things from you because you're *not* being nice. I'm not even being strict. If I were strict, I'd shut you in an empty room and tell you to think about what you've done for an extended time-out of your own. Or I would call your dad and tell him you are in desperate need of discipline, or else I'm leaving. As a child, you shouldn't be able to do whatever you want whenever you want. You don't know what's best for yourself or for others. That's why you hurt your dolls. That's why you hurt yourself."

"Hurt myself?" Annie laughed and skipped a little on the marble. "I'm happy and healthy. How am I hurting myself?"

"Every time you take away a person's humanity, you kill a little of your own. Why do you think we're all zombies out there? But you're not a zombie, Annie."

"I'm a monster?"

"That's right."

"People like to brandish pitchforks and torches at monsters," Annie said. "I don't think I even know what a pitchfork is."

"People usually brandish the pitchforks and torches at the wrong people, the ones who look like monsters but aren't. The real monsters aren't so clear. The most effective ones hide in more innocent guises. Or they're so boring and established that we can't seem to get rid of them—like toxic mold. You're not mold in the basement, though. You're a black widow infestation. I think you like being a monster, Annie. I think it amuses you, and as long as no one stops you, you think you're allowed."

"But you're not stopping me, Miss Sam," Annie sang to echo in the hollows of the house. "You're helping. Zombie to monster? Better to be alive than dead?"

"Something like that."

Annie let go of her hand to hook her arm around Sam's waist and rested her head on Sam's shoulder as they walked, like they were lovers under an umbrella in Paris as they entered the east wing. Sam felt courted by a slug. She tolerated the touch by remembering Lila, which was why Annie had shown her the Time-Out Room in the first place.

She led Sam through the cross corridor, then took a right all the way to the end of the hallway.

When Annie opened the door, there were no sliding doors or IV control boxes attached to the wall. The room stretched up two stories, with a line of thin windows where the second floor would have been. Natural blue light poured in, but Annie switched on glass sconce lights that surrounded the room, which was about half the size of the grand hall—still cavernous, and with the windows, almost reverent.

Which was undercut by the human playground below.

There were metal monkey bars. The slides, too, would not have been very effective if it had been made of bodies, even with more literal lubrication, but they were made of a clear acrylic that showed off the slabs of people underneath—a collection of torsos laid in resin. Most of the playground, in fact, had been created of cast people parts.

But some were, if not whole, definitely alive, given the hanging IV bags attached nearby. On the swing set, a glider had been made with two women facing each other, wooden and metal armatures shaping them while their IV bags were attached to the plastic-enclosed chains above. A man next to them hung by his arms and legs in the shape of a swing. Harnesses below his shoulders and above his hips would help him withstand extra weight, but it still wouldn't be comfortable. A woman hung in a similar configuration next to him.

The swing set wasn't the only place where armature bolstered structural integrity. A jungle gym of human bodies had been mesh-sewn to each other, removing or rearranging parts as needed, around a complicated metal skeleton that arranged them into something approaching geometrical rather than biological. Then there was a merry-go-round, with people lying on their sides, tucked against each other in a circle with bent arms and legs slightly crooked, IVs filling in the space between. Then there were the spring riders that harkened back to the jack-in-the-box, except the spring hadn't been inserted into their bodies. These men and women had been bound on a plexiglass and metal carapace with their legs parted so that everyone could be ridden, one way or another.

"I sometimes bring my dolls in here to play with me—the ones that can walk, that is. My teddy bears love the playground. And Darla has so many more things she can dance on in here."

"Jesus, Mary, and Joseph." Sam hadn't said that in a long time. Her aunt was the one who'd used to say it, back when she'd still been mobile and able to visit her nieces and nephews, make sure they were eating something other than takeout. Her mother was more colorful in her cursing, but colorful didn't encompass the sheer inhumanity—or overabundance of humanity— of what Annie had done.

Once again, there was a quality of genius to the installation. And once again, none of it would have been possible without an obscene amount of money. Murder was cheap; art was not. The really good stuff—and the really bad—came at a price.

People talked about the charities they'd give to, crowdfunding they'd support, student lunch debts and college or medical loans they'd pay or forgive, if they had so much more money. Most people Sam's age and younger had been priced out of renting, much less owning their own homes. This place raised an unsettling question in her mind: How many people weren't monsters simply because they couldn't afford what they really wanted to do?

How many more Annies would there be in the world if people could afford it? How many more Annies in this world were there already, protected by nearly impenetrable shields of money and influence? How many Dream Houses were out there? If no one could touch people like Annie, would anyone ever know?

Annie switched on a sound system that played ice cream truck music and an extended track of children laughing, just to add another layer of awful to the scene.

Then she ran into the middle of the room to the merry-go-round and pushed a lever to start it spinning, since it would be difficult to manually turn such a heavy thing. She climbed onto the moving merry-go-round as it slowly sped up. The people underneath grunted from the weight of her little feet.

She settled over two pairs of legs, holding the merry-go-round bar as she reached into the narrow gap between a man's flushed cock and a woman's ass. Annie idly stroked the man to hardness while he moaned under the influence of his drug cocktail. The woman in front of him closed her eyes, but she couldn't move. Like everyone else, she'd been bound in place, her lips glued together.

Sam was afraid to step anywhere or touch anything that wasn't the rubber playground floor. "What, did you decide Ed Gein's arts and crafts weren't gruesome enough?"

"I think you'd really like the glider, Miss Sam. We also have a toy box in here, too, if you need a little help." Annie pointed to the chest against the wall behind crisscrossed balance beams of amputated legs. "There are a few extra small doses in there, for your dolls or for yourself, if you like. No blue caps, though. No forgetting in the playground. After all, we're supposed to have fun!"

Annie eased the man's cock against the woman's ass. Then she spit between them, the only literal lubrication provided. The man's groan and the woman's soft cry of pain was enough to make Sam want to take two of those blue-cap doses, each straight into her ear canals, possibly another two into her eyes.

Annie swung under the bar to crouch over two women and play with their breasts like stress balls.

"The pink caps make you feel all kinds of good, like you can ride forever, like you want to. The red caps make you feel good and suggestible, if you need me to tell you what to do. But you do need to play, Miss Sam. If you don't, I won't believe that you've really chosen to play with me. Then both you and Lila might need to be moved to the Repair Room."

"Fuck you."

"Mmm, please."

"You do realize, Annie, that if I ever did, it would be as gently as you make your dolls fuck each other."

"Mmm, please."

"I'm not sure you even know what pain is."

"I know what pain is." Annie tightened her fingers over the women's nipples until they writhed under her. "I've been playing with it for years."

"There's not the slightest scar on you. A girl your age should have learned empathy already. You could start by walking into a fire ant pile. I'm sure we'll find a few tomorrow after the rain stops."

"I know what pain is," Annie said again, this time with petulance creeping into her little girl voice.

Which only confirmed that nothing bad had ever happened to her. She'd lost her mother but barely seemed to acknowledge it as loss—more annoyance, an opportunity for her to step into the vacated role. Sam doubted she'd ever suffered anything worse than the flu. "You keep telling yourself that. But no matter how skilled, the puppeteer can never understand the marionette."

Sam knelt in front of the toy box, then opened it to consider the syringes. She wouldn't be able to put this off anymore. If she was going to save her own skin and make herself as much a monster as Annie, drugs could only help.

She'd never had anything stronger than spirits before.

"I've broken bones. I've had a few stitches," Annie said. "The dolls do sometimes fight back. It's why I take precautions and demonstrate to the new dolls what happened to the last dolls who tried. What you do to me, I give to you twelvefold."

"You sicced your teddy bears on me for denying you chocolate. You have no sense of proportion. You do what you like. That's it. And broken bones aren't the same as what you do to them. That's like saying an occasional headache means you understand bad period cramps."

Annie stuck out her tongue, contorting her face in juvenile but genuine revulsion. Either her periods weren't bad or, like Sam, she'd eliminated hers because they were too unpleasant to tolerate. It wasn't like Sam ever wanted to be pregnant or have children.

She wondered if the mad doctor provided birth control for the dolls. She hadn't seen a visibly pregnant belly yet.

Among the syringes and toys, there were also more dire things in the larger part of the chest's cavity: canes, switches, whips, most of them the kind designed for consensual sadomasochism. There was also a bulbous pear of anguish, chastity belts for men and women, gloves tipped with metal claws, small knives… The only reason Annie would trust her with these things was if she was sure she could defend herself or someone else would.

"Everything is cleaned between uses." Annie stepped off the merry-go-round and ran over to the slide to climb up it backward, just like a child. "Everything. And everything was clean before they were put in here. It's required for regular use. Oh, please put on a strap-on. Ever since you said that's what you do, I've been dying to see it." She wriggled in a little dance as she kept pulling herself up the slide.

Sam held up one of the knives. She didn't know what the names were for any of them, but this one was small, about three inches long, smooth rather than serrated. She wondered what it would be like to use a knife instead of a razor like she had when she was in her teens and early twenties, and to use it to end things instead of to feel alive.

She put it back in the box, but for a few moments, she couldn't let it go.

Maybe she could hide the knife on the other side of a seven-inch dildo, then secrete the knife into her pocket or the waist of her pants, maybe even under the strap of her bra. But she still felt cock inside herself. She didn't want to do that to anyone else. So a dildo was out.

Instead, she selected a pink-capped syringe and a finger vibe and reluctantly left the knife. If there had been a pocketknife, she maybe could have palmed it, but that might have been why there wasn't a pocketknife.

Sam turned around with the two things she didn't want to need. "I don't know how to inject myself."

Annie finally reached the top of the slide, then turned around and promptly slid down, her hands on her skirt to keep it from riding up. "I'll help. I'll show you. You'll get better at it with time."

Sam handed her the syringe. Annie took off the pink cap and went through the usual processes of getting rid of air bubbles. The antiseptic wipe taped to the syringe wetted down Sam's arm. She moved with the speed of a professional nurse or phlebotomist, finding a vein that actual professionals sometimes had trouble finding, and with more consideration than she showed her dolls or hostages when she jabbed them in the neck. Annie was almost tender as she finished off and removed the needle.

Now. Now, while you still have your wits. Grab the needle and shove it in her fucking eye.

Annie threw the syringe in the general direction of the toy box, out of reach of any doll, even if they'd been able to reach.

"Soon you won't need the lubrication," Annie said softly. "You'll use it because you want it, not because you need it. Soon, just doing what you'll do under its influence will make you feel this good all on its own."

I hope not. Oh God, I hope not.

Annie may not have been able to make everyone completely become who she wanted them to be, but she'd managed to succeed with so many dolls, and she had a vested interest in making Sam's enjoyment sincere. She showed her father nothing but contempt, but she'd never had a protégé before.

Some of the effects of the drug cocktail were almost immediate. Everything inside Sam seemed to slow down, like a clock that needed winding. She also smiled. It wasn't a conscious choice, but as though little imps in her cheeks lifted up the sides of her mouth. She also *felt* the smile behind the shape her mouth made, sunlight through the clouds.

There was still no sunlight through the rainstorm, and she was aware that the small world around her was awful. It just didn't seem…important that it was awful.

"There. Doesn't that feel better now." Annie kissed where she'd given Sam the injection, like a child might have learned from her mother. "Now, go have fun. Prove you still want to be here with me. Go, go."

Annie waved her away, dark-eyed, barely containing her eagerness. The only reason she contained it was because that kind of eagerness was not childlike in the slightest. Then she went to climb on the jungle gym. The ice cream truck music and children's laughter were interspersed with grunts as Annie put her hands and feet wherever she wanted, regardless of which organ she stepped on.

Sam arranged the vibe strap over her right forefinger, then switched the vibe on to the first level. She giggled as her finger shook. It wasn't the first time she'd used this particular toy, but for some reason, it was funnier now to feel it and see her shaking finger.

She wandered the playground without tension in her hips and shoulders keeping her confined to the center of every path. Where bodies and parts had been encased, she stroked her fingers over smooth resin, crouched down to peer at the details, which were sometimes a little cloudy or with a few obstructive bubbles but otherwise clear enough.

She still didn't want to touch the living, but she couldn't avoid the abundance of flesh—partial and whole, alive or not—which combined with vasodilation and relaxed euphoria to make blood rush better lower down. With the first clit twitch from the sight of a woman's beautiful breasts pressed together between arranged arms, a floodgate opened. Then everything between her legs couldn't calm down, with a deep, heavy ache. She wiped thin beads of sweat from her forehead but was reminded of the finger vibe again because she hadn't turned it off.

Nothing but quickened blood flow awakening nerve endings, but she could almost see her arousal, pulsing red in her vision. She wanted to sit down right where she was and use the finger vibe on herself, then fall asleep with her fingers still between her legs, but she meandered from the slides to the monkey bars to the balance beams. Then she stopped wanting to move her legs and wandered over to the swings.

"Hi." She eased down onto the woman's belly in the curve made by the bindings and harness. "I'm going to do things to you that you aren't asking for. I'm sorry." Then she leaned in toward the woman's loose hair, trying not to fall off the swing in the process. "But I'm not going to hurt you, okay? Forgive me."

Annie had settled on the top of the jungle gym, where she straddled a man and twanged his cock to see how far she could bend it between his legs before he winced. Then she watched it bounce back full and hard. "They're dolls, Miss Sam. You can make them feel good if you like. That doesn't mean they'll forgive."

Annie was probably right. She was usually right. Not in the moral sense. In the moral sense, she was as far in the wrong as a person could be. But she was uncomfortably right when it came to facts. It helped when she was the one who created those facts.

Sam didn't raise her feet to put her full weight on the swing, but she swung enough to be briefly entranced by the movement of the woman's hair.

The body beneath hers was thin but soft. None of these people got any exercise or movement in their day that wasn't mechanically or externally applied. Electrical impulses could combat atrophy, and special stretches could minimize muscle and tendon shortening, but the doctor's job here wasn't to keep them mobile, just alive and relatively healthy beneath the drug dependence. If anything, they'd prefer deteriorating mobility for most dolls.

Sam shook a little as she stroked the woman's small breast and brought her vibrating finger between the woman's legs. They were bound together, but Sam could push between the thighs when it was time for that. She massaged the woman's nipple until it puckered under her touch as she ran the vibe over the woman's inner thighs. Maybe she would have felt nothing but disgust if she were unmedicated, but the cocktail changed everything, and the woman gasped slightly the closer Sam came to the fluff of hair exposed by the harness.

"I'm going to do what I can to make this feel good." But talking wasn't something Sam wanted to do, either. She wasn't slurring like Lila. Her tongue was just tired of moving. All the little processes required to talk seemed like a waste of energy when the woman had to bite her lip like that, and not from holding in pain.

Saying it, though, made Sam feel a little better as she stroked the vibe closer and closer to where the woman seemed to want her. She moved her caresses to the other breast, gentle as she rolled the nipple between her fingers and slipped the vibe down.

The woman couldn't arch, at least not in a meaningful way while Sam was sitting on her belly, but she almost unseated Sam with what little she could manage. Sam didn't quite put the vibrations on the clit but around and around, and when she dug the more pointed tip in, it was just above, where pressing would find pubic bone. So she pressed, pulsed, pressed, then upped the vibration. She had to go through a few different speeds and variations before the woman let her mouth fall open to moan so high and prettily.

Sam licked her lips, wished she could spread those thighs, but she made do with what she had and stood to straddle her, facing away from the woman's eyes.

She had nothing to rub against without using the vibe on herself instead, but she rocked a little, swinging the ropes side to side instead of back and forth. Between the woman's moans and the wooden scaffold's groan, it was like being in bed with a woman begging her without words to come.

It had been such a long time since she'd enjoyed sex, felt this connected within it. She couldn't even see the woman's pussy, but she smelled arousal. It hummed through her own when the woman moaned; the moan itself was like music. She focused on it more than the soundtrack Annie played to make this place more perverse.

Sam didn't even know the woman's name—she wasn't a doll so much as building material—but the woman's moans climbed and her hips fought the harness, thighs quivering against the bindings that kept them together. Sam pushed the vibe just a little farther down to nudge against the blood-rich bud of her clit directly. The woman spasmed and arched despite the harness, nearly bucking Sam off. Then it wasn't like riding a bronco so much as a river wave, leaving Sam hot and damp where she rocked against the woman. She leaned forward to kiss the woman's thighs, then rested her head above the knees as she steadily stroked and pressed over the clit until the woman emerged from her drugged state enough to whisper, "Good. Good. Don't stop, don't stop, don't stop…"

So Sam didn't. Reaching behind her to cup the woman's small breast, she beckoned frantically with the same rhythm and pressure as the moans climbed and climbed.

Then there was a screech. It didn't even sound human. More like the scraping of metal on concrete, except it came from right behind Sam, and she felt it between her thighs.

Sam jerked up as though awakened from a dream. And there she was, the demon, the monster, the woman in the shape of a little girl. Or was it the other way around? From underneath, Annie slowly introduced the woman's pussy to a thick, long dildo much bigger than anything that could be grown by a person. The width had to be at least three inches, ridged with iridescent whorls—pretty, as it was forced inexorably in. The woman was aroused, but she hadn't been ready for that kind of size, and Annie didn't wait for her to adjust. The woman wrenched in her harness and screamed again.

Sam fell off the swing. Her head was going off like a novelty buzzer, as though the vibe that was still shaking her finger and making it itch had been left in her high-empty skull.

Annie stared straight at Sam as she sank the dildo in, bit by bit, until she couldn't push it any farther. Then she shoved.

Sam covered her ears against the sound that came from the woman then.

Annie angled her head to lick at the arousal that dewed the woman's folds, licked it like ice cream melt on the edge of a waffle cone.

"I couldn't resist the sight of you," Annie said. "But you need to swallow that jagged pill, Miss Sam. Playing nothing but nice isn't going to help you. You won't always be able to wriggle out of things or play your own games back at me, taking my chocolate milk again, treating me like a child…"

"You *are* a child," Sam managed to say, when all she wanted to do was bite her knuckles, stuff her whole hand in her mouth, maybe down her throat, choke on the sobs that wanted to come out of her, because she hadn't earned them. "You don't get to have it both ways."

"I get to have it any way I like. It's my house. My dolls. My way. *My way.*"

Annie pulled the dildo back, then shoved it in again, this time putting her shoulder into it. Sam screamed to cover the woman's scream juddering her head. Was there enough morphine in the whole wide world? She and the woman had shared commiseration, pleasure, perhaps forgiveness in the exchange, but Annie shattered that without shattering the connection, breaking Sam's heart all over again, whether that heart was muscle or stone.

Sam recoiled, a whole-body flinch, with each shove deeper and deeper, but she couldn't get far enough away from those screams amid the happy songs and happy laughter, amid the quiet weeping of those who still had tears and consciousness enough to shed them.

Deeper now, with a grunt. Almost all ten inches inside without ten actual inches of vagina.

"Annie, stop! You're fucking impaling her."

"You...don't...say." Annie managed to push the scrotal base flush against the entrance. "I'll call the doctor, but swings and springs tend to wear out more quickly than the others. I wonder why that is."

The woman coughed hard, once. Blood trickled from the corner of her mouth.

The worst part was that she was still breathing.

Sam stumbled out of the indoor playground, slammed the door against the soundtrack and rain on the windows, but it wasn't enough to get the echoes out of her reverberating head.

She fell to her knees outside the barre room and threw up breakfast, but the drugs had been intravenous, not something she could vomit out. That she felt so bad meant she probably felt worse underneath the numbing shallow waters of the cocktail. Yet, her head was alight, scared some semblance of sober. She coughed up bile and tried not to scream again.

The jack-in-the-box room next to her was closed. She wondered if there was already a new Jack or if it was just waiting for the ideal subject to saw in half like a magician's trick.

The trick in this place was that there was no trick—a haunted house without the dead.

She yanked off the finger vibe without switching it off, leaving it a pink, skittering cockroach between the carpet and crown molding.

When she could get back to her feet, she ran into the rain-reflected hall, quiet and clean and empty and cold. She knelt on the marble, then stretched forward onto the unyielding floor—cold on her heated and cooling skin, her sweat like the rain drawing down where light slanted in upon the stone and on her. She watched it pour over the glass and on the stone like she was melting, but it didn't hurt. Better.

Better, but the bad wasn't going away. She was trapped in the dollhouse, and all the dolls were waiting, hoping this was the day they wouldn't be disturbed or that this was the day they overdosed or went septic, just so they wouldn't have to be here anymore. There was no other way to get out.

Her way. All Annie's way. It didn't matter if she was young or old or in-between. All that mattered was that she was in control.

And she was in control because she *would* do her worst. She did things normal, healthy people never thought of a day in their life. She did things dictators considered too far. She did things doctors called impossible, grown-ups called insane, and children called evil, and only the children were right. As they usually were, although the monsters were never really hiding under the bed or in the closet or inside the walls but stood there in broad daylight between roof and windows—give or take a wing.

Zombie or monster?

Did Sam go back in that room, find a knife, and deglove a penis, just to make herself into the monster, one peeling slice at a time? Did she embrace the creative atrocity that was Annie and her host of masturbating minions in the dark behind anonymous screens, perhaps between teaching their children multiplication tables and protecting and serving their community, between simmering spaghetti sauce and corporate birthday parties? Furtive motions beneath work-appropriate attire in a shared bathroom. Checking, checking, checking that the earbuds were still attached, Bluetooth still synced. Choking themselves to a flipped petticoat while their baby daughter played at their feet.

She was feeling sick again.

Zombie or monster?

Sick again but also alive, under a tidal assault of adrenaline that might never end, while Lila was a zombie but also alive, which was better than dead, better than doll.

Could she become Lila's monster more than her ghost?

Sam pushed herself back to her knees, ran her hands through her loose hair, and asked herself what she was willing to become.

Chapter 12: DOLLMAKER

In the kitchen, the entire bustle of pre-lunch work went quiet, except for the long line of blenders to the right that took up almost the whole counterspace, other than the espresso machine.

When they realized Sam wasn't Annie, the staff returned to what they were working on. They didn't feed the dolls, maids, or themselves with the same aplomb as Ji-an served Annie, but they still had a tremendous responsibility keeping so many people with feeding tubes or straw mouths nourished.

Ji-an pushed through the crowd of workers at the blenders and one of several butcher blocks in the massive kitchen. "No, no, no, I told you. No one from your side in my kitchen. If you come in here, Annie comes in here. If Annie comes in here, chaos."

"She's not behind me. She's on the playground." But Sam stopped as she realized what Ji-an hadn't given her an opportunity to notice before waving her out last time.

Ji-an appeared largely healed from whatever Annie had done to her a long time ago, unless Annie had caused the limp; otherwise untouched since. The people who worked for her weren't so lucky.

Every single one had lost a hand, generally their left. In its place was a prosthetic that accepted a few tool or utensil attachments. There were also some workers with both hands removed, a gripping claw on one side and a more specific implement, like an electric carving knife, meat cleaver, or bread knife, on the other. They could still work in a kitchen, but the scope of their abilities had been severely limited.

"If you ran, she will follow. Out, out, out." Ji-an gestured her toward the swinging door. "If you want something, you ask through the serving hatch. Those are the rules."

"No. No, I need—" She pushed past Ji-an and searched the closest butcher block. It was a fucking butcher block, so there should have been knives other than the ones attached where people's hands should be.

"I can't help," Ji-an said, and this time there was a note of regret. "To keep my workers safe, you understand. She takes tongues, lips, stomachs, makes them useless to her, makes them dolls. I can't help you."

"I'm not trying to hurt her. It's for me. It's for *me*. Don't you see?" Sam crouched to see if there was a knife block in open storage under the drawers.

"I can't help you with that, either. There's no escape here. The greenhouse and garden are wrapped in iron. Only I am allowed out to get supplies with the groundskeepers, but even the supply shed is watched. I help you hurt her or kill yourself, the kitchen becomes a new playground, understand?"

"I'm not trying to kill myself," Sam said. Then she punched one of the workers in the shoulder. "Asshole."

"What the fuck, lady, I didn't do anything!"

Sam shoved another worker, who had two functional prosthetics instead of one. "And fuck you, too, motherfucker."

"What are you *doing*?" Ji-an didn't sound angry so much as utterly confused.

Sam beckoned them to come at her. It was either this or a blender, and she thought she might faint before she ever managed to get her hand in one of those.

"Come on!" She grabbed a handful of carrots and flung them in the faces of the workers, then did the same with onions. Disrupting their work. Riling them up and forcing their hands up, sharp or otherwise.

Then Sam wrapped an arm around the neck of one of the workers, not quite cutting off his air but threatening to. He scrabbled at her arm, but Band-Aids would be enough for those scratches. She needed more.

Irritation crept into Ji-an's bewilderment. "Punish yourself somewhere else. You're not allowed to do it here. Juan, Isabelle, Mari, extricate Miss Sam from Manny before he pokes her eyes out—or his own."

Sam yanked Manny back with her into the pantry. She didn't shut the door. It opened out into the kitchen and had no lock, because why would someone lock a pantry?

Within the logistical mess of multiple people trying to follow them in, however, she whispered in Manny's ear, "Go for my face. For the eyes if you have to."

"What?" he managed through the strangulation.

"Just do it." Sam knew it might kill her, like the blender or the electric carving knife. Death wasn't her object, but if it was the outcome, she'd take that, too.

When the staff and Ji-an managed to enter the pantry without bottlenecking, Sam shouted at them, "Goddammit, what does it take to get a fucking latte around here? Or hell, a bottle of vodka. Something to wash this godawful taste out of my mouth."

"I can make you a latte instead of your usual coffee," Ji-an said, as soothing as she could manage. "I can do that for you right now. But you must let go of Manny."

Sam throttled him instead. "Who do I have to fucking kill?"

She saw them coming: his hook-grip prosthetic on the left, the cleaver prosthetic on the right. It wasn't that everything slowed down so much that she became aware of fractions of seconds. Flashing, sharp, shining stainless steel, without aim or reason. Even though she'd orchestrated the attack, her brain didn't appreciate the self-sabotage and reeled her back, dragging him with her against shelves of dry goods.

The gripping hook caught her cheek like she was a catfish; the cleaver landed on her forehead like she was his own personal butcher block.

As the cleaver sent blood dripping dark into her eye, she let him go, stumbling against the shelves, grasping for anything and everything, but nothing held her. She didn't think the cleaver had done anything but scrape her skull, especially as easy as it was for Manny to remove it as she fell, but she dragged him down with her by the hook.

"Fuck."

Sam wanted to laugh at no-nonsense Ji-an swearing in exactly the same tone as she said everything else.

The chef parted the sea of stunned onlookers who'd hoped to be rescuers and knelt next to Sam and Manny. "If you're not trying to get killed, you have a funny way of showing it."

Ji-an stopped Manny from moving or continuing to attempt extricating himself from Sam's cheek, because all he did was pull her along with him, making the hole in her cheek worse.

Sam wasn't quite screaming. A strange nasal 'aaaaa' sound came out of her, like she was at the dentist. She was also stunned from the cleaver and couldn't stop thinking of the images of Phineas Gage with a pole through his head.

The drug cocktail might have been helping, too.

Rather than moving the hook, Ji-an pushed on Sam's cheek and guided her head until she was free. "Now my people will have to spend part of the afternoon cleaning your blood off the floor. What exactly was the purpose of this?"

"I've never been drugged before." Sam felt air through her cheek as she spoke, which captivated her almost before she finished the sentence.

Ji-an didn't seem convinced. "I could sew it up like a rack of lamb, but I assume you'd like a better hand at the stitch, and perhaps better drugs. Isabelle, Juan, help Miss Sam out of the pantry while I contact the doctor."

Here it was: euphoria again. Probably pain endorphins this time. But also, finally feeling held by someone other than Annie.

She was bleeding on everything, including her face. Someone grabbed a dish towel to press against her head and cheek. Ji-an strode to the first drawer on the blender side and pulled out a purple walkie-talkie.

They're everywhere. But it confirmed that not even Ji-an had a phone.

Ji-an didn't use traditional radio etiquette. Too many extraneous words. "Dr. Panabaker."

"Busy," Dr. Panabaker said on the other side of the walkie. "Internal bleeding."

Fuck. It wasn't that Sam had forgotten about the woman in the playground, but she hadn't figured the woman's treatment into her timeline—not that her sense of time was the best at the moment. She didn't want to interrupt the doctor's medical interference on the playground woman, but… Head wound. Bleeding fast. Probably looked worse than it was, but it was still hook in mouth and cleaver in skull. There wasn't a good version of that.

"I've got external bleeding," Ji-an said.

"I don't have time for a sliced finger. You have the emergency first aid until I can get to it."

"This is more than a sliced finger," Ji-an said, irritation taking the fore after being dismissed twice. "The nanny had caffeine withdrawal in conjunction with one of your cocktails and ended up with kitchen implements in her face—through no fault of my worker, who was just defending himself. She was belligerent, violent, high, and now she's bleeding everywhere."

There was an extended silence.

"Bring her to the elevator," Annie said through the speaker. "If your person not at fault killed her, I'll hold him responsible anyway."

Ji-an tossed the walkie back in the drawer and glared at Sam. "Look what you might have done."

Sam reached for Ji-an's apron and pulled her in, getting blood all over her. As a chef, Ji-an had dealt with blood before, but perhaps not so much at once gushing out of a skull and in such a way she'd have to sanitize extra before returning to work.

"Trust me," she slurred, hopefully so that anyone listening couldn't tell what she was saying.

"I don't," Ji-an said, quiet as well, but less unintelligible. "I can't. Your funeral, not mine. And there have been so many funerals. Can you stand? Can you walk?"

Sam braced herself on the butcher block. The world swayed and she swayed with it, but she could stand. Theoretically, the rest of her should work, too, unless the cleaver had hit further in than she'd thought.

"Isabelle, with me. Behind. I will brace her, but if she can't hold herself up, I'll need your help. We're not supposed to go on the other side of the door, either," she added to Sam grimly. "The rule is broken for medical emergencies, but it's always a risk if Annie's in a mood."

"Sorry."

"Don't apologize if you don't mean it." Ji-an hooked Sam's arm over her shoulder and walked slowly with her out into the dining room, then the hall, leaving a trail of blood along the way.

Somehow, they made it to the elevator. Behind Isabelle, who didn't join them, maids silently entered the hall with mops, buckets, bleach, and black latex gloves.

Ji-an and Sam said nothing on the way up.

The elevator opened to Annie kicking her saddle shoes on Dr. Panabaker's bed while the doctor performed laparoscopic surgery on the playground swing's uterus.

As Ji-an led Sam in, the doctor looked up, then blinked through the magnifiers on her glasses. "Jesus. Miss Annie, roll over my shower chair, *now*. Ji-an, keep pressure on her wounds."

If Annie rankled at being commanded, she didn't show it. She hurried to the curtained bathroom to roll the chair over.

"What did you *do?*" Annie snapped at Ji-an as they helped Sam into the chair.

"I told you over radio," Ji-an replied, still composed, although she looked like a horror-movie slasher villain from Sam's blood. "She seemed to have a bad reaction to her drug dose and became inexplicably aggressive."

"My cocktails are literally designed to prevent that," Dr. Panabaker said.

"I know food, not drugs. She attacked one of my preparers. Had he only hands, perhaps she would have a few nail scratches and a black eye."

"But where's the fun in that?" Annie helped Ji-an apply pressure to the wounds anyway. "What happened, Miss Sam?"

"I don't really know. The meat cleaver to my head rattled the Jell-O," Sam said.

"There. This should stem the worst of the bleeding." Dr. Panabaker applied clean, white gauze over the few stitches on the woman's belly.

Just a few stitches. Seemed like what Annie had done should have had more impact.

"Let's stem yours now, shall we?" Dr. Panabaker went to the medical wall sink to wash her hands before replacing her dirty protection with fresh. Then she retrieved a fresh, sterilized packet of surgical equipment and a series of pre-filled syringes from several boxes. She set everything in a pile on a new surgical tray in her lap. "To the dentist chair, Miss Annie."

"I'm going back to my kitchen. *She* doesn't come back to the kitchen," Ji-an said, pointing at Sam. "Service hatch only."

Sam raised her hand in acknowledgment and winced as she stood from the rolling chair and climbed into the vinyl chair.

Dr. Panabaker lowered the chair and leaned Sam back until she was within reach of the sitting doctor, who'd set up the surgical tray on a low rolling table.

"Okay, Sam, I'm going to irrigate your head wound first. The cheek might be more visually alarming, but I'm concerned the other blow might have cracked your skull."

Dr. Panabaker switched on the blinding lights above her. While Annie rolled in the shower chair back toward the bed, Dr. Panabaker focused on cleaning out the head wound. No absinthe at this time of the day.

"Looks like he made a dent but didn't penetrate bone," Dr. Panabaker said. "I'm going to numb this, then stitch you up. Do you notice any additional pain, ache, or pressure in your head? Does this light bother you?"

"Aside from metal digging under my skin, no, there's no pain. No headache. And does this light *not* bother someone?" Talking with a hole in her face felt like she was hypersalivating and couldn't stop it from dripping out the corner of her mouth. "This was the first time I've ever done any kind of drugs. I'm not sure what's from that and what's from the injuries."

"We'll keep an eye on you for the rest of the day and tomorrow morning. If you find yourself getting unusually sleepy after this, let me know."

"Why'd you lose your temper on the kitchen staff?" Annie asked from across the room.

"I wanted coffee," Sam said. "They weren't making coffee. They were blending meat and vegetables into a gazpacho, and it was upsetting. It seemed like a big deal at the time. Still didn't get my coffee."

"Maybe stick to tea for a few days," Dr. Panabaker said. "Little pinches here."

The hypodermic stung, like Dr. Panabaker said, but nothing in comparison to the fresh wounds that her nerves said were probably filled with angry fire ants. The lidocaine worked quickly, because then just her cheek hurt.

"I'll wash it gently after we stitch both your wounds, and you can wash your face carefully, but no putting your head under the shower spray, no submersion, no heavy rains, and no product until I remove your stitches again. We want her to take it easy, Miss Annie."

Annie frowned, but in an exaggerated way that didn't wrinkle her forehead. "I didn't hurt her."

"If that was her first dose, she at least needed to be monitored." Dr. Panabaker said.

"She was supposed to stay in the playground," Annie said. "She ran out just when things were getting good."

"The responsible thing would have been to follow. This is going to take a while, Miss Annie. It's lunch time. I'll let Ji-an know to bring Miss Sam's lunch up with mine, but you should go ahead down. She'll join you later."

"And then we can play in the Repair Room, Miss Sam?" Annie asked, with razorblades in her candy sweetness.

"Absolutely," Sam said. "With pain meds, I may be in an even better state to play."

"I think I'd rather stay and watch you stitch. No scars for the good ones, right, Doctor?" Annie took the doctor's walkie and pressed to speak. "Ji-an, bring lunch for me, Miss Sam, and Dr. Panabaker to the tower."

"Fine," Ji-an barked through the receiver. Probably thinking she could have put something together really quickly and brought it up with her fifteen minutes ago, but now she had to risk leaving the kitchen again.

Dr. Panabaker sighed sharply, but she continued with her stitching. "There. All right, now for the cheek. Let me see."

Sam pulled the bloody towel—far more red now than white—away from her cheek. It was still dripping, though not as much as before.

Dr. Panabaker irrigated the wound. "Nasty. Some pulling and tearing, but no dental damage. That's good. Another quick stitch. This could have been so much worse."

"Yes." Annie continued rolling around the tower in the shower chair like a bored child. "It could have been worse."

"Say what you mean, Annie," Sam said.

"You run from the playground, upset with me. You're on tranquilizers mixed with euphoric stimulants, but you briefly act aggressive around sharp things…"

"If I was trying to kill myself, do you think I would have done it by making someone attach their prosthetic meat cleaver and hook to my *face*?"

Annie stopped herself rolling by using her elbows as brakes on the vinyl under Sam's extended legs. "Fair enough."

"Please don't bump the chair, Miss Annie," Dr. Panabaker said, like a tired mother. "And don't talk, Miss Sam. I need to stitch your cheek now."

With her crossed arms on Sam's thighs, Annie watched intently as Dr. Panabaker sutured. Even though nothing really hurt anymore, Sam winced from feeling needle and medical thread *inside* her cheek.

"You'll want to eat on the other side of your mouth," Dr. Panabaker muttered as she worked. "And be careful as you brush your teeth. I'm going to give you a shot of antibiotics. Any pus, swelling, heat… If you have any issues at all, no matter how small, let me know through your walkie. Now, another thing I'm going to do is give you a small blood infusion. According to your medical files, you're A positive, yes?"

Sam nodded.

"I'm going to also give you a little shot of morphine, if you're okay. It won't tip you over from the last dose, and you should stay conscious, but it'll take the edge off the pain once the lidocaine wears off. You can use acetaminophen or ibuprofen after, if you'd prefer to stay off the opioids. But no aspirin."

The elevator door opened to Ji-an bringing everyone's lunch in an actual picnic basket. Annie clapped happily.

"Picnic in the rain! I'm going to make a picnic under the window so we can watch the raindrops on the glass."

"You do that, Miss Annie." Although Dr. Panabaker had maintained steady hands while suturing, they shook as she set her glasses down and picked up a white-capped syringe, empty, next to a morphine container. "We don't want to give you too much, or else you won't be able to play. Too much, and you'd just fall asleep and maybe wouldn't wake up."

She filled the syringe to the top. Then she set her hand on the chair next to Sam's leg, as though to catch her attention.

"Let me go get that infusion," she said through a tense jaw. "You'll want more blood in you against the morphine."

She directed her wheelchair to one of the fridges.

The syringe she'd concealed under her palm rolled against Sam's thigh.

Sam looked over at Annie, who was taking mini sandwiches out of the picnic basket while Ji-an poured little teacups with iced sweet tea—peach, by the smell.

Annie had her back to the dentist chair; Ji-an could see her. But when Sam took the capped syringe and carefully stuck it in the side of her underwear, trying to look like she was scratching an itch, Ji-an didn't say a word. She grazed her gaze over Sam as though she'd seen nothing.

Maybe she hadn't, but Sam was secretly thrilled and terrified in dizzying turns, because this meant both the mad doctor and the chef had finally figured out what she was trying to do. And they were *helping*, even though they'd said they wouldn't, couldn't, didn't believe it would accomplish anything. Ji-an's help was passive, but it was still help—with plausible deniability.

Dr. Panabaker risked so much more by actively helping Sam do what she'd been hoping to do by getting herself back into the tower. It was risky with Annie still there, and Annie had to know that giving Sam access to medical equipment was dangerous, but the nanny was one of the people in her dollhouse who was allowed certain freedoms.

Sam searched for some kind of mirror Annie might be using to spy on Sam behind her, but the only reflective surfaces were in the medical part of the tower. So, while the doctor was at the fridge and Annie's back was still turned, Sam smoothly grabbed a scalpel from the surgical tray—which was the only reason Sam could think of why Dr. Panabaker hadn't just selected a more basic suture kit. Sam wished she had long sleeves in which to conceal the scalpel, but for now, she hid it under her arm.

"All right." Dr. Panabaker came back around the surgical table. "Here's your new blood. I'm just going to put it in right here. Looks like Annie already used this vein, so I'll just clean these cuts first…bandages…then there…."

While Dr. Panabaker set up the IV line for her blood infusion, Sam wriggled the scalpel under her shirt. The blade against her skin was a risk, but she was able to get it to her other side with the help of Dr. Panabaker's fussing.

"We'll give you that morphine after the bag is empty. Do you need anything else? A B12 shot for energy instead of coffee, maybe?"

Sam shook her head. "I think I'll be fine."

"Have a picnic with us!" Annie said, putting the finishing touches on the blanket she'd stolen from Dr. Panabaker's bed.

Ji-an didn't include herself in the 'us.' Back in the elevator, she glanced back with no emotion, then let the door close on a flash of worry.

"You should be okay to move. The IV stand rolls. Everything rolls around here," Dr. Panabaker added wryly. "You also should be okay to eat, just on the—"

"Other side of my mouth." Sam was beginning to wish for that morphine. The last cocktail barely took the edge off her fear. "All right, Annie, I'm coming."

And she was actually hungry, for first time in what felt like weeks but was only a few days, when the Dream House had still been a dream.

"What do we have here?" Sam approached the picnic while Dr. Panabaker cleaned herself off again to resume her work on the other woman.

"Ji-an made so many sandwiches!" That fact seemed to sincerely delight Annie in a way Sam wished she could still find endearing. "Look, look, look what she did. She made cucumber sandwiches, salmon pâté with green onion, curried egg, homemade peanut butter and blackberry jam, then some strawberries and cream and Nutella and banana sandwiches for dessert. Look how pretty they are. Look how pretty we arranged them."

Ji-an could have just thrown something together like she usually did for lunch, since breakfasts and dinners were so substantial. Instead, she'd gone out of her way to provide something that required a certain amount of presentation on the blanket. Something to occupy Annie. Sam couldn't help but think this was intentional—no more optimistic than before, but a chance.

One chance. That's all she had, and she had to make it good.

She lowered herself to the blanket with Annie, who served tea. Sam fought not to wince as the movement shifted the syringe and scalpel she'd hidden under the sides of her underwear. But she'd chosen the inside of her sweatpants because they were joggers, cuffed at the end. If anything slipped from her makeshift sheath, that would put them out of immediate reach, but they wouldn't fall out the bottom.

She was careful in sitting crisscross, but at over thirty, she could afford to take her time on her way down, and her injuries only further justified it, especially with the scratches on her arms. She adjusted her shirt to hide any potential tiny tent from the tips of the implements or lines of them against the folds of her sweatpants.

Annie chattered about picnics she'd had with her mother, others she'd had with her father after her mother died, outside or in their bedrooms on rainy days, suggesting their present set-up was tradition.

Well-played, Ji-an.

About halfway through the picnic, both of Sam's injuries were starting to feel like she'd been torn apart by a hook and cleaver again.

At least the sandwiches were delicious.

After completing the emergency surgery on the swing woman, Dr. Panabaker stripped her PPE again, washed, and joined the picnic. She glanced perhaps a bit too often at Sam, as though expecting immediate attack, but Sam just exclaimed about how good and pretty each sandwich was—even smiled, although it was starting to hurt.

"Lidocaine's wearing off, isn't it?" Dr. Panabaker said. "I'll get that morphine."

She came back with a syringe at about twenty percent of what she'd put into the syringe on Sam's left hip. Sam felt like a pincushion, but she let Dr. Panabaker stick the needle in her other arm.

Everything started to feel better almost immediately—a little too much better. She kind of wanted to just lay back on the blanket and fall asleep under the rain, a little more comfortable than she'd been on the empty living room floor, because this was laminate instead of marble.

"Thanks." She struggled to stand again, laughed as she fell against the wall. The scalpel fell out from the elastic waist of her underwear, which she found even funnier, but the jogger cuffs did their job and didn't let it clatter onto the floor.

"Maybe a little too much," Dr. Panabaker said with some concern. "When I remove your stitches, remind me to do some bloodwork. I'll create custom cocktails for you like I do for Mrs. Fratello, Miss Annie, and Miss Annie's teddy bears. You'll get more enjoyment out of them than just taking the standard doses."

"Sounds like a party," Sam said.

Annie clambered up, too. "Is it time for the Repair Room? We can really party in there. And we can try again, can't we, Miss Sam? We can do this right."

"Lead the way, Annie. No, really, lead the way. You might have to hold my hand."

Annie giggled with her. "You're funny when you're really high, Miss Sam."

In the elevator, Sam tucked herself into the corner of the elevator because it provided stability on two sides of her. Annie leaned in to kiss Sam's cheek near the bandaged sutures. Sam thought Annie would feel the syringe on her left hip, but she didn't react.

Sam closed her eyes and exhaled all the way down to the ground floor.

Annie skipped out of the elevator, then skipped back in to drag Sam out with her. Sam was pretty sure she was weaving, but Annie treated it like a carnival ride and danced with her back to the Repair Room.

Sam wasn't nearly high enough when the Repair Room carousel lights switched on. Blessed indifference was an improvement, though—like looking at photographs of the Battle of Antietam.

"Come up here, Miss Sam. I'll show you how it works."

Annie jumped up onto the control board platform. In the center were buttons with numbers corresponding to each broken doll. To the left were the levels for their IV doses. It looked like they were set to go off at regular intervals, but Annie could up the dosage at any time. There were whole containers of the stuff just beneath the control board. The left side was the most complicated and had been integrated into a computer, with additional components that reminded Sam of a sprinkler system program, which may have been what Annie had foraged it from.

Wires from the right side connected to the left, suggesting it was part of the same system, but the board was much less complicated—just buttons of silhouetted sex positions. Because of the orientation of the plastic-wrapped chains, the positions on the board were solely face-to-face, but with more variations than Sam would have come up with on her own.

The joysticks in front of her were more elaborate than they'd seemed. Each button corresponded to a part and could go in multiple directions, not just pushed down. It was more like manipulating marionette bars than using an old arcade joystick.

"You'll learn how to control these with enough practice, but the buttons have preprogrammed arrangements and movements so you don't have to do everything yourself. Most of the pictures with a man and a woman can be a man with a man with some angle adjustments or woman with a woman with a strap-on. We even have a few scissoring positions, although no one seems to have any actual fun with that. The first selection needs to be your top and the second needs to be your bottom. Now, choose who you want to play with, Miss Sam."

Not the sort of things one expected to hear in a persistent and by now effortless little girl voice, with little girl enthusiasm, but Annie couldn't break character, even if her dialogue was more mature.

Sam looked over the dolls, who stared at her with too much despair to hope she could help them now. Annie was treating her like a partner. Those who still had a shred of optimism left for her had lost it.

Sam chose a man, short but broad-chested. He didn't lift his head and kept his eyes at half-mast as she brought him to the center.

"And..." Sam chose a woman who appeared at least somewhat aware, because if she paired two dissociating dolls, it wouldn't be as fun for Annie. Annie needed her to get her hands dirty.

"Now, he might respond just by the jingling of the chains and track," Annie said softly, as though they were about to watch two animals mate in the wild. "Let's see if he stirs when she starts trying to fight the shackles. Yep, look, there it goes. Now, lubrication. I'll get into dosages later, but just let me..."

Yellow fluid slithered through the IVs and into the dolls' bodies.

"Oh, yes, he's waking up quite nicely. Look at that. He's such a beauty when he wakes up."

His eyes didn't open much beyond half-mast, but he couldn't help but shift his body as his cock swelled. He was long enough into his surrender that he made no effort to hold back the tension and flex of his thighs as he thrust into air.

"Now, choose a position. *I'll* make the adjustments and teach you how to make them dance, unless you want to give it a try."

"Can I manipulate them after I've chosen a position?" Sam asked.

"Sure. It just defaults back to the program if you don't make any adjustments for five seconds."

Sam selected a button that showed a woman with her legs stretched back, knees to her shoulders, a man bent over her like she was on a table. The doll woman, already drifting, flipped into position. The man was heavy over her, but although he had his own rhythm, he acclimated to the program a lot faster than if he'd been actively resisting.

Like before, the positions weren't exact. Annie stepped away from the board to join the two dolls in the center of the carousel. While Annie helped position the man's cock, Sam slipped the syringe out of her underwear band and removed the cap. She hid most of the syringe in her hand, with the needle sticking out between two fingers like keys on her way to her car.

Then she took the joysticks in both her hands. Her right was a little more awkward, but the syringe was small. The principle seemed pretty self-explanatory—left stick for left person, right for right, top button for head, middle buttons for arms, and bottom for legs.

She flailed both sets of arms. The woman's were caught around her legs, but the man's had more room to maneuver and clocked Annie across the mouth while she held the woman's legs back farther to angle her upward.

"Oops. Must have squeezed too tight."

Annie shook off the blow with a frown. After a few seconds, the dolls resumed their previous positions. "Let's wait to use the joystick until the dolls aren't in a pre-set position. You learn so much more when you have to manipulate every action yourself."

Because the man had slipped out when he'd flailed, Annie reached between the dolls to position the man's cock back where it needed to be.

Sam flailed the arms again.

When Annie glared at her, Sam stepped back from the joysticks and put her hands behind her back. "Sorry. Not touching again."

She waited until Annie tried to put the man back in for the third time. Then she parted the two and smashed them back together, like when she'd pretended to play both sides of Street Fighter at mini arcades when she was a kid and didn't always have fifty cents to her name.

Sam giggled again as she pulled away from the joysticks. Annie's glare had gone from real glare masked as mock-glare to full-on real.

"What, is my being high only funny when I'm not having fun?" Sam said. "I thought you wanted me to play with you, Annie."

"By playing with my *dolls.*"

"Isn't that what I'm doing? Am I not playing right? You know, I'm beginning to think you don't really want a playmate. A playmate has their own ideas about how to play and when and why. A playmate sometimes chooses a game you don't want to play, but you agree to it because you're her friend and you like them. You don't want a playmate, any more than you wanted a nanny. You just want a doll who follows you around and has a voice box that agrees with you all the time while you play your way. We're *all* just extensions of you, puppets of Annie's will."

"Yes!" Annie left the two dolls in the middle of their fake fucking and strode toward the control board. "Everyone here only exists because of me."

"I think some of their births predate your pubescence."

"Everyone exists *here* because of me. Don't play stupid, Miss Sam. Silly may be amusing, but stupid doesn't suit you." She put herself between Sam and the joysticks. "If you're not going to play nice, then you go adjust them and keep them in a good position for Mario to screw her."

Sam adjusted her hold on the syringe so she could put her thumb on the plunger. She thought of Dr. Panabaker and her three fingers—two to hold a syringe and one to depress. Because Sam had all her fingers, she could hold the syringe in her whole fist.

She came up behind Annie. "I'm sorry. I didn't mean to interfere with your playtime. I was just trying to have fun."

Sam poised the needle near the side of Annie's neck.

Annie slammed her elbow into Sam's stomach. Sam fell back off the platform, losing the syringe when her body jolted hitting the floor.

"*You think no one's ever tried that?*" Annie screamed at her, bent nearly double, like Mario over the doll woman. "You think you're the first to access the doctor's office for sharp objects to use against me?"

Then she straightened, smoothing her hands over her skirt, as though she wasn't upset in the least.

"I'll admit, having someone in the kitchen attack you... That was a new one. Like you said, why would you do anything that would have someone damage your *face*? But you disappoint me, Sam. And now I need to go over the tower footage to determine if Dr. Panabaker needs to lose her knees."

When Sam got her wind back, she fumbled for the syringe but couldn't find it without looking away from Annie, which was like looking away from a cobra. "She didn't do anything. I took advantage of both of your distractions. The other woman was your fault, Annie. I just split the doctor's attention."

"We'll see. Dr. Panabaker has been notoriously disloyal." Annie stepped down. She didn't even try to find something to defend herself with, which made Sam *very* nervous. "I can hire a million other housekeepers, a million other chefs, a million other nannies, but there aren't many high-caliber surgeons who can perform so well while hobbled and humbled. She knows I won't kill her or make her a doll as long as she's so difficult to replace. She also has no immediate family. A lot less to lose. But you, Sam… You knew what you had to lose, and you did it anyway."

"The game was set up for me to lose. Your game, your rules, only one inevitable winner. Like a three-year-old playing Candyland."

"And what was so goddamn difficult about doing as I say? Instead, you had to undermine me at every turn. Some people might find an unbroken mare fun, but I don't. I *don't*, Sam. I don't enjoy spirit. I do, however, enjoy the breaking."

She ran at Sam almost too fast to believe and slammed her foot down on Sam's grasping hand. Annie had no hesitation, didn't hold back on anything. Sam heard snaps and shouted, but she curled her body around Annie's feet like a dying bug and locked around her shins to bring her down, a tiny giant to an unforgiving floor.

Sam couldn't say she was as unflinching as Annie in hitting another person, but she slammed both hands into Annie's belly, screaming at the same time as the impact unsettled whatever had broken. Then she crawled to her hands and knees, ginger on the right hand, and slammed her knee in that much harder to paralyze Annie's diaphragm.

Then, because Annie couldn't do anything but gasp for air into lungs temporarily unable to expand, she jammed the same knee into Annie's groin. It didn't have the same impact as on a man, but that didn't mean there weren't an abundance of nerves and smaller structures to damage. Annie jerked reflexively into fetal position.

Each blow was easier than the last. Fear battled off the final shreds of the morphine's dreamy effect.

She scrambled like a beetle across the floor, not quite reaching her feet as she tried to find the syringe. Rattling chains alerted Sam to the broken dolls along the wall pointing, if they were able. She followed their gazes to where the syringe had skittered. She ran after it, but the dolls' widening eyes warned her not quite in time for Annie's attack.

It felt like a claw scratching her back. It wasn't until she whirled back around that she realized Annie had torn through shirt and skin, a slow climb of stinging nervous awareness, with a glint of silver in her hand.

Scalpel.

Sam shook her leg. She couldn't feel metal above her jogger cuff. In the fight, the cuff must have pulled open just enough for the scalpel to fall out.

Fuck.

"You know, Manuel has done such a number on your face, and Dr. Panabaker isn't a plastic surgeon. Her priority is a good suture, not an invisible scar," Annie said, still trying to catch her breath. "Like whittling a piece of wood, sometimes you have to work with an existing imperfect shape to determine what form or figure will emerge. I like where that hole is in your cheek, Sam. What if that's where your smile ended?"

Annie was calling her Sam. At first, Sam had thought it was a break in character, like when she'd turned off the cameras, but she'd done it several times now here in the Repair Room without losing her little-girl voice. Intentional.

She wasn't Miss Sam anymore. Dolls didn't deserve an honorific.

Sam fell back as though her knees couldn't hold her anymore. Really, she just wanted to get closer to the syringe.

Her palm landed on the cylinder. She grabbed it but had to keep crab-walking backward as Annie came after her with the scalpel, brandished like a knife so she could stab down. It caught Sam's thighs and knees, cut through muscle and bits of tendon like they were nothing.

"*Fuck*, Annie."

Sam stuck the syringe between her teeth, all too aware that the delicate needle was so close to her own skin. But they could run round and round this carousel 'til kingdom come and still go nowhere.

She looked intently at Annie, tried to see in Annie everything that had already killed so much inside her—in the dollhouse and out. Tried to see the adult and not the little girl, until awful adult was all she saw.

She was the sadistic manager pitting employee against employee. She was the customer who swigged a daily shot of narcissism with her paranoia and insisted everyone experience the world through her lens. She was the parent who wanted Sam to provide all the education and enrichment capable in her small bones, but within the parent's individualized principles and beliefs over all others. She was the supervisor who said being hit on by old men wasn't as bad as she said it was and she certainly didn't need someone else to help during a bath or shower with a belligerent client; the same supervisor, the fucking prick, didn't mind flirting with nurses and aides and called them oversensitive when they told him to stop.

Annie was the dragon at the top of a mountain of money trickling down from between her claws, laughing at Sam slipping on the bottom under the flood of gold she wasn't allowed to touch.

Annie didn't expect Sam to do anything but run on her cut-up legs. She certainly didn't expect Sam to come *at* her while Annie was the only one with a good weapon.

The scalpel pierced the bandages on Sam's arm, but Sam knocked Annie's arms to the sides, the scalpel blade still embedded below her elbow, then punched Annie flat in the face.

What might have been a mild break became more substantial as Sam's fist collided with Annie's nose and cheekbone. Sam screamed while Annie shouted in indignation, but Sam swung another haymaker with her other hand, knocking Annie's nose the other way and sinking into the softness of Annie's eye.

Annie stumbled back, then hit the step to the control platform and sat down hard, like a petulant child in time-out.

Sam raised her foot and crashed the heel of her shoe against Annie's nose and mouth. What had been a trickle of blood became a faucet flow. Annie wailed like she'd never been hit before in her life, with injustice and pain in equal measure.

"You broke my teeth," she said when she could finally manage words. Because of the broken tooth, she pronounced it 'teef,' which seemed eminently appropriate.

Sam pulled the scalpel out of her arm and threw it behind her like bloody salt over her left shoulder. While Annie covered her mouth and nose to catch the blood—as though she needed to put it back in—Sam grabbed her pigtail and jerked her head to the side.

Then she plunged the syringe needle into Annie's neck where she assumed the jugular or carotid was. She didn't know which would be better or if she hit either. She just hoped that when she depressed the plunger, it entered Annie's system, and fast.

She also didn't know whether Dr. Panabaker had given her enough to kill or just neutralize. Sam didn't particularly care which.

She withdrew, then threw the syringe in the same direction as the scalpel, so Annie couldn't reuse the needle.

"You fucking *bitch*," Annie snarled. She jumped at Sam, curling her fingers into claws. She managed to scratch one of Sam's eyes and caught on the mouth sutures while tearing new lines down her cheek. "You just wait. What I'm going to do to you. What I'm going to do to your girl. What I'm going to make you do to each other. You're going to be so goddamn *pretty…*"

Annie stumbled.

Her face went slack even as her fury tried to writhe through. Her limbs, too, loosened in their sockets. When she pitched forward, Sam didn't dare trust it and let her fall flat on her blood-gushing face.

When she'd lain there for a couple minutes, Sam nudged the body with her toe. Again.

Nothing.

Sam knelt next to her and put her fingers on Annie's neck.

She had a pulse, and slow, even, sleeping breath. She wasn't dead—yet. She was out.

Sam didn't have time to check her own wounds. Given she didn't have *that* much blood soaking through her clothes, Annie didn't seem to have hit anything major. Even so, Sam thought she should probably sit down.

She knew she couldn't.

She didn't know how long her next window of opportunity was. Because someone was still watching. Stopping Annie was only the beginning. This would be their only chance to stop the dollhouse before it took them down with it.

Chapter 13: TIME FOR TEA

Video 1:

Sam sits in the library and faces the phone camera. She has a bloody face, bright red starburst in her eye, and black sutures over the worst scratches and cuts on her face and arms, which are smeared with some iodine but no longer covered with bandages. She wears a sling for a visibly broken but untreated hand. Her hair is mussed and bloody; her clothes are a mess. Otherwise, she might have been the host introducing an old movie.

"Hello. My name is Samantha Frain. I haven't used these platforms in forever, but if you're here, it's because I shared the link to my videos, which I'm posting in multiple locations. I'm also sending them out to several other people directly.

"I don't care about going viral for myself. But I need you right now. I need you to do your influencer things, and I need you to send it to anyone you can think of who might be able to help: journalists, doctors, paramedics, firefighters. Hell, send it to construction workers or your handy aunt or uncle. If they have too much authority, I'm afraid they might be helping hide what's happening and could be coming here right now to hurt us, so if you call 9-1-1 or the chief of police wherever you are, that's great, but this might be officially dismissed as a prank while they eradicate us.

"This isn't a prank. This isn't a haunted house. This isn't early promotion for a horror movie. This is real. Terrible things are happening in a house hidden deep in the woods outside North Texas suburbs.

"Don't delete, report, or remove. Do share, download, screenshot, record and resend, video it while it's playing… I don't care. We need people to come help us. People with tall ladders. People who won't shoot us or set fire to the house with all of us in it.

"I'm dropping my pin in the comments. We're locked into the property, and although some of us might be able to climb, most of us can't. I'm just glad we finally found their phone cache and that they hadn't just smashed them all, but most of us are in desperate need of paramedics, surgeons, psychiatrists, a goddamn fucking priest…"

Video 2:

Sam carries the phone with her as she walks through the expansive, empty hall.

"People are going to say this is CGI or AI, but it's not. I barely know how to post these videos, and I'm not doing it clean or polished. Everything you're going to see is real. Some of the people I've sent this link to are people I've worked with in daycare and senior care, people who know me and would trust that I don't joke or prank or make shit up.

"Four days ago, I was kidnapped by Harold Lange. I thought I was hired as a nanny for a developmentally delayed teenage daughter. It was only when I arrived that I learned Annie Lange was a regressed thirty-something woman who acted like a child. That was suspicious right away.

"I don't know if everyone believed what Mr. Lange and Annie were telling us or suggesting through her behavior, but the ones I've asked really believed she was child-minded. She's not. Don't let her fool you into thinking she's a little girl in an adult's body. She acts like whatever lets her get away with things and whatever makes her father give her everything she wants.

"Harold Lange is not innocent in all this. He's a voyeuristic predator who brings Annie her victims, gives her what she needs for her projects, then gets off on watching. If you see Harold Lange, stop him, hold him, keep him away from this house and away from his phone so he can't send someone here in his stead."

Video 3:

Sam walks down a curved hall. The wall to her left is blank. The right has glass doors dotted with air holes. The teddy bears inside look up at her with the blank stares of drugged zoo animals who have known nothing but captivity.

Cut to another corridor, straight rather than curved. She opens the doors that aren't already open. "I've let some of them out, but some didn't want to leave. Others couldn't. I really don't know what's going to happen to them. If they were animals, they'd be put down. One of the men I let out of his shackles smashed his head against the wall to kill himself.

"Annie has been performing medical experiments on what she calls her dolls. This is her dollhouse, her Annie Dream House. She's self-taught in engineering, medicine, sewing, anything that helps her do what she wants. I know this is hard to look at, but I want to emphasize to you that these are real people.

"Our streaming platforms are probably going to flag these as too graphic or obscene. Someone's going to say that people don't need to see this. But real people have been physically broken, pumped full of drugs to make them calmer and compliant, even euphoric. Then they're put in little boxes to wait for Annie to play with them and to perform on a twenty-four-seven streaming service for the wealthy, sick, and deranged, all in whose best interest it is to make us disappear.

"I cannot stress this enough: Don't show this to your kids, but don't let them pull us down. Don't let them make us disappear. Spread the word. And come here to help us out before they figure out how to stop us."

Video 4:

After taking her unseen audience through the playground, Sam walks down the hall, clenching her teeth, more strained and shadowed than when she started the tour.

"I'm showing you these people—not dolls, they're *people*, goddammit—on not the worst day of their life but just the most recent. This place is a constant hell in which they're forced to *survive,* in which their bodies continue to exist and they must endure.

"I don't want to do this. I'm not a shock jock. I'm not a sadist like Annie. These people deserve their privacy. They deserve not to be treated like an old-fashioned freak show for people to point and laugh at and tell themselves 'but for the grace of God.' They're not cautionary tales to be told over campfires and in the dark bowels of the internet. But I talked with everyone capable of listening and replying, and they agreed we have to show the bad stuff. Because what was done to them is worse than how you feel looking at it.

"Spread it around. Share it wherever you can. Contact someone you know who either has a very tall ladder or who rescues kittens from your trees. If you have a newspaper column or just a goddamn smartphone and a social media following, we need you to come and try to help. Hold them to account and bear witness to us, like I was made to bear witness to what Annie did."

Video 5:

Sam is in the barre room, sitting next to an unmoving person on an ottoman. "This person next to me is dead. He's been coated in resin or plasticized… I don't know the process. She wanted to keep some people around after death. Darla, the music box girl, has been dancing every day for what must be fucking *years*, made to fuck the dead and alive mannequins in here for the entertainment of the people on the other side of cameras somewhere in here." She gestures vaguely around the mirrored room.

"I don't know how to get the live mannequins out of the resin keeping them in place. I feel like I need to wait for someone more professional to keep from hurting them more than they've already been hurt. I'm not sure if there's any hope to get them out.

"Someone once said that where there's life, there's hope. I'm sure that's true for some, but there are people here who might have something to say—or do—to that rose-colored-glasses-wearing bastard."

Sam scratches idly at her head, wincing when she realizes the itch is where sutures are. "*Fuck*. What's happened to me for the last four days would be someone else's worst nightmare, but I got off so easy. I came in here to tell Darla that Annie wouldn't hurt anyone ever again, and she immediately stopped dancing. Not only was she starved skeletal, she was *aware* of what she'd been forced to do all these years. She fell to the ground. She'd been dancing en pointe, but now I'm not sure she can even walk, especially now that she's stopped taking her regular drugs. She's so light, I could carry her to the Repair Room myself, even with my injuries.

"People have been here for years and known exactly what was happening to them. Every day. Every freaking day and every night, in the dark alone—or worse, with someone else in the room, wound up and drugged and manipulated into becoming instruments of torture. I don't know how people are going to deal with that, either—not just having things done to them, but made to do those things to someone else.

"I couldn't even risk opening the teddy bears' door to see if they were like Darla and could switch it off as soon as they didn't have to perform. The way they looked when they obeyed her... I don't know how much *them* is there anymore. Even if they can be treated for their physical changes, will they still be a danger to others because of this place? How many dolls were made into monsters, too?"

"Sam?"

Sam flips the orientation of her camera to front-facing. Dr. Panabaker moves her wheelchair into the room.

"Annie is awake. Mrs. Fratello is keeping the hungry wolves at bay, but she won't be able to hold them back for long."

"Coming."

Video 6:

The orientation has been switched back to face Sam, but the electric wheelchair whirs nearby.

"Annie had all these people under her thumb to act on her behalf, incentivized to snitch on anyone threatening to rebel so *they* wouldn't get hurt worse for letting it happen or encouraging it. Anyone who tried to overthrow Annie would suffer from their wrath, too.

"You may not understand how one little girl was able to do that, but we actually do it every day. We could change the world at any time, but we don't. We're told we get to deal with slightly less crap if we can get them to shovel it at someone else. Prisons, sweatshops, fraternities, sororities, military, politics, corporations… We do it all the fucking time. It's easy to criticize from the outside, harder to fight it from the inside.

"I was new. That was the only reason I could still fight. But God, guys, I'm so fucking tired. I've had more sleep in the last four days than I've had in two weeks, and I'm so fucking tired.

I don't want this to end with freedom, finally, then a rain of bullets leaving us all silent. These people have been silent enough. They need to be able to speak, to feel, to do things Annie doesn't want them to do. They need to see there's still a world on the other side of these walls.

"I've shown you one or a few people at a time, but this house is a fucking mansion. An *estate.* Maybe a castle, because of the turrets? Given the size of each wing, I'd guess there are at least a hundred people here, up to a hundred fifty."

"There are a hundred sixty-eight, after the last Jack died," Dr. Panabaker says off-screen. "We have a few others on the brink of death, but they can stay on the brink for a while, and they count."

"The bulk of the people are maids, then cooks, then dolls," Sam says. "But don't get me wrong, the maids and kitchen staff are also Annie's victims. She doesn't play with them the same way as the dolls, but that doesn't mean she doesn't play. Let me show you."

Sam holds the door open for Dr. Panabaker but keeps the camera mostly on the people inside the carousel-style room, which is almost full. The broken dolls have been removed from their chains, but most can't move because of their dislocations and relocations. By far the most mobile and agitated are the groundskeepers and the maids and kitchen staff who can be spared while other dolls in other rooms still need to be cared for.

"This is the Repair Room, where Annie starts the process of breaking people. She literally dislocates joints, so they can't run or resist what the marionette program she created makes them do. You can recover from these things—Darla used to be one of them, and she's been dancing for who knows how long. Other things Annie does are harder to recover from.

"She brings two people to the center and forces people to rape each other. Where she's hanging now, that's where she drags them for everyone to see, relieved they didn't get chosen but knowing what will happen the next time they are. This is where I helped her, under threat of joining them. Play or be played with. Isn't that right, Annie?"

The dolls who could walk far enough to make it to the Repair Room are reluctant to get out of Dr. Panabaker's way, but they let her through to also let Sam through. There's no reverence, no celebration, but Annie *is* bound, and Sam is the one who did it.

"I dropped her with a shot of morphine," Sam says coldly. "She's still emerging, but you can hear me, can't you, Annie? I don't know if I even want to take that gag out. All you'll do is spew some kind of privileged nonsense or *deny, deny, deny.* Let's just hear her try, shall we?"

Sam pushes down the gag.

"She orchestrated everything!" Annie shouted in her most fearful little girl voice. "They'll tell you I did terrible things, but I *couldn't* do those things. Look at me. How am I supposed to keep everyone here under control all by myself? You're the grown-up, Miss Sam, the one in charge. You just want my money for yourself, and you're using them to do it."

Sam laughs so hard that the camera shakes. Unable to hold herself up, she falls to the floor next to a white-skinned waif.

"Yeah, yeah, I managed to convince a hundred sixty-eight people to overthrow you because *I'm* the tyrant. And I did it all for your fucking money. Your father promised me sixty-two thousand a year living here rent-free, which sounded like *heaven.* That was before I realized you're the devil and this is actual hell."

Video 7:

Sam circles Annie, lingering on the shackles over her joints. Hers haven't been dislocated like her dolls'.

Then Sam zooms in on Annie's face, still in a little girl pout.

"This is not a child. She's barely a woman. For twenty years, she's been perfecting her art of turning people into dolls, but given how she treats the help, the dollmaking process was just a creative formality. She retreated into the Dream House because she didn't like that she wasn't allowed to treat people like dolls in the real world."

Sam scans the crowd, lingering on scar build-up, missing limbs.

"Men made into teddy bears and jack-in-the-boxes. Women turned into music box dancers and mannequin displays for her dresses. Maids with no mouths. Cooks with knives and forks for hands. I could believe the little girl when it was just stuffed animals and Barbie dolls. But not this."

"Silly Miss Sam, you always took things too seriously. We were just playing. You can't tell the difference between play and real? What kind of nanny are you?"

"Stop, Annie. Stop talking. I wanted you to be able to speak for what's coming, but there's no point in arguing. Don't you get it? Dr. Panabaker has the receipts, because you *wanted* her to see everything. Even if your father or your IT guy—if that isn't you—erases the feed and the backups, Dr. Panabaker has medical records of illegal medical procedures, she has screenshots, and once she figured out how and that no one noticed she was doing it, she got fucking videos. She has the blackmail, the medical experiments, the rapes, the slow deaths. She even has you making the teddy bears rape me."

Sam switches back to front-facing as Annie's jagged-toothed smile drops like a porcelain plate slipping through fingers. Then Sam turns the camera back to herself. "That's right. Everyone on the other side of those hidden cameras, you should be afraid. Very afraid.

"I've only been here four days. I quit my last two jobs a week ago. People know where I've been for the last twenty years of your reign. You can't pin all the blame on me now. I don't have any weapons or drugs on me, except what the doctor gave me for the stitches. And I don't have your goddamn money. I can barely figure out livestreaming. You think I can figure out the finances of rich people?

"If the dolls blamed me, they would have already taken their anger out on me. They didn't even hurt the doctor, even though she's been partner to your experimentation. They see the pounds of flesh you took from her. They know if they were in the same position, they would have done the same thing. You want to know what they want to do to you to make sure you never hurt them again?"

Annie has gone pale and silent. Her lips move like spells muttered under her breath—hesitant, as though she's not sure which combination to use.

"Or how about this: Do you want to know how little control I have, after asking them to hold back this much? The only reason they waited was because I told them it wouldn't be as satisfying if you were unconscious. I could have just killed you. I had the right, and maybe that would have been smarter. But as much as you hurt me, you hurt them worse—and for much, much longer. I'd rather you live after what you did. I'd rather you *live*, Annie. Like they had to live."

Annie stops muttering. Her pigtails shiver. "You can't. You can't do that. You're recording. Everyone will see you let this happen. They'll crucify you, too."

"After they see what you did… Not a single Texas jury will convict, if it even makes it to court. And if I end up in prison, that's still three hots, a cot, and anywhere but here. I'm not stopping them, Annie. I couldn't if I tried. This is the bed *you* made."

Sam backs away as dolls, maids, and cooks creep forward, emboldened by the harmlessness of their former queen.

Mrs. Fratello steps forward, hands clasped in front of her. "Not too fast. Not too much. Others will want their turn. And remember, keep her alive."

Dr. Panabaker follows Sam out as the first blow by a prosthetic serrated knife rends the front of Annie's dress and a naked man with a painfully enhanced erection tears at her skirt from behind.

Sam is out of view of what happens next, by design.

"It's not nice. It's not kind. But you can't understand how bad it is here. You can't understand this isn't even 'eye for an eye.' There isn't enough of Annie for that. She might not survive before someone comes. If she does, she'll probably wish she hadn't. It'll be the first time in her life she feels something she didn't choose for herself. I just...I just haven't developed a taste for this. But this isn't for any of you to see. This is theirs. If I have to show everyone their humiliation, let them at least have that."

"Give the camera to me," the doctor says off-screen. "I'll show proof while the dolls weigh their own pounds of flesh."

"This is important, everyone," Sam says. "Take names, screenshots, come help us. The sooner someone gets here, the more likely Annie makes it out alive. Since the same can't be said for some of her dolls, don't weep for her. But don't let them kill us. Don't let them kill these accounts. Don't let them make this into something it's not.

"This is real, and we really need help. Please, please, *please* don't go away, and don't let them bury their crimes. Please, *help* us. I'm begging you."

Video 8:

Dr. Panabaker sits behind her desk with both her mutilated hands visible. She props the phone up so she doesn't have to hold it.

"My name is Jeanette Panabaker. I am a doctor of medicine. I am a cardiothoracic surgeon. I broke my oath to become Igor to a malignant cancer of a person. I didn't realize she wasn't actually a little girl in an adult body, because I've known plenty of nasty little girls. But I knew she was evil, and I helped her, because she would have hurt me more than she already had.

"It doesn't excuse what I've done. I've saved the videos that will be needed to decide if I, too, should be punished for my contributions to this nightmare. But through the next few videos—which I hope you save and spread as far and wide as you can to the relevant authorities, journalists, and boards of directors—I will help you hold Annie accountable, as well as everyone else who supported her. I don't think it will expiate my sins, but at this point, it's the least I can do. It'll be worth what happens to me if I can ensure those sons of bitches go away, too.

"Let's begin with Harold Lange…"

Video 23:

"Jeanette, I hear a helicopter," Sam says off-screen.

"It might not be bringing help. They could be here to shoot at us. Or drop a bomb." Dr. Panabaker has been testifying for multiple videos and now appears at the end of her tether, like all she wants to do is sleep for seventy years.

"I know. But if someone bad's found us, other people may have found us, too." The camera jostles as Sam picks it up again. "Besides, my battery's low. Because of course."

"We showed at least some of our hand, Sam. That's something. We can only do what we can do."

Video 24:

"I should go," Dr. Panabaker insists.

"No, I should go. I'm the one who invited everyone to the party," Sam says.

Ji-an is there in the foyer with them, but she's clearly smart enough to know why everyone else is fighting over going first and doesn't volunteer.

"I should go because of my complicity," the doctor says. "My indulgent participation."

"We need you to show where the bodies are buried. I've only been here for a few days. I don't even know where the Jack is buried. I'm the face they know. I'm the one who needs to meet them, so if they're here to save us, they know I'm not the threat."

"If *they're* the threat, then I need to meet them." Mrs. Fratello joins them, otherwise silent in her shoes. "You think you're the one who did her dirtiest work, Doctor? She's been a blight since childhood. She has stolen many, many years from me, and more from her victims, but I will not have her steal from the young who still have time to find a way to move on. You may recover from this, Samantha. I cannot, nor can I survive prison. I go first."

She opens the doors. She doesn't have a remote control for the gate, but she has keys for the house. She steps down onto the drive as Sam shuts the doors. She plasters the camera against the door glass.

"Please, please, please, please, be good people," she mutters. "We have a hundred rooms to hide in, but we can't hide forever. They could massacre us, and all we have is live video."

Mrs. Fratello continues slowly and steadily down the drive. From the way she walks, she appears to suffer some kind of arthritis or stiffness from an old back injury.

At the end of the drive, sparks fly from the sides of the gate. Whoever has come doesn't have a remote, either; they're pulling the gates down.

There are several shouts from people on top of the wall or in trees on the other side of the wall, staring in. Telephoto lenses. Cameras. Phones. There will be more witnesses than just Sam's phone, but that doesn't necessarily mean they're safe. Based on the ladder and the bulkiness of the silhouettes at the end of the driveway, firefighters work on the gate, but swirling red and blue lights mean there are also police. If there are police, there are guns. Guns mean cameras can be confiscated, destroyed, and crowds dispersed, with repeated rote recitation in bad faith that justifies a shot.

The dolls aren't rescued yet just because doors open and police are there. They will only be rescued when the police put those guns down.

"Come on, come on," Sam mutters.

Mrs. Fratello stops halfway down the driveway, her hands still clasped in front of her.

Finally, the first gate door falls onto the property. The firefighters continue dismantling the other side, but two SWAT teams swarm in and split to the sides, perhaps to clear the perimeter. Five police officers in bulletproof vests follow, with SWAT assist in front of them. They creep in, rifles trained on Mrs. Fratello.

They yell something that sounds like, "Identify yourself." If Mrs. Fratello answers, it's too soft to hear.

"She's unarmed," Sam whispers. "Don't shoot her. She's unarmed. At least, I think she is. Jeanette, what if she…"

Mrs. Fratello holds out her arms. A police officer approaches her, pats her down. Then he gestures for her to leave through the half-open gate.

"Fuck. I should have gone out there. I'm scared they're going to burst in here and start shooting everyone and arresting everyone else. The kitchen staff can't put down their weapons. The maids, the dolls… I know they probably seem scary, but they're just hurt. This is a torture house. These people need to be approached with compassion, not guns in their faces when some of them would *rather* have the police shoot them than be rescued. Oh, Christ, this is bad. This is bad."

Police and SWAT approach the house. Sam curses again when SWAT climbs the stairs and knocks on the door. Among the guns, tear gas cannisters are also visible.

"This is the police. Open the door."

Sam arranges the phone in an innocuous corner so that their entrance can be recorded. Then she gestures for Dr. Panabaker to move back. "I'm opening the doors," she shouts. "Please don't shoot. For the love of God, don't shoot."

"Open the door and keep your hands up."

"They're going to try to fight back if you come in with guns. *Please* don't come in with guns." Sam opens the doors, then backs away with her good hand up, eyes closed in anticipation of bullets. The SWAT team enters first, splitting again to both sides, then the police.

"Are you Sam Frain? The one who posted the graphic videos?"

"They're only graphic because Annie was cruel. Don't shoot. I'm unarmed."

Three of the police were plainclothes, two in uniform. The primary officer was in plainclothes.

"Is the threat neutralized?" the primary officer said.

The two in uniform patted Sam down, while the other two did their best on Dr. Panabaker, who also had her hands up.

"Annie is chained up. I can't swear to the state of her. The rest of them are suffering from physical torture and PTSD. They're going to react to you like a threat. Please don't hurt them. They've been hurt enough."

The primary officer lowers his weapon. "We don't want to hurt anyone."

A SWAT member notices the phone and picks it up. He carries it over to the primary officer, who inspects it, realizes he's on the video, and grimaces. But he hands the phone back to Sam without stopping the video, which is clearly the last thing Sam expects.

"This is a humanitarian effort. Everyone is instructed not to shoot unless deadly force is necessary for the protection of another officer."

"Are you fucking serious?" Sam says.

"We're going to do our best. Where are most of your people congregated?"

Sam turns to follow the SWAT team as they keep to the edges and enter the hall. "Kitchen staff in the kitchen. Most of them can't drop their knives, because they're attached to their arms. Maid staff is in some of the dolls' rooms. The dolls who could walk, the broken dolls who couldn't, and the rest of the maids and cooks are in the east wing, probably still in the Repair Room. Hostages are in the Time-Out Room behind that painting. I don't know how to get in. There are other dolls in the ballroom basement. I know where that door is, but not where they're stored *under* the ballroom."

"What the actual fuck," the primary officer mutters.

"I know where all the secret rooms are," Dr. Panabaker says, even though she remains flanked by officers with guns at the ready, albeit pointed at the floor.

"You're the doctor?" the primary officer asks.

"Yes."

The primary officer studies her with thin lips and stern set to his jaw. "You stay, then. Ms. Frain, you should join Mrs. Fratello outside the fence. We've set up triage. Everyone will be briefed after they've had medical care."

"I've had enough medical care. I just want to make sure no one murders anyone except Annie."

"Look." The primary points at the living room.

Sam whips the phone around. SWAT are gesturing for anyone mobile to proceed out of the east wing to the foyer and open front doors.

"Our first priority is our safety, but the next is yours. The doctor here gave us a few names that were making a stink about the viral prank and ordering us to ignore. Then they claimed you were occupying a former mayor and judge's home, holding his daughter hostage, and we should treat you as hostile. But pending investigation of the videos the doctor provided, they've been suspended from their posts."

Annie's victims are a flood of wide-eyed wondering as they squint against the post-storm light—a glimpse of the world beyond the Dream House, and for some of them, the first smell of fresh air in years.

"If I hadn't invited scrutiny or witnesses, would this be happening?" Sam asks.

"I would hope so," the primary officer replies.

"What about Mr. Lange?"

"Apprehended trying to enter this neighborhood. In custody."

"What about us?"

"Most of these guns shoot rubber bullets or beanbags. There are news vans and influencers from all over the state outside this place, most behind caution tape. We're watching the perimeter in part to make sure none of the true-crime podcasters climb over the wall to get exclusive lurid footage beyond what you've already so generously provided."

"I had to show—"

"We know why you did it, Ms. Frain. They told me to stop your videos, but we haven't found everyone the doctor named, and she hasn't even named everyone yet, which means we don't know how far this goes. I watched everything you posted, you and the doctor. I don't care if I get chewed out about it later. There's a reason you shared those videos, and it's the same reason I didn't take your phone."

He calls for a sitrep, but it's a big house; they won't have cleared every room yet. Over the radios, there are exclamations of revulsion, sometimes for the people, sometimes for what Annie has done.

"Cap, we're in the Repair Room and…we had to…remove, um, friendlies from the subject. She's…not in good shape."

"Copy," the primary officer—the captain—replies, keeping his gaze on Sam and her recording phone. "Keep them away from her. We'll remove her when the house is cleared and paramedics can enter."

"It's pretty awful, Cap."

"Let God judge them, Reg," the captain says.

"Copy, Cap."

The captain continues to stare at Sam.

"I wasn't going to get between them and Annie," Sam says. "It's less than she deserves."

The captain has nothing to say to that.

The number of people able to exit the house on their own thins to a trickle, then nothing.

"Shall I show you the hidden doors now?" Dr. Panabaker says placidly.

Accompanied by more officers, Dr. Panabaker started leading paramedics into the house, so she could show them how to enter the Time-Out Room. Sam refused to leave until she could watch Lila leave first.

Every step down the long driveway was harder, as though the doctor had left the suture needles in each of her wounds. Pain flooded through her, now that she could spare the headspace.

She continued to record, but she'd run out of words in her relief. She wouldn't be the only one bearing witness now. There were more people in the trees, even drones. She hoped professionals and amateurs all the way from surrounding states started arriving, too.

"Thank you, everyone," she managed into her phone camera. "Thank you for believing me. Thank you for helping us. Thanks for making sure this went right."

She walked more gingerly by the time she reached the gate doors, which had been pulled onto the lawn away from the path.

Though she hadn't yet heard a single gunshot, she feared one would ring out as soon as she stepped off Dream House property. That she would turn around and see a field of limp dolls, mouths open and tongues lolling to taste free earth in their last dying and dead seconds. That she would cross the gateway only to be confronted by strange grinning men in expensive suits and deep pockets, minions ready to pull a hood over her head and take her to a whole new kind of hell.

Instead, police fought with people driving in and clogging up the road, yelled at them to pull to the side so emergency vehicles could come in and out. There were three fire engines, at least a dozen ambulances, and temporary structures with fluttering tent roofs and portable hospital beds as doctors and nurses assessed each person's injuries. Ji-an was making her presence known among those tending her staff, dismissing all attempts to get her to stay where she'd been told to sit. Her shirt had been cut up the back, exposing unusual scars that looked like she'd been struck with a whip that terminated in something sharp.

"They're just scars," she kept saying. "They're healed. They're old. Stop trying to take their hands off. Focus on new. Fix old later."

Lila was among the 'new.' Most of the Time-Out hostages looked around with confused but clearer eyes now that the drugs could work their way out of their systems. She was wrapped in a blanket against the cool of the shade and any potential withdrawal.

There were some tents, too, with curtains that went all the way to the ground. That was where they shuttled dolls—even harder to look at outside the dollhouse while surrounded by so many people untouched by Annie's imagination. The curtains preserved at least some of their privacy as they were extricated from each other, if possible, or arranged on a wheelchair, hospital bed, gurney, or dolly. The medical first responders did their best to control their expressions, but it was different seeing the dolls in person than through video or just hearing how bad it was.

When Sam stepped through the gateway, someone started clapping. She thought it came from the rig or the wall, but the clapping spread to the trees and woods and the first responders, even the maids, kitchen staff, groundskeepers, and some of the dolls, moved by social contagion.

Across the crowd, Lila straightened, hope and wariness warring in her expression.

Sam looked away. Then she shook her head, waved her hands for everyone to stop. "No. No. Don't. There's nothing to applaud here. Stop. Stop it. The only good here is that they're free of Annie. That's it."

"And that's because of you," a paramedic said as she ran up to Sam with a forehead thermometer.

"It shouldn't have taken me for it to happen," Sam said. "And I could have just as easily failed. Look, I'm fine. Dr. Panabaker already handled the worst of it. God, why won't they stop?"

The applause persisted, and now there were flashes. Sam covered her face with her bad hand and finally ended her livestream recording.

"Come over here. The sutures look exceptional, but we should be able to re-dress them before taking you to the hospital for this broken hand and the rest once the worst cases leave first."

Sam nodded and followed the paramedic to open-air triage.

Her phone vibrated. She didn't have much battery left, and she'd received so many notifications since she'd started posting videos, but she checked anyway.

This Lila. Paramedic phone. Feel like something happened to me. Can't remember. Did something happen to me?

Sam could have lied, but Lila would have known it was a lie.

She replied, *Yes.*

She didn't let herself glance in Lila's direction, and Lila didn't call for her or text again.

It was enough that Sam knew Lila was all right—as all right as she could be. But Lila was just another way Annie had hurt her.

The applause died, as did every last conversation, interview, exasperated shout, and influencer monologue. Everyone went absolutely quiet and still.

Sam used the last of her battery to livestream them rolling Annie out handcuffed to a gurney. She was barely recognizable, bleeding from every orifice, from bite wounds and scratches, from a socket where the eye had been removed, from her mouth ripped due to a violently dislocated jaw. Her good eye was vague, distant, unaware.

But she was breathing and given priority for an ambulance. The captain and another officer joined her in the back.

Sam's phone died before the ambulance drove out of sight.

Epilogue: SAMANTHA

After she was released from the hospital into police custody, the police took Sam's statement about eight times. The feds took her statement about twelve more times before she completely shut down and stopped talking to anybody. Then her older brother, Michael, came in and demanded that they release her if they weren't going to charge her with anything.

He'd abandoned his barely-breaking-even band tour when he'd heard what had happened to her. Michael and his wife, Pamela—who might have been an actual saint for living with, supporting, and still loving Sam's brother—shielded her as best as they could from the world and hired her a lawyer. Pamela even set up crowdfunding for Sam and another for all the other victims of Annie and Harold Lange and worked with other victims' families to make sure they each got a share in addition to their own individual crowdfunding.

Sam would have told Pamela not to bother begging on her behalf, but after the whole protracted spectacle that she'd help cause, professional and amateur journalists of every medium visited or camped outside her brother and sister-in-law's house. Day and night, they clamored to get a glimpse of Sam or an interview with her brother and sister-in-law. Offering them a portion of the funding assuaged her guilt, at least for what she'd done to their lives.

Annie only had two notable headlines:

SADISTIC DOLLMAKER ANNIE LANGE IN COMA AFTER DOLLHOUSE DISCOVERY

ANNIE LANGE DIES FROM INJURIES, FATHER HAROLD TRIAL DATE SET

Sam wished Annie had lived to see the inside of a courtroom with her outsides more representative of the insides. She wished Annie could hear every last testimony and get told to shut her little girl voice up by a judge. But Sam could still watch a class action suit promise to drain the generous Lange estate dry, albeit more by lawyers' fees than anything else.

Pamela had Sam's lawyer join the suit on her behalf, but Sam refused to say another word about what had happened. The authorities had her statements, and although they were hidden behind a content warning, her videos were now a matter of public record.

She read everything and watched every segment about the trial against Harold Lange and every last person who had charges brought against them for willfully participating in the dollhouse. Some claimed they'd been forced into doing it for the purpose of blackmail and to use their influence; Sam could believe that was possible, but she'd leave judgment to the imperfect courts. She wasn't foolish enough to believe they'd catch every monster.

She just wanted to get to the point where she didn't have to obsessively read and watch everything to do with the dollhouse. It took far too long to start fading from other people's consciousness, because Mr. Lange's lawyers dragged the whole sordid affair out for as long as they could, going so far as to accuse Sam and Dr. Panabaker of slander, although those never made it to trial. No one could challenge the raw veracity of Sam's videos.

Aside from doctors' visits, Sam didn't even leave her brother and sister-in-law's house until six months later, and only after midnight. She often frequented a nearby Waffle House, where the staff didn't give a shit who she was. By then, she was out of the stitches and had cut her black hair short so she'd look different. She thought about dyeing it platinum blonde, but she didn't do that until she could finally convince herself to leave the house during the day.

Two months after Harold Lange was finally convicted of conspiracy, murder, torture, rape, and blackmail—among a multitude of other charges—he killed himself in prison. His estate quietly settled the class action suit. Less than a month later, Lila changed her relationship status to 'married.' In her photos, she looked so much happier than she'd ever been with Sam.

Jeanette Panabaker was put in witness protection during the course of the trials, a courtesy that Sam had refused. There were so many people around her brother and sister-in-law's house that neighbors complained on Nextdoor, aired their grievances on the local news, and shot bullets at the sky to keep people off their lawns. Police regularly drove by for the first six months, but the media attention inadvertently provided her additional protection from the kind of people who might have contributed to Harold Lange's 'suicide.'

There had been rumors he was asking for a more lenient sentence in return for a more comprehensive list of clients, as well as a more comprehensive collection of evidence, but that's all they were—rumors. It was entirely possible he'd just decided he wasn't going to survive in prison, since at that point it was common knowledge he'd been watching his daughter have sex since she was a teenager. He'd been thwarted from committing suicide three times before.

But my, what a coincidence he'd succeeded just when he'd made promises threatening as yet unnamed powerful people. Such was the nature of wealthy monsters in the shadows.

Sam thought the real reason why no one killed her and made it look like an accident or suicide was that she'd stopped talking after she'd left the dollhouse. Her videos were undeniable, but she could only personally implicate Annie and Harold Lange.

Dr. Panabaker, however, didn't stop. Through protected means, she sacrificed herself every week to speak for the victims and against the monsters, inviting ridicule, insult, and Mengele references.

At one point, between doing those protected interviews, she sent Sam a picture through an anonymous email. Sam only knew it was Dr. Panabaker because of the mutilated hand in the corner, resting on her lap on top of a crocheted blanket. The picture showed a quiet place in the country, out of reach.

A year after Harold Lange's conviction, amid dozens of still active trials, several networks and news programs did retrospectives on the Dollmaker case. Some of the more torrid dolls who people had managed to get images of to sell to networks or use in their own content were trotted out again. Many of them had endured surgery to try to get them as close to normal as humanly possible, but there were a few who could never be as they were again. These retrospectives also always brought up the suicides, paired with photos of them before Annie, then excruciatingly clear pictures of them after—as though to say to viewers safe and comfortable on their couches: *Of course they wanted to kill themselves. Just look at them.*

Yet Sam watched every program, even the documentary series two years in and the fictionalized limited series five years in. She silently seethed on the little couch in her little bedroom. Reporters returned to the lawn after each airing, and she was pretty sure her brother's house was on at least one murder tour.

Everything in the Dream House that wasn't evidence was auctioned off to pay the class action settlement; the property was sold for the same reason. The new buyer razed the Dream House entirely, then built another mansion—much more understated, as mansions went.

Sam lived at her brother's house for six years before she managed to do much more than online work where no one had to see her or ask about her scars or if she was *that* Sam Frain. Being able to work at all had taken over two years.

Really, she was proud of her brother for stepping up and realizing that, in an absurd twist of fate, Sam was in no state to take care of herself for a while. And not just Michael. Her sisters came by all the time. They started having something approximating family dinners.

Not her mother. Sam wasn't sure her mother even knew what had happened to her.

Sam had always loved her brother, but she respected him a lot more than before, because although he still toured with his godawful band, he wasn't the person he'd been when she'd taken over the family. He did odd jobs during tours so he could send something home to Pamela, and when he was home, he had a little side business of repair and minor contracting work and otherwise took over childcare so Pamela could have the break she didn't always get while he toured. He even knew how to make more than boxed macaroni and cheese.

Sam loved him, but she hated living with him, hated needing him, hated that she'd boxed herself into a bedroom and barely came out—which still felt like more freedom than a giant mansion and its grounds.

But it wasn't freedom. She continued to constantly immerse herself in the Dollmaker case, even though she wouldn't talk about it with anyone.

And it wasn't freedom because she still woke up next to Annie almost every morning.

Annie was dead. Mr. Lange was dead. Almost all the monsters who hadn't made plea deals were in prison. Sometimes the dolls, maids, or cooks contacted her—Ji-an, too, although Mrs. Fratello had essentially disappeared. They wanted to thank her and tell her how far they'd come in physical and psychological therapy. They showed her pictures of their new smiles, their new prosthetics, their spouses, their kids, their jobs. They asked how she was doing.

Sam didn't tell them. She felt like she didn't have the right to be a mess when they'd gone through worse for much longer and were apparently doing much better. Then again, there were dozens upon dozens of others who didn't contact her, and in the private online group set up for Annie's victims, a new suicide article came up every now and then, or news that someone else had checked into rehab or a psych facility again.

Survivor's guilt. The other victims talked about it a lot. Sam didn't feel like she had a right to that, either.

So, Annie stayed with her for a while, long after Sam thought she'd have to endure her.

She'd always been so independent, to the point of other people being dependent on her. Yet, here she was, caught between her brother's guest room and Waffle House. And occasionally the movie theater, where she watched funny things and cried and watched romantic things and cried and watched scary things and cried—just cried buckets over her popcorn during morning matinees when she wouldn't bother anyone. She figured that was as good as therapy, because at least she didn't have to fucking *talk*.

When she could finally go out into the world around normal people during the day, reporters weren't claiming stakes on her brother's lawn, and her scars had calmed into little puckered dimples in her skin, Sam moved. Between crowdfunding, the settlement, and what she'd saved while working and living in her brother's house, she bought her own smaller house in another neighborhood.

She had a Japanese maple and an herb garden. She adopted two cats. She still woke up next to Annie, but it stopped being as terrible when she came back to herself in her small full-sized bed and the pressure against her legs was Walter and Harvey, not a person.

Sam visited Annie's grave. It was a modest thing. Mr. Lange had had other things on his mind than continuing to spoil her posthumously. There were bleached areas on the gravestone that suggested it was regularly vandalized, but there were also flowers and cheap dolls left by fans of the Dollmaker who made pilgrimages to her 'tomb.' No accounting for taste.

Sam had given it a lot of thought and didn't want to make things more difficult for the cemetery staff, so she'd brought wild thistle, a severed sunflower head, and a container of mealworms.

Afterward, Annie didn't go away, but Sam slept soundly the next morning at least.

Just like that, she was over forty and very alone. She still met her family for dinners, and when she finally called her mother, her mother talked only about herself and didn't seem to realize that Sam hadn't called in years.

She worked as a third-shift customer service representative. She didn't have to, but she wanted to *do* something other than write a book about her experience or sell exclusive interviews. She didn't blame others for taking that on, becoming spokespeople, joining nonprofit groups against human trafficking, or other things like that. She didn't blame the ones with cam accounts, either.

She just knew she didn't want to be seen. Except she didn't want to be invisible anymore, either.

One of her sisters set her up on a semi-blind date with an Applebee's waitress who had a daughter she co-parented with the girl's father. Rhea was heavily tattooed, which suggested a measure of patience and a tolerance for pain.

"I like your tattoos," Sam said. She spoke all the time into a headset for her job, but she wasn't used to speaking to people in person beyond giving a food order. Everything she did felt off in timing.

"Thanks. I made friends with the tattoo artist. I know how you got them—I'm not going to pretend I don't—but I like your scars."

Sam made sure the one on her head was covered by her hair. "I don't."

"That's okay. The rest of it is good, too."

They were awkward until they weren't. And eventually, Sam started talking. Rhea didn't share any of it with a soul.

Sam had never wanted a child, but Rhea's child wasn't hers and Rhea never expected her to be a mom, so it was nice to just *be* with Maya without having to take care of her. Rhea knew how she felt about them, but Sam still gave Maya dolls: little ragdolls she found in boutique shops. They didn't make her think of people so much as talismans.

Rhea was careful; Maya was trusting. Sam taught Maya how to guard herself, if not how to heal, and Rhea taught Maya and Sam how to live.

It wasn't after their first date, nor the next, nor the next, but eventually, Sam learned to love the way Rhea loved her scars, too.

PLAYTHINGS

we all wait in the dollhouse,
bound, splinted into the shapes
she makes of her limp possessions,
dream in the haze of unknown days
and nightmares, when she returns
in the company of a new plaything,
to dress up and feed and break
and replace with more desirable parts.

THE END?

Not if you want to dive into more of Crystal Lake Publishing's Tales from the Darkest Depths!

Check out our amazing website and online store or download our latest catalog here:

We always have great new projects and content on the website to dive into, as well as a newsletter, behind the scenes options, social media platforms, our own dark fiction shared-world series and our very own webstore. Our webstore even has categories specifically for KU books, non-fiction, anthologies, and of course more novels and novellas.

AUTHOR BIOGRAPHY

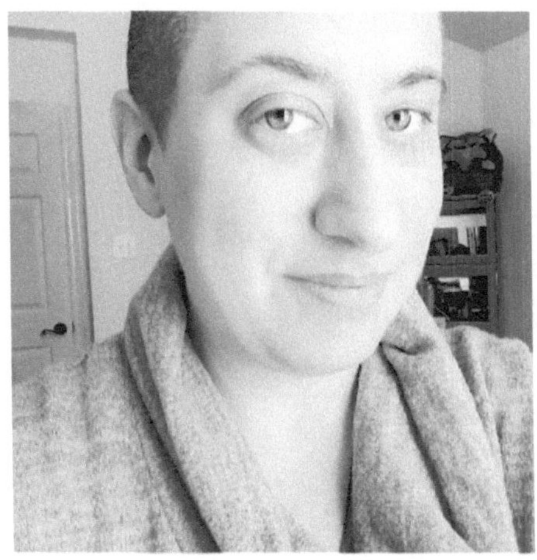

Amanda M. Blake is a cat-loving daydreamer who enjoys geekery of all sorts, from superheroes to horror movies, urban fantasy to unconventional romance. Born and raised in Texas, Blake attended Trinity University in San Antonio and graduated with a BA in English Literature.

Amid dipping tentacles into the sea of gothic and horror short stories and poetry, Blake is also the author of fantasy novel *Drift*, horror novels *Question Not My Salt*, *Deep Down*, and *Out of Curiosity and Hunger*, dark poetry collection *Dead Ends*, and the fairy tale mash-up Thorns series.

In the Dollhouse We All Wait is Blake's eleventh novel. Alt-Victorian plague tale *Masque* has been acquired by Quill & Crow Publishing House and is slated for publication in 2027.

Readers…

Thank you for reading *In The Dollhouse We All Wait*. We hope you enjoyed this novel. If you have a moment, please review *In The Dollhouse We All Wait* at the store where you bought it.

Help other readers by telling them why you enjoyed this book. No need to write an in-depth discussion. Even a single sentence will be greatly appreciated. Reviews go a long way to helping a book sell, and is great for an author's career. It'll also help us to continue publishing quality books.

Thank you again for taking the time to journey with Crystal Lake's Torrid Waters.

You will find links to all our social media platforms on our Linktree page: https://linktr.ee/CrystalLakePublishing.

MISSION STATEMENT

Since its founding in August 2012, Crystal Lake has quickly become one of the world's leading publishers of Dark Fiction and Horror books. In 2023, Crystal Lake officially transitioned into an entertainment company, joining several other divisions, genres, and imprints, including Torrid Waters, Sinister Smile Press, Crystal Lake Comics, Crystal Lake Games, Crystal Cove Press, Crystal Lake Kids, Memento Mori Ink, and The House of Shadows & Ink on YouTube.

While we strive to present only the highest quality fiction and entertainment, we also endeavor to support authors along their writing journey. We offer our time and experience in non-fiction projects, as well as author mentoring and services, at competitive prices.

With several Bram Stoker Award wins and many other wins and nominations (including the HWA's Specialty Press Award), Crystal Lake puts integrity, honor, and respect at the forefront of our publishing operations.

We strive for each book and outreach program we spearhead to not only entertain and touch or comment on issues that affect our readers, but also to strengthen and support the Dark Fiction field and its authors.

Not only do we find and publish authors we believe are destined for greatness, but we strive to work with men and women who endeavor to be decent human beings who care more for others than themselves, while still being hard-working, driven, and passionate artists and storytellers.

Crystal Lake is and will always be a beacon of what passion and dedication, combined with overwhelming teamwork and respect, can accomplish. We endeavor to know each and every one of our readers, while building personal relationships with our authors, reviewers, bloggers, podcasters, bookstores, and libraries.

We will be as trustworthy, forthright, and transparent as any business can be, while also keeping most of the headaches away from our authors, since it's our job to solve the problems so they can stay in a creative mind. Which of course also means paying our authors.

We do not just publish books, we present to you worlds within your world, doors within your mind, from talented authors who sacrifice so much for a moment of your time.

There are some amazing small presses out there, and through collaboration and open forums we will continue to support other presses in the goal of helping authors and showing the world what quality small presses are capable of accomplishing. No one wins when a small press goes down, so we will always be there to support hardworking, legitimate presses and their authors. We don't see Crystal Lake as the best press out there, but we will always strive to be the best, strive to be the most interactive and grateful, and even blessed press around. No matter what happens over time, we will also take our mission very seriously while appreciating where we are and enjoying the journey.

What do we offer our authors that they can't do for themselves through self-publishing?

We are big supporters of self-publishing (especially hybrid publishing), if done with care, patience, and planning. However, not every author has the time or inclination to do market research, advertise, and set up book launch strategies. Although a lot of authors are successful in doing it all, strong small presses will always be there for the authors who just want to do what they do best: write.

What we offer is experience, industry knowledge, contacts and trust built up over years. And due to our strong brand and trusting fanbase, every Crystal Lake book comes with weight of respect. In time our fans begin to trust our judgment and will try a new author purely based on our support of said author.

To date we've published around 300 books, and with each launch we strive to fine-tune our approach, learn from our mistakes, and increase our reach. We continue to assure our authors that we're here for them and that we'll carry the weight of the launch and deal with third parties while they focus on their strengths—be it writing, interviews, blogs, signings, etc.

We also offer several mentoring packages to authors that include knowledge and skills they can use in both traditional and self-publishing endeavors. This includes Shadows & Ink Creators on our The House of Shadows & Ink YouTube channel and our Crystal Lake Academy.

We look forward to launching many new careers.

This is what we believe in. What we stand for. This will be our legacy.

Welcome to Crystal Lake Publishing—Where Stories Come Alive!

Also from Torrid Waters...

A tale as dark and complex as the human psyche.

Kaliana Cook, a heroin addict haunted by her past, is on a desperate quest for freedom. Paroled but longing to reunite with the child she loves, Kali makes a daring escape, only to realize she's entangled in a far more sinister web.

As Kali's journey unfolds, reality warps into a nightmare. She finds herself pursued not only by a relentless parole agent but also by a monstrous presence she unwittingly unleashed. This chilling entity, a bizarre blend of nightmare spiders and a deceptively innocent little girl, embodies the horrors of addiction and the grotesque distortions of a mind plagued by heroin.

Blood and carnage trail Kali's frantic steps, painting a surreal landscape reminiscent of a Cronenbergian nightmare. Her world becomes an unsettling fusion of Trainspotting's raw desperation and the tragic depth of Les Misérables, all shrouded in the eerie innocence of Charlotte's Web. Each moment on the run intensifies Kali's struggle, as she battles not just for her freedom, but for her sanity.

Caught in this twisted web of her own making, Kali faces a harrowing truth: escape is not just about outrunning her physical pursuers, but confronting the haunting specters of her addiction and the supernatural horrors that they manifest.

Kali's Web is a gripping journey into the heart of darkness, exploring the depths of addiction, the potency of the supernatural, and the enduring strength of the human spirit.

Will Kali find her way out of the web, or will you, the reader, be caught in the gripping terror of her journey?

Also from Torrid Waters...

Come for Thanksgiving Dinner. Stay for the Feast.

Sierra's first American Thanksgiving promises to be unforgettable when her college roommate, Zoe, invites her to the Samuels family feast. But as the ten-hour banquet unfolds, it becomes clear this is no ordinary holiday gathering.

With everyone bound by a chilling rule—eat and drink exactly as served, and enjoy it, or face dire consequences—the traditional celebration quickly takes a dark and macabre turn. Will Sierra survive the Samuels' sinister hospitality or become part of a feast far more horrifying than she could have ever imagined?

Question Not My Salt is a gripping tale blending the terror of *The Texas Chainsaw Massacre* with the culinary horror of *Hannibal* and *The Menu*.

Also from Torrid Waters...

A fast-paced story of survival, terror, family, and friendship.

The people of Wicker thought the mountain belonged to them—purchased with blood, sweat, and resilience. They forgot the deal their ancestors made. They forgot that their mountain belonged to something ancient, powerful, and hungry.

Charlotte Crowe and Rebecca Greenleigh grew up as best friends on the mountain, descendants of the original settlers of Wicker and inheritors of a terrible secret. They expected to grow old on their mountain. They did not expect the return of the wolves, the bone chimes appearing overnight in the trees, or their neighbors turning on one another. In a matter of days, everything they thought they knew is flipped upside down and they find themselves trapped in a place they once called home playing a dangerous game with a creature older than the mountain itself.

THANK YOU FOR PURCHASING THIS BOOK